BURHAN SÖNMEZ is an internationally prize-winning novelist whose works have been translated into over twenty languages. Sönmez was born in Central Anatolia in 1965 and later moved to Istanbul where he worked as a lawyer. He was a founder of the social-activist cultural organisation TAKSAV (Foundation for Social Research, Culture and Art) and wrote on literature, culture and politics for various newspapers and magazines. Sönmez was seriously injured following an assault by Turkish police in 1996 and had to receive treatment in Britain, where he remained in exile for several years. He now lectures at METU University in Ankara and lives in Istanbul.

www.burhansonmez.com

ÜMIT HUSSEIN is a British translator and interpreter of Turkish Cypriot origin. She has translated the work of Nevin Halıcı, Mehmet Yashin and Ahmet Altan, among others.

'A writer of passion, memory and heart, Burhan Sönmez does what very few novelists achieve: he gives a voice to the voiceless and revives not only the stories of a land but also its bruised conscience.'
Elif Shafak, author of *The Bastard of Istanbul*

*'Istanbul Istanbul* turns on the tension between the confines of a prison cell and the vastness of the imagination; between the vulnerable borders of the body and the unassailable depths of the mind. This is a harrowing, riveting novel, as unforgettable as it is inescapable.'
Dale Peck, author of *Visions and Revisions*

'A wrenching love poem to Istanbul ... An ode to pain in which Dostoevsky meets *The Decameron*.'
John Ralston Saul, author of *On Equilibrium*

# İSTANBUL
# İSTANBUL

# BURHAN
# SÖNMEZ

*Translated from the Turkish by*
ÜMIT HUSSEIN

TELEGRAM

Published 2016 in Great Britain by Telegram

Published by arrangement with OR Books LLC, New York

© Burhan Sönmez 2016
© Kalem Agency, Istanbul
Translation © Ümit Hussein 2015

ISBN 978-1-84659-205-8
eISBN 978-1-84659-206-5

A full cip record for this book is available from the British Library.

Printed and bound by CPI Group (UK) Ltd, Croydon, CR0 4YY

Telegram
26 Westbourne Grove
London W2 5RH
www.telegrambooks.com

*For Kıvanç*

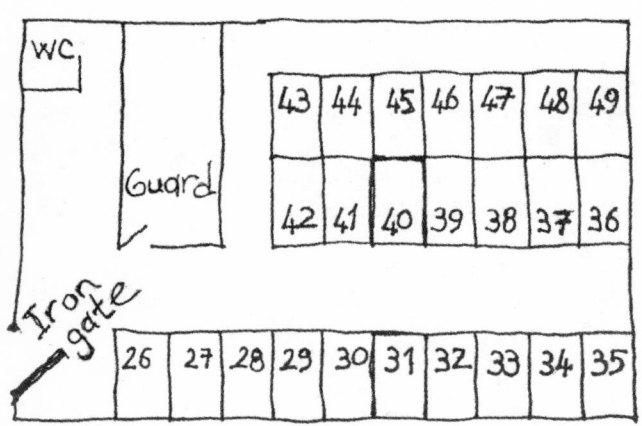

# CHAPTERS

# 1ST DAY

*Told by the Student Demirtay*

## THE IRON GATE

"It's actually a long story but I'll be brief," I said. "No one had ever seen so much snow in Istanbul. When the two nuns left Saint George's Hospital in Karaköy in the dead of night to go to the Church of Saint Anthony of Padua to break the bad news, there were scores of dead birds under the eaves. That April, ice cracked the Judas tree flowers, while the razor-sharp wind bit the stray dogs. Have you ever known it to snow in April, Doctor? It's actually a long story but I'll be brief. One of the nuns sliding and stumbling in the blizzard was young, the other old. When they had almost reached the Galata Tower the young nun said to her companion, a man has been following us all the way up the hill. The older nun said there could only be one reason why a man would follow them in a storm in the pitch darkness."

When I heard the sound of the iron gate in the distance I stopped telling my story and looked at the Doctor.

It was cold in our cell. While I was telling the Doctor my story, Kamo the Barber lay curled on the bare concrete floor. We had no covers, we warmed ourselves by huddling together, like puppies. Because time had stood still for several days we had no idea if it was day or night. We knew what pain was, every day we relived the horror that clamped our hearts as we were led away to be tortured. In that short interval where

1

we braced ourselves for pain, humans and animals, the sane and the mad, angels and demons were all the same. As the grating of the iron gate echoed through the corridor, Kamo the Barber sat up. "They're coming for me," he said.

I got up, went to the cell door and peered through the small grille. As I tried to make out who was coming from the direction of the iron gate, my face was illuminated by the light in the corridor. I couldn't see anyone, they were probably waiting at the entrance. The light dazzled me and I blinked. I glanced at the cell opposite, wondering whether the young girl they had shoved in there today like a wounded animal was dead or alive.

When the sounds in the corridor grew faint I sat down again and placed my feet on top of the Doctor's and Kamo the Barber's. We pressed our bare feet closer together for warmth, and kept our hot breath near one another's faces. Waiting too was an art. We listened wordlessly to the muffled clinking and rattling from the other side of the wall.

The Doctor had been in the cell for two weeks when they threw me in with him. I was a mess of blood. When I came to the next day, I saw he hadn't stopped at cleaning my wounds, he had covered me with his jacket as well. Every day, different interrogation teams marched us away blindfolded and brought us back hours later, semiconscious. But Kamo the Barber had been waiting for three days. Since he had been inside they had neither taken him away for interrogation nor mentioned his name.

At first the cell, measuring one by two meters, had seemed small, but we had grown used to it. The floor and the walls were concrete, the door was of gray iron. It was bare inside. We sat on the floor. When our legs grew numb we stood up and paced around the cell. Sometimes when we raised our heads at the sound of a scream in the distance we examined one another's faces in the dim light that filtered in from the corridor. We passed the time sleeping or talking. We were permanently cold and growing thinner by the day.

Again we heard the rusty grating of the iron gate. The interrogators were leaving without taking anyone. We listened, waiting, to be certain. The sounds died out when the door closed, leaving the corridor deserted. "The motherfuckers didn't take me, they left without taking anyone," said Kamo the Barber between deep breaths. Raising his head, he gazed at the dark ceiling, then curled up and lay down on the floor.

The Doctor told me to go on with my story.

Just as I was launching into my tale with, "The two nuns, in the thick of the snow . . . ," Kamo the Barber suddenly gripped my arm. "Listen kid, can't you change that story and tell us something decent? It's fucking frigid in here as it is, isn't it bad enough freezing on this concrete, without having to tell stories of snow and blizzards as well?"

Did Kamo see us as his friends or his enemies? Was he angry because we told him he had been ranting in his sleep for the past three days? Is that why he glared at us with such contempt? If they took him away blindfolded and ripped his flesh to ribbons, if they hanged him for hours with his arms outstretched, he might learn to trust us. For now he had to make do with tolerating our words and our beaten bodies. The Doctor held his shoulder gently. "Sleep well, Kamo," he said, coaxing him to lie down again.

"No one had ever seen such heat in Istanbul," I started again. "It's actually a long story but I'll be brief. When the two nuns came out of Saint George's Hospital in Karaköy in the dead of night to go to the Church of Saint Anthony of Padua to break the good news, there were scores of birds chirping happily under the eaves. The buds on the Judas trees were about to burst into bloom in the middle of winter, the stray dogs to melt and evaporate in the heat. Have you ever known it to be as scorching as the desert in the dead of winter, Doctor? It's actually a long story but I'll be brief. One of the nuns staggering in the intense heat was young, the other old. When they had almost reached the Galata Tower the young nun said to her companion, a man has been following us all the way up the hill. The older nun said there could only be one reason why a man would follow them in a deserted street in the dark: rape. They ascended the hill with their hearts in their mouths. Not a soul was in sight. The sudden heat wave had made everyone rush to Galata Bridge and bask on the shores of the Golden Horn, and now that it was late at night the streets were deserted. The young nun said, the man is getting closer, he'll have caught up with us before we get to the top. Then let's run, said the older nun. Their long skirts and cumbersome habits notwithstanding, they sprinted past sign painters, music sellers, and bookshops. All the shops were closed. Looking behind her, the young nun said, the man is running too. They were already out of breath, sweat streaming down their backs. The older nun said, let's separate before he catches up with us, that way at least one of us will get away. Each of them ran into a different street, with no idea of what would befall them. As the young nun dashed to and fro through the streets she thought she had better stop looking behind her. Remembering the Bible story, she fixed her gaze on the narrow streets to avoid sharing the fate of those who stopped for one last glimpse of the city from the distance. She ran in the darkness, constantly changing direction. Those who had said today was cursed were right. The mediums who took the heat wave in the middle of winter to be a portent of disaster had spoken on television, the neighborhood idiots had spent the entire day beating tins. Realizing after a while that she could only hear the echo of her own footsteps, the young nun slowed down at a corner. As she leaned against a wall in an unfamiliar street, it dawned on her that she was lost. The streets were deserted. Accompanied by a dog gamboling under her feet, she crept along very slowly, following the line of the walls. It's actually a long story but I'll be brief. When the young nun eventually reached the Church of Saint Anthony of Padua she found out that the other nun had not returned. She lost no time in relating her misfortunes, throwing the church into an uproar. Just as a search party was about to go out to look for the older nun, the gate opened and in she rushed, out of breath, her hair disheveled. She sank onto a stool, took several deep breaths, and drank two cups of water. Unable to contain her curiosity, the young nun demanded to know what had happened. The older nun said, I ran from one street to another, but I couldn't shake the man off. Eventually I realized there was no escape. The young nun asked, so what did you do? I stopped at a corner, when I stopped the man stopped too. And then what happened? I lifted my skirt up. And then what? The man pulled his pants down. And then? I started running again. And then what happened? It's obvious. A woman with her skirt up can run faster than a man with his pants down."

Still lying on the floor, Kamo the Barber started laughing. That was the first time we had seen him laugh. His body rocked gently, as though he were frolicking with weird and wonderful creatures in his dreams. I repeated my last sentence. "A woman with her skirt up can run faster than a man with his pants down." When Kamo the Barber started to roar with laughter I leaned over to cover his mouth. Suddenly he opened his eyes and stared at me. If the guards heard us they would either beat us or punish us by making us stand up lined against the wall for several hours. That wasn't how we wanted to spend the time remaining before our next torture session.

Kamo the Barber sat up and leaned against the wall. As he took deep breaths his face turned serious and reverted to its usual expression. He was like a drunk who had stumbled into a ditch the night before and woken up with no idea where he was.

"Today I dreamt I was burning," he said. "I was in the lowest circle of hell, they were taking sticks from everyone else's fire and using them to stoke mine. But damn it, I was still cold. The other sinners were screaming, my eardrums burst and healed a thousand times over. The fire kept getting bigger and bigger but I couldn't burn hard enough. You weren't there, I searched every face, but there was no sign of a doctor or a student. I craved more fire, crying out and begging, like an animal going to the slaughter. The wealthy, the preachers, the bad poets, and cold-hearted mothers burning in front of me stared at me through the flames. The wound in my heart wouldn't burn and turn to ash, my memory refused to melt into oblivion. Despite the fire that was turning metal to liquid, I could still recall my cursed past. Repent, they said. But was that enough? Were your souls saved when you repented? All you inmates of hell! Bastards! I was just an ordinary barber, who brought food home and liked reading books, but didn't have any children. Toward the end of the time when everything in our lives went awry, my wife didn't reproach me. I wanted her to, but she begrudged me even her curses. When I was drunk I told her what I thought when I was sober; one night I stood in front of her and said I'm a poor wretch. I waited for her to humiliate me and shout at me. I searched for a scornful look, but as my wife turned away I saw that the only expression on her face was one of sadness. The worst thing about a woman is that she's always better than you. My mother included. You think I'm weird for saying these things, but I don't care."

Kamo the Barber stroked his beard, turning his face

toward the light coming from the grille. Independently of his not having been able to wash for three days, it was obvious from his filthy hair, his long nails, and the stench of rancid dough that accompanied him on the first day, that he shied away from water even when he was outside. I had got used to the Doctor's smell and grown quite protective of my own. Kamo's smell kept imposing itself, like the foreboding of ill omen oppressing his soul. Now, after a three-day silence, there was no stopping him.

"I met my wife on the first day I opened my barbershop with a sign saying 'Kamo the Barber' on the window. Her brother was about to start school and she had brought him in for a haircut. I asked the boy his name and introduced myself: My name is Kamil, but everyone calls me Kamo. Okay, Kamo Ağbi, said the boy. I asked him riddles and told him funny stories about school. When I asked her, my future wife, watching us from where she sat in a corner, told me she had just finished secondary school and now worked at home as a seamstress. She averted her eyes from me and looked at the photograph of the Maiden's Tower on the wall, the basil under it, the mirror with the blue frame, the razor blades and scissors. When I held out some of the cologne that I rubbed on the boy's hair to her, she opened her hand and closed her eyes as she raised her small palm to her nose and inhaled. At that moment I dreamed it was me she saw under her eyelids, I wanted no eyes but those to ever touch me again for as long as I lived. As my wife was leaving the shop, wearing lemon scented cologne and her flower print dress, I stood in the doorway and watched her depart. I hadn't asked her name. She was Mahizer, who had entered my life with her small hands, and whom I thought would never leave it.

"That night I returned to the old well. There was a well in the back garden of the house where I had grown up in the neighborhood of Menekşe. When I was alone I would lean over the top of the well and stare down into the darkness below. I never realized the day had ended, I never remembered there was another world that had no connection with the well. Darkness was serenity, it was sacred. I grew drunk on the smell of damp, I was dizzy with pleasure. Whenever anyone said I looked like my father, whom I had never met, or my mother called me by my father's name, Kamil, instead of Kamo, I would run to the well, panting. As I filled my lungs with air in the darkness I would lean right down into the well and fantasize about plunging in. I wanted to break free from my mother, my father, and my childhood. Motherfuckers! My mother's fiancé had made her pregnant then committed suicide, she had had me, even though it meant being disowned by her family, and named me after her fiancé. Even when I was old enough to start playing outside, I remember she would sometimes hold me to her breast, put her nipple in my mouth and cry. I tasted my mother's tears instead of milk. I would close my eyes and count on my fingers, repeating to myself again and again that it would soon be over. One night as it was growing dark my mother found me leaning into the well and yanked my arm to pull me out. Just then the stone she was standing on suddenly slipped. I can still hear her scream as she fell in. It was midnight when they took her body out of the well. After my mother's death I went to live in Darüşşafaka orphanage, and fell asleep spinning daydreams in dormitories where everyone told their own interminable life story."

Kamo scrutinized us to see whether we were listening to his tale.

"During my engagement to Mahizer I gave her novels and poetry books. Our literature teacher at school used to say that everyone had their own language, and that you could understand some with flowers and others with books.

Mahizer would cut out patterns at home and sew dresses, sometimes she would write poems on small scraps of paper and give them to her brother to bring to me. I used to keep her poems in my barbershop, in a box in the bottom drawer, with the perfumed soaps. The business was doing well, with the number of regular customers growing constantly. One day one of my customers, a journalist who had come in for a haircut and left with a big smile, was shot as he went out of the door. The two assailants ran to the journalist lying on the ground and, after firing another shot into his head, shouted, you either love or you leave, pal! The next day a large crowd gathered on the still-bloodstained street to pay tribute to the journalist. I joined them, in honor of the haircut, and went to the funeral. I had no faith in politics, the only political person I had ever felt close to was Hayattin Hoca, my literature teacher at school. Although he never mentioned politics we used to find socialist journals poking out of his files. My skepticism was absolute, how could politics, made up of people, change the world? Anyone who claimed that kindness would save society and make it happy didn't know anything about people. They acted as though selfishness didn't exist, the motherfuckers! The basis of human nature was self interest, greed, and rivalry. When I said these things my customers protested and argued hotly to try and make me change my mind. How can a poetry lover think such things, said one of my customers, as he waited his turn. He stood beside the mirror and read out loud several verses from *Les Fleurs du Mal* that I had put there. The violence showed no signs of abating, we heard people in neighboring streets getting shot. Once a young customer of mine rushed into my barbershop in a terrible state and asked me to hide his gun before the police caught him. I may have occasionally helped someone out, but that didn't mean I gave a damn about politics. The only existence for me was saving up to buy a house, fathering children, and spending my nights with Mahizer. But somehow Mahizer couldn't get pregnant. When we went to a doctor in the second year of our marriage we found out it was me who couldn't have children.

"One night as I was closing up I saw three people attacking a man. It was Hayattin Hoca, my literature teacher from school. Grabbing my knife I rushed out to them and slashed their hands and faces. The attackers, caught unawares, retreated and disappeared into the darkness. Hayattin Hoca hugged me. We talked nonstop as we walked. We went into a tavern in Samatya. We told each other about ourselves. After Darüşşafaka Hayattin Hoca had changed schools twice, reduced his teaching hours and now spent more time on his political activities. He was worried about our country's future. He had heard that I had gone to university to study French language and literature. But he hadn't heard that I had dropped out in the second year because I had to work, it saddened him when I told him. When he asked if I was still interested in poetry I mumbled several verses from Baudelaire that I had memorized in his classes. He beamed at me proudly and reminded me of the time I had won first prize in the poetry reading competition. We clinked our glasses of rakı. Hayattin Hoca was happy to hear of my marriage, but he was still single. Apparently he had fallen in love with one of his students a few years previously but hadn't declared himself, and once he heard that the girl had married after leaving school he had resigned himself to complete solitude. We drank until dawn. I recited poems from heart and he read out poems he had written for the girl he loved. I don't know how I got home, it wasn't until I had sobered up the next day that I remembered hearing Mahizer's name in Hayattin Hoca's poems.

"I didn't go to Hayattin Hoca's funeral a month later. He was shot in the head with a single bullet as he was leaving school. In his file they found a poem dedicated to me, about brave horse riders in a storm. A friend of his brought it to me. That night I clung to Mahizer and begged her not to leave me. Why would I leave you, my foolish husband, she said. I had brought home the box that I had kept for years in the soap drawer at the barbershop. I opened it and took out the scraps of paper with the poems that Mahizer had written me when we were engaged and asked her to read them to me. The scraps of paper smelled of rose and lavender. As Mahizer was reading the poems, I undid her blouse and sucked her breast. I wanted to suckle milk but I could taste the tears flowing down onto her chest. Three months passed. One night Mahizer cried again as she fired questions at me, her voice trembling. She asked who had shot Hayattin Hoca. He never took any liberties with me, she said. For several nights I had been talking in my sleep, saying he had deserved to die. Who else have I talked about? I asked. You mean there are more? asked Mahizer. I swore on my mother's life. I had nothing to do with it, I said, words spoken in dreams don't mean anything. I put on my coat and went out into the cold. What a delusion! My weary soul. Foolish old man. My soul that used to have wings of fire. It would take flight at the slightest impetus. Oh, gasping sick man, worthless workhorse. Is there anything in the world that won't end in ashes? My soul, miserable, senile, bleeding wretch. Neither the zest of life nor love's torrent can reach you now. Time skips a beat. As I breathe, I feel myself—my self—dissolving, losing my bearings. How did I reach the top of the well, how did I lift the stones and raise its cover, I wasn't in my right mind. I leant down into the well and shouted. Mother! When you forced your breast into my mouth why did you give me tears instead of milk? Mother! When you clung to my puny body why did you feverishly repeat my dead father's name instead of mine? I knew you were thinking of my father when you called me Kamil instead of Kamo. On your last night too you cried out Kamil. I knew the stone you were standing on was loose. You were bound to fall, mother! You said I was born thanks to my father, that I owed this life to him. Damn it! The dead were dead and gone! You didn't understand how cruel the light was. The light only showed things from the outside. It stopped us from looking inward."

Kamo the Barber said the last words as though he were mumbling to himself. First he bent his head forward, then tossed it back and banged it against the wall. "An epileptic fit," said the Doctor, quickly laying Kamo down on the floor. He placed the piece of bread that we had been saving for our new cellmate, who could arrive at any moment, between Kamo's teeth, to stop him from biting his tongue. I held his feet. Kamo had lost all control and was convulsing, his mouth foaming.

The cell door opened. The guard towering above us yelled, "What's going on?"

"Our friend is having an epileptic fit," said the Doctor. "We need something with a strong smell to bring him around, like cologne or an onion."

The guard stepped inside, saying, "Tell me if your ass of a friend dies, so I can clear out the body." But to be on the safe side he leaned over Kamo and checked his face. The guard stank of blood, mold, and damp. The reek of alcohol on his breath made it clear that he had been drinking before going on duty. He waited a while, then straightened up and spat on the floor.

As the guard was closing the door, I saw the face of the girl they had brought in today in the grille of the opposite cell. Her left eye was closed, her lower lip was split. It was her first day here but it was clear from the color of her wounds that they had been torturing her for a long time. Once the door had closed I crouched down onto the floor. Clinging to Kamo's legs, I pressed my face down on the concrete so I could observe the guard's feet from the crack under the door. The guard had returned to the girl and was waiting, motionless. I could tell because his feet weren't moving. Hadn't the girl left the grille, wasn't she sitting in the darkness of her cell? The guard wasn't swearing, he wasn't banging on the girl's door and threatening her, or bursting into her cell and throwing her against the wall. Meanwhile Kamo's body relaxed and tensed alternately, he struggled to free his legs from my grip. He had stretched out his arms and was thrashing them against the cell walls. After a final convulsion Kamo's spasms ceased and he stopped wheezing. The guard surveying the opposite cell left the girl alone and departed, his footsteps growing distant in the corridor. I stood up and looked out. When I saw the girl at the grille I nodded to her, but she didn't move. After a while she went back inside, disappearing into the dark.

The Doctor leaned against the wall and stretched his legs. He placed Kamo's head on his lap. "He'll be able to sleep for a while in this position," he said.

"Can he hear us?" I asked.

"Some patients can hear when they're in this state, others can't."

"It's not a good idea for him to tell us so much about himself, let's warn him."

"You're right, he should stop."

The Doctor looked at Kamo the Barber as though he were putting his own son, and not a patient, to sleep. He wiped the sweat from his forehead and smoothed his hair.

"How's the girl in the opposite cell?" he asked.

"She has old scars all over her face, it's obvious they've been torturing her for a long time," I said.

I looked at Kamo the Barber's tranquil visage. His customer was right to find him strange, how could a man like him love poetry? He was sleeping like a child exhausted from playing outside all day. Beneath his eyelids he was now leaning over his well, staring down into the darkness. He had held on to damp stones so many times he didn't trust the stable ones, he descended with the aid of a rope he had lowered down into the well, and let himself go in the water. There Kamo is both north and south, he possesses the east and the west. His outside existence has been wiped clean, he has become a well in the well and water in the water.

"How long was I unconscious?" murmured Kamo, half opening his eyes.

"Half an hour," said the Doctor.

"My throat's dry."

"Sit up slowly."

Kamo sat up and leaned against the wall. He drank from the plastic water bottle the Doctor held out to him.

"How do you feel?" asked the Doctor.

"Shit, I feel tired but rested as well. I should have told you what I've got. It started in the spring right after my mother died. It didn't last long, a few weeks later I was better. But they say the past comes back to haunt you. After Mahizer left me the fits started again."

"Demirtay and I will take care of you here. I'm going to tell you something important, Kamo. It's good to chat, but there are rules in these cells. We don't know who is going to give in to the torture and confess all their secrets, or who is going to tell the interrogators whatever they hear in here. We can make small talk and share our troubles to pass the time, but we have to keep our secrets to ourselves. Do you understand?"

"Aren't we ever going to tell each other the truth?" said Kamo. Gone was the tough man of a moment ago, in his place was this docile patient.

"Keep your secrets to yourself," replied the Doctor. "We

don't know why they brought you here, and we don't want to know."

"Don't you wonder what kind of a person I am?"

"Look, Kamo, if we were outside I wouldn't want to meet you or be in the same place as you. But in here we're at the mercy of pain, we're constantly embracing death. We're in no position to judge anyone. Let's heal each other's wounds. Let's not forget that in here we're the purest form of human there is, the suffering human."

"You don't know me," said Kamo. "I haven't told you anything yet."

The Doctor and I looked at each other and waited in silence.

It was clear that Kamo the Barber selected each word carefully and weighed it cautiously before he spoke.

"My memory that I was just complaining about is like a greedy moneylender, it hoards every word. You, student kid, do you know that it was Confucius who was supposed to have said those words in that story you just told? In my barbershop, above the mirror, in line with the national flag, there was a poster of a half-naked woman. Those words were on the bottom of the poster. The girl was wearing a brightly colored skirt that she had pulled up. She was running as fast as her long legs could carry her, with her head turned shyly toward me and my waiting customers. In between her legs were the words 'a woman with her skirt up can run faster than a man with his pants down.' Sometimes my customers would stare at the girl's beauty and think that couldn't be true, fantasizing that if they ever got to be with her they would be so happy together they wouldn't give a damn about anything else. When one day a writer customer of mine looked at the poster and sighed 'Ah Sonya!' we all heard him and thought that must be the young girl's name. When it was his turn for a haircut the writer sat on the chair and launched into a long conversation. Eventually he started telling me about myself. He said I had a soul like the Russians. Seeing my surprise he repeated things I had said on his previous visits that he had retained.

"If I had been born in Russia I would either be a member of the Karamazov family, or live like an underground man, or be as wretched as Sonya's father, Marmeladov. Everything the writer said about those Dostoyevsky characters was true of me. Dostoyevsky depicted them with the same mental condition, first Marmeladov in *Crime and Punishment*, then in part one of *Notes from Underground*, and finally in the whole of *The Brothers Karamazov*. There wasn't a big difference between them, but it was big enough to take them on incredible journeys during their lives. Sonya's father Marmeladov was a broken man, he knew he was pitiful, and was full of self condemnation. He was a miserable wretch who was a victim of his fate. Sonya adored her miserable father. Ah Sonya, that beautiful, destitute prostitute! Who wouldn't commit brutal murders for her sake if it meant being worthy of her love? As for the Underground Man, he revealed his own wretchedness so he could expose the wretchedness of others, and manifested it as wrath. His obsession with finding people like himself, with holding a mirror to their faces, led him to tear his soul to shreds. The Karamazovs' journey on the other hand was another thing entirely. They were at odds with themselves, with others, and even with life itself. They neither felt desperate like Marmeladov, nor regarded their wretchedness as a tool for exposing others like the Underground Man. Their wretchedness was their inescapable destiny, a constantly suppurating wound. They strove not to accept life, but to dispute it, and, when they suffered, to spill their blood and smear it over the face of life. That life has opened up a new page for me too now. Damn you! Take that look off your face, stop staring at me like those people burning in hell. I have lent you my ear for three days, listened to your stories and heard your groans after you were tortured. Now you can lend me your ears."

Kamo gave us a contemptuous look, raised the water bottle to his lips again, and continued.

"I don't know what lies ahead, will they release me, or take me away to be tortured like you? Pain turns the body into its slave, while fear does the same to the soul, and people will sell their souls to save their bodies. I'm not afraid. I'm still going to talk to the torturers and tell them the secrets I haven't told you.

"I'll tell them whatever they want to know, I'll answer their questions by putting my whole soul in their hands. Just as tailors turn a jacket inside out and rip out the lining, I'll rip out my liver and lay it open before them, I'll tell them more than they want to know. At first they'll be interested, they'll write down everything I say in case it's useful, but after a while the things I tell them will make them uneasy. They'll realize that I'm telling them things about themselves that they don't want to know. What people fear most in this life is themselves. They too will be afraid and will try to silence me, the men who tortured me to make me talk will hang me with my arms outstretched, give me electric shocks and soak me in my own blood to make me hold my tongue. They will be just as horrified by the truth as I am. I'll tell them everything about myself and make them face up to the side of their own selves that they don't want to see. They will stare in disbelief, like lepers who look into the mirror for the first time, they will retreat until they hit the wall, and because they can't do anything to change themselves they will think the only solution is to smash the mirror, in other words, my face and my bones. But cutting out my tongue won't do them any good, my groans will deafen them and imprison their minds in one single truth. Damn it, even in their own homes, they'll wake up in the middle of the night in a cold sweat and gulp down bottles of the strongest drink. But there's no escape, the truth runs in your jugular vein. They either accept it or slit their wrists. They all have loving wives who will take them in their arms and comfort them, then light a cigarette and put it between their trembling fingers. They live in mortal fear of discovering their own truth. Now I know why they haven't taken me away for interrogation these past three days. They're afraid of me."

Kamo the Barber was talking from the deepest pit, from the edge of the pit, from the darkest corner of that pit. He had hidden for too long, he had been crushed and was profoundly damaged. There was no way of knowing whether he had gone into hiding because he was damaged or if it was going into hiding that had damaged him. The darkness that was so dear to Kamo stifled me. When they blindfolded me and led me out of the iron gate they were taking me out of the world I knew. I appreciated the value of direction, I struggled to cling to the chaos of words in my mind. It wasn't easy to think in the dark. Life was right beside me and I wanted to return to it.

Kamo was peering out of half-open, weary eyes. Even the tiny ray that was casting its light into the cell made him uneasy, perhaps that was why he wanted to sleep all the time.

"There was only one time when my mother didn't tell me off for standing over the well," he said. "That day she had dreamt of burning sticks. It was a sign that she would overcome something that was troubling her. Strange, the first time I ever dreamt of burning sticks was in this cell. What trouble could I have overcome while my past remained frozen?"

"This time will end too, just as the old days ended," said the Doctor. "Your dream is telling you that you will get out of here and that you'll be free again."

"Free? Nothing has been the same for me since I lost Mahizer, there's not a single stone inside me that's not loose."

"You're tormenting yourself. Everyone goes through this kind of thing at some point." The Doctor waited for a moment, before continuing. "You need to think positively in here, Kamo. Dream that we're all outside. For instance, imagine we're chatting on Ortaköy beach and contemplating the shore on the other side."

The Doctor liked to take us out of here and transport us to the outside world. He taught me how to do that. It was better to dream about the outside world than to dwell on our troubles. Time, which stood still in the cell because our bodies were trapped, started ticking again once our minds went outside. Our minds were stronger than our bodies. The Doctor said that could be proven medically. In here we often dreamed about the world outside, for example we shared the happiness of people walking on the seashore. We waved to the people dancing to loud music on a boat near Ortaköy shore. We walked past lovers with their arms around each other. As the sun was setting on the horizon the Doctor bought a bag of green plums from a street vendor. Smiling, he offered me the first one.

Last week they pushed me into the cell, half-conscious. I was muttering incomprehensibly because my lips were dry. The Doctor, thinking I was asking for water, sat me up to try and give me water, and opened my eyes. "I don't want water, I want green plums," I said. We laughed about that for two days.

The Doctor asked Kamo if he too would like some green plums.

Kamo wasn't impressed by the story. His mind didn't work on the same plane as ours. "The past, Doctor," he said, "our past . . ."

The Doctor brought down his hand that was poised in the air as though he were offering him a plum. "Our past is somewhere that's too far away to reach. We should concentrate on tomorrow instead," he said.

"Do you know what, Doctor, God can't change the past either. God, the all powerful, rules over the present and the future, but can't touch the past. Where does that leave us, when even He is powerless to change the past?"

For the first time the Doctor eyed Kamo with pity, then he smiled. "Every barber I know likes talking. They talk about football or women. Why do you talk about these things? If I were your customer I wouldn't go back to your shop. Maybe barbers shouldn't go to university, otherwise where would we men go to chat about football and women?"

"I'd still ask the same questions even if I didn't have an education."

"Think of it this way, Kamo. Your childhood with your mother was unhappy, but meeting your wife set you free of your past. The same thing will happen again, once you find new happiness in the future you'll forget the old days."

"New happiness?"

The Doctor took a deep breath. He rubbed his cold hands together. He looked up at the ceiling, as though trying to decide on the best way of dealing with a difficult patient in his consulting room. Just then we heard the heavy sound of the iron gate.

We looked at each other. We could hear the interrogators' lighthearted banter as they entered. We listened hard to hear what they were saying in the corridor.

"Did he spill?"

"Give it a day or two and he will."

"What was it today?"

"Electric shocks, hanging, high pressure water."

"Did you get his name and address?"

"We know that already."

"Is he a big shot or some little shit?"

"This old codger, he's a big fish."

"Which cell?"

"Number 40."

That was our cell.

We piled our cold feet on top of each other, trying to get one last bit of warmth. At any moment we could leave and never return. Or we could leave sane and return mad, go from being human to animal without a soul.

"They're coming for me," said Kamo, turning to face the grille. "Perfect timing."

The footsteps grew closer. The cell door opened. Two guards supported a heavily built elderly man by the underarms, they struggled to carry him. The man's head had fallen onto his chest, his face and body a bloody mess. "Here's a new friend for you." The Doctor and I stood up, brought the man inside and lay him tenderly on the floor. The guards closed the door and left.

"He's practically frozen," said the Doctor. He examined him to see if he was still bleeding or had any fractures. Lifting his eyelids, he checked his eyes in the dim light. He took one of the man's feet and started rubbing it. I took his other foot between my two hands, it was like ice.

Kamo the Barber said, "I'll lie on the floor, you can put him on top of me, we have to protect him from the concrete."

The Doctor and I held the man and lay him on Kamo's back. We lay down on either side of him and held him. In the past people used to snuggle up to their cows and dogs to keep warm. The cell took us back to the beginning of time. We were embracing a complete stranger in an attempt to give him life.

"Are you all right, Kamo?"

"I'm fine, Doctor. It's as though this man has been buried naked in snow."

"Snow?"

"Yes, the day I was arrested it snowed nonstop," said Kamo the Barber.

"Apparently winter has come early this year. The day I was arrested the weather was beautiful."

I listened while the Doctor and Kamo the Barber chatted. They didn't stop long enough for me to join in. For the past three days Kamo had either been ignoring or berating me. He occasionally referred to me as "student," but more often it was "kid." I was eighteen years old and would have liked him to treat me with at least some of the respect he showed the Doctor. When I was arrested I had a good idea of the trials that lay ahead of me, but I never imagined that a problematic cellmate would be one of them. Pain had no boundaries, you either resisted it or it defeated you, but I had no idea how to react to Kamo. When I was arrested one of the civil policemen kept calling me "kid," as he crushed my fingers in the car. "It will be a shame to waste your life, kid, you'd better talk now," he had declared. When I said "I'm not a kid," he put his two hands around my neck and tried to choke me. The other policemen must have stopped him, either that or they were playing their usual tricks. They knew my real name and asked who I was going to meet. I was more surprised by their knowing the time and the place of the meeting than by their knowing me. "I'm not a kid, I'm a university student. I was on way to class, I don't know what meeting you're talking about." "Why were you running away then?" As soon as I realized they were following me I took the first turn and started running. "I was late, I was just trying to get to class on time."

Half an hour later they took me to the meeting place, the bus stop in front of the University of Istanbul library. They

ordered me to wait at the bus stop and said they would shoot me
if I tried to escape. The civil policemen got out of the cars and
dispersed. From their vantage points they set about observing
everyone waiting at the bus stop with me. I looked at my watch,
it was three minutes to two. Our rules for meetings were very
strict. We had to arrive at the earliest three minutes before
the designated meeting time, if the meeting didn't take place
we couldn't wait any longer than three minutes. As I looked
at the people getting off the bus in front of me I feared seeing
the person I was waiting for. I was surprised to see so many
people at this bus stop where I came so often. Everywhere
there were students, tourists, men in suits. Time was ticking
on, it was two minutes to two. I checked out the people on the
other side of the road looking over to my side. In the crowd
everyone looked alike. The person I was meeting may well
have been one of the people weaving their way hastily through
the cars and crossing over to this side of the road. Perhaps
they would realize this was a trap, perhaps sense something
odd about the civil police surveying me. They would perceive
I had been caught from the distressed look on my face and
immediately dissolve into the crowd. I consulted my watch,
it was one minute to two. On an impulse I leapt out in front
of the approaching bus. The impact sent me flying. I heard
screams. Several people put my arms over their shoulders and
carried me to a car. They started punching me in the back seat.
"Who was it? Tell me which one it was, bastard." They put the
barrel of the gun in my mouth. I couldn't open my eyes, my
head was spinning. "You've got five seconds before I pull the
trigger." Five seconds later they took the gun out of my mouth
and squeezed my testicles. I wanted to scream but they covered
my mouth. Tears ran down my face.

No matter how much you think you have braced yourself,
the reality of pain numbs your mind. Pain brings time to a

standstill and you lose all sense of future. Reality disappears and the whole universe is restricted to your body. You feel as though you will remain frozen in this moment forever, that there will never again be another moment. It was like Kamo the Barber's imprisonment in the past. I understood him. But why now, why out of billions of years of time, do we have to be at the precise moment in which I am suffering pain, I thought, asking myself meaningless questions. It was like the child who is wary of everything after it has burnt its hand on a hot glass. I knew no other definition except pain, and could think of nothing except time. If I thought he would answer my questions I would ask the Doctor. The Doctor believed not thinking about pain would make us more resistant than thinking about it. When endless time came and convened on my body I couldn't stop myself from thinking: out of all the billions of years during which time had flowed, why were we now at the precise moment in which I was being oppressed by pain?

The Doctor raised his head and asked me too, "Are you all right?"

"I'm fine."

"We should get up, before Kamo freezes."

We removed our jackets and spread them out on the floor. Kamo the Barber didn't have a jacket. We lay the elderly man on top of the jackets. The Doctor took the man's pulse and touched his neck. He wet his fingers and pressed them to the man's parched lips. The man coughed, his chest heaved violently.

The three of us sat in a row with our backs against the wall. We looked at the elderly man's face and long hair. His feet practically touched the door. His bulk took up the entire cell as he lay there like a corpse in a grave. We had already been buried in that same grave. Cities were built on the ruins of old cities, while the dead were buried in the soil of the old dead. Istanbul breathed in unison with the underground cells where we lived, while our skin bore the odor of the dead. The wreckage of old cities and the people of old was stamped on our minds. Our burden was heavy. Which is why pain attacked our flesh so viciously.

"Will he live?" asked Kamo the Barber. "If he doesn't we'll have more room, like we did before. There was barely space for three, now there are four of us. How are we supposed to lie down now?"

The Doctor did not reply to Kamo. He placed his hand on the elderly man's heart, as though touching a sacred book. He closed his eyes and waited. There was a serenity about him that would resurrect the dead and heal pain. "He'll come around, he'll come around," he murmured. When they brought me in unconscious did he look at me in the same way, did he calmly wait for me to come around too? Did he listen to my breathing more than he listened to his own?

I stood up and put my face to the grille. The girl in the opposite cell was at the grille too. I nodded to her. I searched for a change in her expression, some response. We couldn't speak, the slightest whisper would echo through the corridor and reach the guards. I pointed at her and tried to mime, "Are you okay?" She scrutinized me, then nodded. She looked rested, as though she had slept. The blood on her lower lip had gone but her eye was still closed. She raised her left hand to the level of the grille and started tracing letters in the air with her index finger. I didn't understand what she was asking about, when she realized she wrote again. "How is the new arrival, Uncle Küheylan?" she asked. She knew the man's name, she knew who he was. Likewise I traced letters in the air. "He'll live," I said, then introduced myself. "My name is Demirtay."

As the girl was tracing her name with her slender finger, the sound of the elderly man's groans made me turn back. The man opened his eyes. He tried to work out where he was. He looked at the Doctor and Kamo hovering above him. He observed the walls and the ceiling. He brushed his hands over the concrete he was lying on.

"Istanbul?" he rasped. "Is this Istanbul?"

He closed his eyes, and fell asleep with a strange expression that suggested happiness rather than someone about to lose consciousness.

# 2<sup>ND</sup> DAY

*Told by the Doctor*

## THE WHITE DOG

"Uncle Küheylan, did you think this cell was Istanbul? Right now we're underground, everywhere above us there are streets and buildings. The city stretches from one end of the horizon to the other, even the sky finds it hard to cover its totality. Underground, there's no difference between east and west, but if you observe the wind above ground it meets the waters of the Bosphorus and you can gaze at the sapphire-colored waves from a hill. If your first view of Istanbul, which your father told you so much about, had been from a ship's deck instead of inside this cell, you would understand, Uncle Küheylan, that this city does not consist of three walls and an iron door. When people arrive by ship from distance places, the first thing they see are the Princes' Islands on the right, draped in a cloud of mist. You think those silhouettes are flocks of birds that have landed there to rest. The city walls on the left, which snake along the entire length of the coastline, eventually meet with a lighthouse. As the mist lifts, the colors multiply. You contemplate the domes and the elegant minarets as though you were admiring the wall rugs in your village. When you are engrossed in the picture on a wall rug you imagine a life that you know nothing about is weaving its course without you in another world; well, now a ship is transporting you to the heart of that life. A person consists of the breath he takes during a sigh. Life is not enough, you tell yourself. You think the expanding city, with its city walls on the horizon, its towers and its domes, is a new sky.

"On the deck, the wind snatches up a woman's red shawl and carries it to the shore ahead of the ship. You dissolve into the crowd and wander through the cobbled streets, just like that shawl. When you arrive at Galata Square in the midst of the cries of street vendors you take a packet of tobacco out of your pocket and roll a cigarette. You watch an old woman advancing slowly along the road, holding a sheep by a lead. A young boy calls out to her, old woman, where are you going with that lead around that dog's neck? The old woman turns and looks first at the sheep, then at the young boy. You blind boy, you think this sheep is a dog, she says. You walk behind the old woman. A youth walking in the opposite direction says the same thing: Old Woman, are you taking your dog for a walk? The old woman turns and looks at her sheep again, grumbling, it's not a dog, it's a sheep, have you been drinking this early in the day? A little further ahead someone else calls out, why have you got a lead around that mangy dog's neck? Then the street becomes deserted and the voices fall silent. When the hunchbacked old woman notices you she asks you, have I lost my mind, Old Man? Have I mistaken a dog for a sheep? Once my mind cleared, the whole world cleared too, all that's left are you, me, and this poor animal. As the old woman talks you look at the animal on the end of the lead. Do you see a sheep or a dog? You're afraid that your day in Istanbul that began with doubt will pledge you a lifetime of doubt.

"The old woman slowly walks away, tugging at her lead. You look not at her but at the things around you, at the things created by mankind. Men have built towers, statues, squares, walls that could never have sprouted out of the earth of their own accord. The sea and the earth existed before men, whereas the world of the city was created by men. You understand that the city was born of men, and that it is reliant on them, like water-dependent flowers. As with the beauty of nature, the beauty of cities lies in their existence. Irregular stones become a temple door, broken marble a dignified statue. You think this is why in the city you mustn't be surprised by sheep being dogs.

"You stroll until the sun plunges behind the rooftops. You drink cool water from an ancient street fountain. When you hear a dog barking you raise your head and look in the direction of the sound. You see the red shawl, it's fluttering on a breeze blowing from Galata toward the sea. Life is such a strange adventure. The shawl that came from the sea returns to the sea; you wonder where a person in the city will return. You walk at a leaden pace toward the street where you heard the dog barking, as though the sign you were searching for is there. You are guided first by a scent, and then by rising smoke, to a dilapidated courtyard further ahead. You approach and peer over the wall. The three youths are sitting on the ground roasting meat over an open fire, laughing and joking as they drink wine. One of them is gently humming a tune. When you see the sheepskin and lead beside them you realize it's the old woman's sheep. These are the same youths who have been following the old woman around all day and teasing her. The old woman eventually fell for their trick and released the sheep, finally convinced it was a dog. The three lads grabbed the sheep, hotfooted it to this courtyard and prepared their banquet."

Uncle Küheylan, who had not taken his eyes off me while I told my story, laughed. I imitated the student Demirtay and repeated the final sentence: "The three lads who grabbed the sheep lost no time in preparing their banquet." Uncle Küheylan laughed harder.

"You speak well, Doctor," he said, "but a voice inside me still tells me this cell is Istanbul. My father used to talk about

Istanbul so much that sometimes I couldn't tell what was the truth and what was make-believe. When I was a child I never knew whether the stories about the underground city with its city walls that stretched from one end to another, or the missing people who lived in the cemetery and only came out at night were real things he had seen, or part of the Thousand and One Nights. As you say, Doctor, living is such a strange adventure. Two weeks ago they blindfolded me in the military police station of a distant village, then I went through a dark corridor and I opened my eyes in my father's Istanbul."

As Uncle Küheylan spoke, he moved his hands, he groped the air and placed two fingers in front of his mouth as though he were holding a cigarette.

"In the evenings my father used to make shadows on the wall in the lamplight with his hands, he would build cities with his skilled fingers. And use them to describe Istanbul. He would make long shadows for ferries and longer ones for trains, then he would project a shadow of a young man waiting beside a tree. When he asked what the young man was waiting for we would all chorus, for his sweetheart. But he insisted on making things otherwise, locking the young man up in dungeons, throwing him into dens of thieves; it was only when we despaired that he would reunite him with his sweetheart. Istanbul is vast, he would say, there is a different life behind every wall, a different wall behind every life. Like a well, Istanbul is both deep and narrow. Some are intoxicated by its depth, others are oppressed by its narrowness. Then my father would say, I'll tell you a true Istanbul story that I witnessed with my own eyes. As he told the tale he would cast picture shadows on the walls with his fingers, taking us out of our tiny house and transporting us to that unknown city that was born in the lamplight and enveloped our nights with its vastness. I grew up on my father's stories, Doctor. I know this door, these walls and this dark ceiling well, this is the place he described."

"It's still only your first day, Uncle Küheylan. Don't be so quick to decide, give it a few days first."

"Doctor, while you were telling your story I felt as though I'd been here for a long time. Is it day or night now?"

"I don't know. We know it's morning when the food arrives."

Usually the interrogators went out on operations at night, in search of new prey. The moments when they captured their new victims were the only times when we could sleep or breathe freely. This was not a rule, they had a different formula for each person. There were times, like the first five days after they brought me here, when they tortured prisoners uninterruptedly day and night, without bringing them to the cell.

"I wonder what's for breakfast today," I said.

"You mean we get different food?"

"Of course, the bread and cheese are never the same. Sometimes the bread is stale and sometimes it's very stale. And some days the cheese is moldy and other days it's rotten. The cook varies our diet all the time."

Uncle Küheylan smiled. For the past two hours he had been leaning against the wall with his legs bent. The wounds on his face were swollen and he was bruised all over. Only his eyes shone. He leaned forward and smoothed the jacket covering his shoulders. "Isn't anyone coming?" he asked Demirtay, who was standing at the grille.

Demirtay came back and crouched down. He shook his head despondently. "We'd hear the iron gate if anyone was coming," he said.

"Didn't the girl say anything when they were taking her away?"

"Not a word."

While Uncle Küheylan was asleep they had come for the girl in the opposite cell. He was worried about her and kept questioning Demirtay.

Uncle Küheylan had been tortured for two weeks in a military camp, then he had made the long journey here. The girl, handcuffed like him, had accompanied him on the journey, together with four armed guards. He worked out from whispered conversations overheard from the guards that they had been traveling for some time, that the girl had come from even further than he had. The girl had not said a word throughout the entire journey, not once moving her blood-encrusted lips. She had not eaten the bread they gave her when they stopped to rest, only drinking water. Uncle Küheylan had told her about himself and his village, and said to the girl listening to him wordlessly, "I trust your silence." The girl had answered with her expression, nodding her approval. These two people who had met for the first time were journeying from one dark hole to another. Because time flows differently on the edge of pain, they had trusted one another.

"Didn't she tell you her name?" asked Uncle Küheylan.

"She did," said Demirtay, "or rather she wrote it."

"What did she write?"

"Zinê Sevda."

"Zinê Sevda," repeated Uncle Küheylan. His face lit up. "Do you think she's mute? Maybe she can speak but prefers not to because she's a prisoner. She wrote you messages in the air with her fingers. Why didn't she answer me in the same way during our journey? Was it because the guards were there?"

Uncle Küheylan held his fingers to his lips as though he were smoking a cigarette, and took a deep drag. Then, exhaling like he was blowing out the smoke, he leaned his head against the wall. He stared into space for a long time. He scrutinized the darkness of the ceiling from wall to wall. He held his fingers to his lips again and inhaled. His actions looked like the things people fantasize about doing when they're alone. He used his hands and lips to pretend he was smoking. As he was taking a drag of his make-believe cigarette he turned his head toward me and our eyes met.

With a completely straight face he mimed the action of taking his cigarette case out of his pocket. He offered it to Demirtay and me. For a moment I was taken aback, but I didn't reject his offer. I made as if I were taking a cigarette paper from the tobacco case in his empty hand and placed a few strands of tobacco in it. I smoked but I couldn't roll cigarettes. I watched how Uncle Küheylan did it and copied him. Uncle Küheylan put his hand in his pocket again, mimed taking out a box of matches and lit our nonexistent cigarettes. Kamo the Barber was completely oblivious of our little game. He had been asleep for several hours. He was leaning against the wall with his knees bent, his head on his chest.

"The biggest problem for me is finding somewhere to stub out the butts," said Uncle Küheylan. "Most of the time I look for a hole in the wall and put my butts there. If I can't find one I have no choice but to throw them on the floor. Once, I woke up in a pitch black cell. I couldn't even see where the door was, I had to feel my way to it. I leaned my back against the wall and rolled a cigarette. But no sooner had I struck a match than the cell lit up. I saw human teeth, jawbones, and chopped-off fingers embedded in the plaster. They plastered the prison walls with their dead victims. I touched the walls in surprise, and inspected the entire cell. At that moment I forgot that the match was still burning in my hand. When my finger got hot I yelped in pain and threw the match on the floor. My burnt finger hurt for two days."

I realized that Uncle Küheylan was not fantasizing, that those events in his head had really taken place. It was obvious from all his gestures that he thought the cigarette between his fingers was real; from the way he brushed away the odd strands of tobacco that fell onto his lap as he was rolling his cigarette, the way he blew on the tips of his fingers when the match had burned out. I too liked playing with the truth, but although I fantasized about strolling in Istanbul with Demirtay I still remained anchored to the cell, I knew it was my boundary. My mind held onto the reins of my fantasies at all times. And it had never occurred to me to play the game by myself. But there was no question of illusion for Uncle Küheylan, it was all real. He could play when he was alone too, endowing the walls and the darkness with a different life. And he was also being serious when he said that this cell was Istanbul. As far as he was concerned there was no such thing as unreal. Feeling no need to go outside, he brought the world inside, transcending place as well as time here. So, this cell was Istanbul and there was cigarette smoke everywhere.

The smell of cigarette smoke grew more intense, filling the whole cell. I fanned the air with my hands to try and clear the air. I wanted to believe what I was doing. It was like not wanting to wake up from a beautiful dream. We were regressing to our childhood.

As I was looking around for somewhere to stub out the cigarette, Demirtay held out his hand. "Here's an ashtray," he said. His empty hand remained suspended in the air for a few moments, then he put the invisible ashtray on the floor between my legs. I stubbed out my cigarette first, followed by Demirtay.

"Demirtay," said Uncle Küheylan, with a look of amazement, "you've just taught me an illusion by producing that ashtray. I've been squirming for days looking for somewhere to put my butts. You've solved the problem for me."

Uncle Küheylan looked thoughtful. He stroked his beard. He turned to me.

"Doctor," he said. "In a city how can you tell that a dog is a dog? Here people raze hills and erect giant buildings in their place. Streetlamps do the work of the moon and stars. To what extent is a dog a dog when people can change every aspect of nature?"

"In here existence depends on people. If you know people then you know all living things, including dogs," I said. I doubted the truth of my words. I too asked myself similar questions and wondered what the most correct answer was.

"How well can you know people, Doctor? Did you really get to know the patients whose bodies you opened up and whose hearts and livers you examined? When I was a child and my father described Istanbul by projecting hand shadows onto the wall in the lamplight, he said people in Istanbul consisted of similar shadows. He'd say people had left one of their forms behind and taken their other to the city. He saw nothing bad about that, he found it exciting. The appeal of shadows was irresistible, it was impossible not to succumb. My father, who on some nights talked about exotic fruits in our humble home, asked us to imagine them. Once he described an orange, he showed us its color on a piece of fabric, and then he described the segments as he mimed peeling its skin. All together we would indulge in large make-believe banquets. City dwellers build illusions, whereas we were built within the illusion. We could smoke when we had no cigarettes and savor the aroma. Was it because we were poor, or because we had a different perception of existence? My father never told us."

I had witnessed the poor's interest in daydreaming during their illnesses. They waited despondently in the corridors of hospitals that smelled of disinfectant. They would fall gravely ill and die very quickly. In their last breaths they only half looked at the world. There was no reproach in their expression, there was curiosity. I could see their desire to live in Uncle Küheylan.

"Humans are the only living things who aren't content to be themselves, Doctor. A bird is just a bird, it reproduces and flies. A tree just turns green and produces fruit. But humans are different, they've learned how to fantasize. They can't be satisfied with what already exists. They want to fashion earrings out of copper, build palaces from stone, their eyes are constantly turned toward the invisible. The city is the land of dreams, my father used to say, it has endless possibilities, and people there aren't a part of nature, they're its sculptor. They build, they assemble, they create. In this way they mold themselves, while making tools they shape themselves, too. People started out as a humble piece of marble, but in the city they converted their existence into a magnificent statue. That's why they make fun of their original unrefined selves. In the city ridiculing others is sacred, they feel superior to anyone who isn't like themselves. They strive to turn soil into concrete, water into blood, the moon into a destination, they change everything. And as they change it, time accelerates, and as it accelerates, human desire becomes irrepressible. As far as people are concerned, yesterday is dead and gone, and today is uncertain. Dogs and love and death are uncertain. People regard them all with the same suspicion and enthusiasm. And my father, who was used to all that, was a different person in the city, he always returned to the village as a stranger. He was reluctant to embrace us and waited until he had reverted to his old self.

"My father used to compare this tendency to the depth intoxication suffered by deep sea divers. City intoxication he called it. Those were the only times he drank wine. Apparently the most dedicated wine drinkers and the most incurable dreamers are also sailors. Once my father was locked up in a cell with an old sailor and witnessed his nightmare. The elderly sailor dreamt that his ship was sinking and woke up in a cold sweat. According to him a white whale roamed the dark seas, dragging ships toward storms in its wake. Every sailor's dream was to see the white whale, pursue it through the waves and harpoon it to death. A captain who navigated distant seas was the only one who succeeded in finding the white whale. The captain harbored a passionate hatred of this sea monster, which had torn off one of his legs many years previously. When their paths crossed again the white whale's fury clashed with that of the captain. Eventually the whale destroyed the great ship, sending the captain and all his crew to the bottom of the sea. Only one deckhand survived to tell the tale of the long chase in the sea and the last battle amid the waves. Since that day every sailor dreams of sighting the white whale, even more than they dream of sighting a mermaid. As my father projected the shadow of the whale onto the wall of our room with his fingers, making it swim up and down for us, he would say that the Istanbul sailors had gone to ruin on the same road. The ones who roamed from north to south and east to west returned months later to the misty port, dejected, empty-handed, and utterly defeated. Many was the sailor who lost his mind to fantasies of the white whale, who plunged daggers into his own flesh, whose sleep was haunted by nightmares. The elderly sailor in my father's cell was one. It was true, Doctor, like all my father's stories, it held hidden secrets, and very few people had ever heard it."

Uncle Küheylan took a deep breath. He sat up straight, as though about to make an important statement. He turned to face me and said, "I already knew the story about the old woman that you just told us. I heard it from my father. He laughed as he told us about the old woman who mistook her sheep for a dog, and about the youths who snatched it and feasted on it."

"Is your father still alive?" I asked.

"Do I look that young? My father died a long time ago," he said.

He raised his hand and felt the wall with his fingers as though to confirm the cell existed. He was probably thinking that his father had also been in this cell many years ago. He searched the walls for evidence of his presence. Although there was no evidence of his father there was plenty of evidence of our other predecessors. I also touched the wall, exploring it very slowly with my fingers.

"Uncle Küheylan," I said, "If you know the story about the old woman I know your story about the white whale too. I could have told you many a tale, from when the captain sailed the seas for forty years attempting to harpoon the whale, to the life of the sole surviving deckhand."

"You already knew the sailors' adventure?"

Seeing Uncle Küheylan's surprise, Demirtay joined in.

"I knew it too," he said.

A faint sound came from the corridor. Demirtay motioned to us to be quiet, crouching down, he looked out from the crack under the door. The guards sitting in the room at the top of the corridor occasionally did the rounds of the cells, trying to catch prisoners talking. Each guard had his own rules, some eavesdropped silently and gathered secrets, while others burst in and disciplined whoever was talking. Demirtay sat up. "It's all right, he's gone," he said.

"So you knew about the whale," said Uncle Küheylan.

"In this cell we tell each other stories that we already know, Uncle Küheylan. At first it was just Demirtay and me, there were times when we told the same story twice. We'll tell it a third time for you."

The student Demirtay, who was sitting by the door, motioned to us to be quiet again. We heard the faint sound of footsteps. The guard's shadow was cast onto the bars of the grille, then slowly drifted by. The footsteps did not go much further before they stopped. The guard was listening at each cell in turn. We looked at each other. Demirtay and I had grown used to these inspections and would sometimes sit for long spells in silence. When the guards' rounds went on for a long time we tried to sleep instead of waiting, then we would hear a cell door opening. We would hear the sound of beating. Some prisoners would beg, others would protest. Once the guards had gone back to their room, Demirtay and I would dream we had left this place and go far away. We would board a cargo ship with a Panama flag that was passing through the Istanbul Bosphorus and heading toward the Black Sea. A cool breeze would blow on the deck, as we cruised in the company of the choppy waves and the seagulls. When night fell we would go down into our cabin. We would watch television with a deckhand whose hands were blackened with oil. We would tell each other about whichever film was on. If the film lasted two hours we would make the story last two hours. The cabin was as tiny as this cell; when we felt tired we would curl up and go to sleep. It was cold there too.

If Kamo the Barber had woken up while we were listening to the guards' footsteps and seen us sitting in silence, lost in faraway thoughts, like old men in coffeehouses, what would he have done? Instead of wondering whether anything had happened while he had been asleep, would he be thinking of how unbearable everyone except himself was, and wondering why he was forced to put up with us? He would not speak nor feel the need to ask questions. Wearily he would let his head fall onto his chest once again and nod off to sleep. Before going to sleep he would avail himself of some excuse to reproach Demirtay. He was permanently down a well, while we were outside it. He knew himself, that's what he said, whereas we had grown too arrogant and now had to face up to ourselves here. We had dabbled too much in the light. That's why we went through life in such a state of confusion and foolishness. We were hopeless cases. Kamo had no other option but to curse and let us be.

The day Kamo arrived I was alone in the cell. He was as on edge as a cat enclosed in a hut with a dog. I asked if he was wounded, he did not reply. I introduced myself, but he fired questions at me as though he hadn't understood. "Who are you? How long have you been in this cell? Why have they put me in with you?" He was filthy, he stank, he was hungry. He hesitated in accepting the bread I offered him, he stared at me as he reached out his hand to take it. We had met in the wrong place. I had arrived first, he was new. He was ready to sit and wait in silence for hours, but also to fly at my throat and choke me. Was this the hold of a ship that had lost its route, or the bottom of a precipice that he had no idea how to get out of? There were just three walls, one door and a blood-soaked man. He thought if he closed his eyes he would wake up in a different place, that the place would be transformed in an instant. He stared with curiosity, trying to comprehend his own existence all over again. When we heard a scream from outside he raised his head. Whose voice was that echo? Was it his own? How far away was the wall where the voices came from? There was a very fine line between believing in himself and losing himself; was Kamo afraid of his head spinning on that line?

Knowing in your mind that you couldn't share pain was one thing, but discovering it with your body was something else entirely. Whenever we came around after suffering unendurable pain, we thought months or years had passed. "Was it a brief, fleeting moment?" We puzzled over that, and were terrified that the moment might turn out to be the longest ever. When it came to pain, time got deeper instead of longer. It was as though Kamo the Barber already knew that from experience. When he entered the cell his face was in a mess, his mind in a daze. He had crashed into life's wall too many times and fallen down again and again. If suspicion was a defense mechanism, I could understand his icy attitude. I gave him bread and water and talked to him. I was no stranger; like him, I stood at death's threshold. Kamo the Barber examined the bloodstains on the walls, inhaled the smell of death hanging on the air and said, "A person has no island but himself." Was it indifference talking? Despair? In those cases I could always find the right words to soothe any problem. "Hope is better than what we have," I said, pointing to the light shining in through the grille, "hope is better than what we have." He stared at me blankly. I too had gazed at the walls in just the same way the day they had put me in the cell. Our borders here were walls and people.

Kamo the Barber's uneasiness and aloofness did not abate as the days passed. He had exhausted all the seas that would beckon to him, all the chasms he would clear, before he came here. His ill humor masked an ancient wound.

"So, this is what the depths of Istanbul are like," he said, looking at the ceiling. "Just as I imagined."

What had he imagined? Why was he so attached to this city when he had the choice of leaving? It takes three days to become acquainted with a city, but three generations to really know it. It took time to clear the solid walls separating acquaintance and in-depth knowledge, it couldn't be achieved in a moment. Those same walls existed in both cities and people. If the depths of the city were dark, so were the depths of people. Damp and cold. No one wanted to descend into the darkness inside them and come face to face with themselves. No one except Kamo the Barber. He looked inward. He had got to know the depths of the city by examining his own soul. "Just as I imagined." For some people suffering was the only teacher they needed. Kamo didn't need three days, or three generations, for him to know the city intimately; three deep wounds had sufficed.

Uncle Küheylan, on the other hand, had come to a city he had dreamed about. Here he saw a whole new nature, a new man, in stark contrast with the nature of the village where he grew up. He spoke in the tones of delirious poets, wild-eyed explorers and crazed lovers, setting greater store by a reality he had never seen than his own reality. That's why the underground was good for him, if he had seen Istanbul from the surface he may well have been disappointed. Misfortune did not lurk in every corner of this city that had turned into a site for seeing, tasting, and pleasure, but gone too was the enchanted world of tales of old. The city that the first generations had assailed with all their energy and creativity had been replaced by lust. The driving force of love for people, for art, for dogs, was lust. Like children running into the forest and getting lost, eating everything they lay their hands on but still feeling hungry. I couldn't tell Uncle Küheylan those things. In a cell you had to know when to keep quiet. I couldn't say that beauty in one place is immediately lost in another, or that so many youths search in vain for a dream city.

When I was a child the lifeblood of Istanbul pulsed in the streets, but it quickly filled first with roads, then with squares, then with growing numbers of cars and grand buildings, and disappeared from our lives. Perhaps it had started to disappear before, and I just hadn't noticed. As I left childhood behind me, growing taller by the year, architecture got taller too; progressively higher buildings sprang up on every corner. And now, were the streets dirty or grimy? Were our lives, which we lived in the streets before there were tower blocks, dingy? In the past, when the city used to sprawl out in all directions, houses would never presume to grow vertically in floors and block out the sky. Buildings were limited to the threshold of where the sky was visible. I could sense that even as a child. I could see the sky in whichever street I happened to raise my head. At that time the city's skyline stretched out, undulating like a line of small hills that were all joined together. There were large squares beside the domes and towers. No square was crushed beneath giant shadows.

When I had visited Ragıp Paşa Library two weeks previously I noticed that it was no longer the same eye-catching landmark it had been in my childhood. The Ragıp Paşa Library, which used to preside over Laleli hill like a solitary diamond, had grown smaller, and now cowered amongst the crowds, the billboards, and the cars. The ascending pavement meant that its main entrance was now two meters below street level. Passersby did not turn and look at it, or wonder what might lie behind that door. The moment I set foot in the library's courtyard I noticed the absence of the bustle from the street. I felt as though I was in an ancient city. The marble laid hundreds of years ago, the carved stone, and the bronze engravings were part of a forgotten era. The birds flapped their wings gently, the rose bushes shed their leaves in preparation for winter. As I looked around me in wonder, it struck me that people had a right to live without stress, and that the place where they happened to be could make that possible. Time in this cool library flowed differently from time in the city. Here it moved neither forward nor backward but drew circles around itself, as though subject to a different gravity. I pondered questions that had never occurred to me before. How could the world in this courtyard be so different from the world that lay just outside? How could a door transport us from one time to another, as though we were moving from fire to water? Especially when these two worlds were inside each other, when we could see one through the other's window and strain our ears from one to hear the other.

I crossed to the other side of the courtyard to look for the person I was meeting in the library. I walked up the steps and went into the reading room. I remembered the small dome perched on four pillars. The walls were decorated with blue and white tiles. I looked at the books and the handwritten manuscripts in the wooden cabinets. When I used to study here as a child I would raise my head from my books and let my gaze wander inside. I had no idea how long I remained musing. The air on my face felt cool. Suddenly remembering why I was here, I shot a look at the desks in the reading room. All of them except one were occupied by students hard at work. I didn't know who the girl I was meeting was, according to my brief I would recognize her because she would be studying a book on anatomy. Several people glanced in my direction and turned away. I walked slowly, peering at the desks, but the girl I was looking for wasn't there. I consulted the brown wooden clock on the wall. It was ten minutes ahead of mine. Was that clock wrong, or was I late for my appointment? My fear only lasted a moment as I recalled the past. The clock had been the same when I was a child, it had always been ten minutes fast.

I returned to the courtyard.

As I contemplated the courtyard separating the library from the street lying just beyond it, I thought of the sea flowing into the Bosphorus. Istanbul resembled the waters of the Bosphorus that flowed from north to south on the surface, but did the reverse on the seabed. It showed lives that were led in the same place but worked in different ways, lives that were lived side by side but in different eras, it showed that place can rule over time and that, like a vortex, time can be carried to different places. Architects perfected the art of playing with time before physicists. Architects, who built places in the form of tunnels, could make time pass through that tunnel and transport people from one era to another. And time in that small library adjacent to the crowds flowed in a different direction, like an invisible vortex in the depths of the Bosphorus, living its calm, gentle existence in the city's undercurrent.

The hair and clothes of the girls around me all looked the same. I always thought young people looked alike, but that was even more true today. Was it because of my advancing years? Doubtless, given the growing number of gray hairs on my head. I stood on the porch and looked out onto the courtyard. I couldn't see anyone carrying an anatomy book. Perhaps she was there with all the other young people and I hadn't noticed her. But she could see me and would be able to recognize me. I took Jack London's *The Sea Wolf* out of my jacket pocket, ensuring the cover was facing outwards so she could see the title. Several people looked at me. Were they wondering what this man old enough to be their father was doing there? I returned to the reading room. I walked up and down, ostentatiously displaying the book, and looked straight at the girls. They returned my look. Suddenly everyone stood up, pulled out guns and started shouting, "Don't move or you're dead meat!" Several people ran into the reading room from the courtyard and held a gun to my head. "Are you the doctor? Are you the doctor?" When I didn't reply they hit me on the back of my head. I fell down. *The Sea Wolf* tumbled out of my hand and they kicked it away. My ears rang. My head spun.

I felt as though time in here had suddenly stood still, like a broken clock, but when I left the courtyard and heard the clamor of Istanbul I came back to my senses. The police who had laid this trap had surrounded the entire area. A large inquisitive crowd stood on the pavement and watched. Was I a murderer, a thief, a rapist? The crowd pushed and shoved to get a better look at me. As the civil police frog marched me to a car, I looked at the people's faces. Was I living in the same time as them? Uncle Küheylan was right in saying that when people built cities they sculpted themselves at the same time, as though they were made of marble, but if he had seen the people looking at me in the street he would have pondered, then asked: "What has time in the city turned these people into?"

We heard the sound of the iron gate. I stole out of my daydreams and returned to the cell.

"Do you think they've brought Zinê Sevda?" asked Uncle Küheylan.

As the iron gate creaked slowly we wondered which cell the interrogators would choose, who they would take away. There were so many cells here. No soldier in the war thought he would die and neither did we. We were all thinking the same thing: In a moment they would take someone out through the iron gate, but who would it be? The best way of evading that question was to think about better things. Maybe it was morning and our bread and cheese had arrived.

Kamo the Barber raised his head and looked at the grille. "I wish they'd hurry up and come," he said.

"They must have brought food. Are you very hungry?" I asked.

Kamo didn't reply, he took no notice of the smile on my face. He focused on the light coming through the grille.

"Were you able to sleep?" I asked. "We talked for a long time."

"Your talking didn't bother me, but that dog's barking kept waking me up."

"Barking?"

"Didn't you hear it?"

"No," I said, "what would a dog be doing here?"

"You were too busy chatting, you didn't notice it. The sound came from far away, beyond the walls."

"You were dreaming."

"I know the difference between dreams and reality, Doctor. Every time I heard the dog barking I opened my eyes to make sure I was in the cell. The barking was as real as this cell."

Uncle Küheylan placed his hand on Kamo's shoulder. "You're right," he said, "the barking must have come from far away and we didn't notice it."

Kamo looked first at the hand on his shoulder, then at Uncle Küheylan's face. "It sounded like the barking of the white dog. The white dog's loud bark."

Uncle Küheylan removed his hand.

When we heard talking outside we all turned toward the door.

"These are the ones I'm taking," said one of the speakers. As he didn't say their names he must have been showing the guard a piece of paper.

"They're all in the same cell," replied the guard.

"Which cell?"

"Number 40."

We looked at each other. We put our hands under our arms, for one last shred of warmth. We waited in silence.

The footsteps clattered on the concrete floor like stones. It was difficult to tell how many of them there were but there were more than usual. The corridor stretched endlessly, the interrogators' words echoed on the walls and in our ears. We hoped they would walk past but they stopped at our door. They slid the iron bolt and opened the gray door. Light flooded in.

Kamo the Barber stood up before any of us.

Pushing him, the guard said "You stay put, asshole. Everyone else, out."

## 3RD DAY

*Told by Kamo the Barber*

## THE WALL

"As the sun was near to setting, a traveler clad in a black khirkah, clutching a long staff, arrived at the village nestled amongst the mountains, shrouded by clouds, which, from a distance, with its stone houses and treeless gardens, resembled a rocky wilderness. First he greeted the walls, then the dogs, and then the old men sitting in the shade of the wall. When they asked his name he replied, I am the prophet. He politely declined the villagers' invitations to their houses. Seeing the cracked skin of the bare feet of the traveler, who had come from afar, and the trail of bloodstains he had left in his wake, they pressed him to accept, and offered him food. He drank only water and announced in soft tones, I will be the guest and eat the food of whoever believes I am a prophet. The children eyed him with curiosity, and the elders laughed. The traveler spent the night outdoors. In the morning he told them once again that he was a prophet and cried out passionately to the villagers who asked him to perform a miracle: Words that reflect the heart are the greatest miracle! Don't look for any other miracle, believe in the word! No one believed him and the traveler spent that night too outdoors. He drank water and slept side by side with the dogs in the shade of the wall. When he spoke the next day, the children joined in with the elders' laughter. The traveler remained serene. If that wall spoke would you, who refuse to believe me, believe the wall? he asked. Yes, we would, they all replied in unison. The traveler was a man with a black khirkah, patched trousers, and bare feet. He had no possessions except for his staff and the saddlebag slung over his shoulder. He turned and addressed the wall: Hey wall! Tell the old men and the children that I'm the prophet! Although they were skeptical, the villagers waited in silence. The wall began to speak: He's lying! This man is not the prophet!"

How long have I been in the cell by myself? They took the Doctor, the Student, and Uncle Küheylan and left me here. As I was alone I spoke to the wall. I sat and looked at the opposite wall and told stories, laughing by myself. Time passed much more pleasantly when there was no one else here. I didn't have to deal with anyone else's suffering, or put up with their bullshit. I knew about human souls. They wanted the truth but they didn't understand it. What could they believe, after all that sweat, all those possessions, and all that worship: the miracle of the wall speaking or the words the wall said? "He's lying! This man is not the prophet!" Weren't people themselves lies?

If the Doctor and the Student were listening they would say, "We know that story too, we tell each other stories we already know, we share what already exists." Was there any other way? Are there any untold stories, or unspoken words left in the world? I told the customers sitting in my barbershop one spring day when no one wanted to go outside during a sudden spell of rain that lasted for hours, then I told them the story about the traveler. Of all my customers, the Architect Adaza laughed the most at the villagers' bewilderment in the mountain village, spilling his tea over his tie. As Adaza looked into the mirror and laughed at himself too, he didn't know that he would lie awake wide eyed that night. He left in a happy mood and returned early the following morning with bloodshot eyes.

"Kamo, tell me the truth. It's been playing on my mind all night. Tell me, was that traveler the prophet?"

I calmed him down, and made him sit in the chair in front of the mirror with the blue frame. I ordered two glasses of tea from the tea shop next door.

"Adaza," I said, "you're asking me to explain, but will you take my word for it?"

"Yes I will."

Our tea arrived. I took a sip, he paused.

"If I said I were the prophet would you believe me, Adaza?"

He didn't answer. I offered him a cigarette and lit first his, then mine.

"You wouldn't believe that I was the prophet," I continued. "Okay, if that wall spoke, would you believe it?"

Adaza looked at the wall. He studied the picture of the Maiden's Tower, the boat, the seagulls. He scrutinized the basil under the picture and the small radio at great length. His gaze switched to the flag and the poster above the mirror. He became lost in the ingenious smile of the girl in the poster, whose face and not her legs was what all the customers looked at. He became engrossed in the picture, as though he had lost touch with the girl for failing to turn up for their last rendezvous, but still cherished unforgettable memories of her. If he had honored their assignation, would they have lived together happily, somewhere far away from here? Adaza the Architect tore his eyes away from the poster, encountering his own face in the mirror with the blue frame. "Lies!" he said, looking at himself. He paused. He took a deep drag from the cigarette and exhaled toward the mirror. As his face grew hazy in the smoke he repeated, "Lies!" A tear trickled down his face. Without another word he exited through the open door.

He never returned to my shop after that day. I thought he had found a new barber. My wife and his were close friends.

One day she came to our house and told us that Adaza had left home and that no one knew where he was. After he left, their two daughters had fallen ill. His wife asked me to help her, to find Adaza and bring him home. When my wife Mahizer also pressed me to go, I went out to look for him. I looked in architects' clubs, searched the bars in Beyoğlu, scoured the news on page three of the newspapers, and discovered at last that Adaza was hobnobbing with the homeless in the shade of the city walls. After searching the tunnels winding from Sarayburnu to Kumkapı like moleholes, meticulously checking every secret passage, asking glue-sniffing children and cheap prostitutes, I eventually found him one night at Cankurtaran, beside a fire near the railway track section of the city walls. A dozen homeless, penniless outcasts whom fate had spurned were sitting around the fire, passing around a bottle of wine, listening to the arabesque song that one of them was warbling. "Oh how pitiful is a fate like mine." I stood beside a tree and watched them, keeping my distance for a while. As the song continued, "The world is all darkness, where is human kindness," a train passed over the tracks. The ground beneath my feet shook. A flash of yellow light swept over the trees and vanished. By the time the sound of the train had died down, the song was also over. Someone said, "Hey traveler, talk to us like you did last night, tell us some new things."

The traveler was none other than the Architect Adaza. With the support of his long staff, he rose to his feet. He was wearing a black khirkah. Like the traveler in the story, his feet were bare. He was like an orator addressing a venerable audience. He examined everyone carefully, then started speaking.

"They lied to us. That fire we see before us was not named by the first person who used it. Later generations named it and said humanity had discovered fire. What existed existed already, how could anyone discover it? They didn't say anything about the first person creating fire rather than discovering it. As long as fire burned and went out of its own accord, it was nothing. One day someone roasted his meat on it and heated his cave with it. That wasn't discovering fire, it was creating it. They kept the truth from us."

"Bravo, Traveler!"

"Well done, Traveler! Keep talking, never mind if we don't know what you're on about."

"Drink wine, so your lips don't go dry."

The Architect Adaza was drunk, but he recalled the words he had heard from me perfectly. The sentences he was stringing together here were the words I had spoken in my barbershop to pass the time while I was cutting hair.

"We are city victims," he continued. "We're either poor or unhappy, and quite often we're both. We're conditioned to hope. For the sake of hope we tolerate evil. But if we're not masters of today, what guarantee is there for tomorrow? Hope is the lie of preachers, politicians, and the rich. They deceive us with words and cover up the truth."

The drunks replied with the same zeal.

"Down with hope! Long live wine!"

"Good on you!"

"Hope is the opium of the people!"

Adaza interrupted the shouting and whistling with a question. "My brothers, is this city dead or alive?"

I think he was reminiscing about his university years, he spoke as though he were addressing young insurgents. He was delving into his magician's hat and producing the words he had been stashing away for years. He missed his revolutionary era and regretted abandoning it for fear of the police. Once, when he was drunk, he opened his heart to me. "You may abandon the past, but the past will never abandon you," he had said.

The layabouts were bickering amongst themselves.

"This city is dead and alive."

"If anyone says it's alive I'll smash a bottle over his head."

"Dead!"

Adaza was excited. As he spoke he stood on the tips of his toes, then lowered himself back down again.

"My homeless brothers! You, the poor defeated! The heartbroken!" he said. As he spoke his voice became more confident. "We did not create this city, we found ourselves in it. And we're not the ones who killed it either. There's no way out, our predecessors burned the boats. Like the first people who created fire, who will be the first to create the new city, who will give it life?"

"Speak, Traveler, let rip."

"Tell us about the moon, too."

"And about the stars."

They all raised their heads in unison. I walked two paces away from my tree and raised my head likewise. The stars were so endless that none but the homeless and drunks could ever have the time to contemplate them. Here there were no city lights, the sky glittered with starlight. The stars in this enormous city that dentists, bakers, and housewives never looked at, had congregated in the shade of the city wall and were palpitating in space as though they might fall out of the sky at any moment.

"What a long night!"

"We need more wine!"

"Traveler, recite us a starry poem."

Recite a poem? This time I couldn't just sit back and take his terrible poems. With heavy footsteps I approached the drunks gathered around the fire.

When the Architect Adaza saw me he hesitated, then he took a swig from the bottle he was holding. He drank as though he had discovered the secret he had been searching for, as though he had finally found happiness after so many years spent in vain. He laughed.

"Here," he said, "is the man I was telling you about, Kamo the Barber."

Everyone turned and looked at me. The closer I got the more ugly they seemed, and the more scars I saw on their faces. They had taken over the area, like rats in a rubbish dump, and admitted the Architect Adaza into their circle. Adaza was happy, his drunken mouth drooping. On another such evening, when he had looked as happy as now, and when Istanbul had grown dark early, we had gone to a tavern together. After two double rakıs he announced that he was going to recite his latest poem. He had stood on his chair and made everyone in the room repeat the verses he read out loud. It was unbearable. Listening to that bad poetry weighed on my heart.

The Architect Adaza, speaking by the fire in the shade of the city wall, a bottle of wine in one hand, managed to stay upright with the aid of his long staff, which he clutched with the other.

"Kamo," he said, "the traveler in that story wasn't lying, he was demonstrating the lie. Wasn't he? Words are the only path to the truth, that's what the traveler was trying to explain."

"Mr. Architect," I said, "Adaza, it's time to go home."

The drunks around the fire stirred and sat up. They looked at each other and at Adaza.

"Kamo," continued the Architect Adaza, "we're seeking the truth of the era when the first person did not give fire the name fire. What do we possess except poetry? Poets go beyond not just reality but fantasy too, and get close to the time before fire. They didn't teach us that at university, they didn't give us poetry to read. Every day they told us lies."

Instead of returning home to the warm embrace of his family, the Architect Adaza was dawdling over words that he would forget in a few minutes. He had a wife and two pretty daughters who loved him. Fools were lucky, they didn't appreciate what they had. What more were they after? What more could they want, when they already had the happiness that everyone spent a lifetime searching for?

The drunks were staring at me, wondering what I was going to do. They were unkempt, ugly, and emaciated. There was not one among them who was decently dressed and brushed. The Architect Adaza looked just like they did now. The man before me was no longer the person who regularly came into my shop for a shave, and who was careful not to cross his legs so that the trousers his wife had ironed wouldn't crease.

"Kamo," he said, "you said clinging to a belief with your heart turns a person into the devil, do you remember? Look, I'm also clinging to a belief."

Yes, clinging to a belief turned a person into a devil. The person who regarded his own beliefs as superior looked down on others. He gathered all of life's value in the palm of his hand and saw the source of goodness in himself. According to him, evil was a part of others, and was a stranger to his own heart. Sometimes I tested my customers with words like those. While they agreed with me wholeheartedly, or argued amongst themselves, I would take the opposite standpoint without anyone noticing, and argue against everything I had been saying. I would weigh up who was the most tenacious when it came to defending their beliefs.

"Did I say that? I don't remember," I replied to Adaza.

"Don't underestimate him as a simple barber, Kamo goes to university. He knows more than the professors and he's the one who understands my poetry the best."

Why hadn't this man got run over by a car while he was drunk? His wife would have cried for a bit and then made a new life for herself, and found a better father for her children. People like him never learned, the foolishness they practiced at home persisted after they left home. I had known that since I was a small boy. No matter what you said they would fall into bad ways and get up to crafty tricks. While praising you and showering you with kindness, they aggrandized their bad poetry by burdening you with it. These types graduated from university, built cities, became heads of state, and talked about the justice in this country. And they wanted you to live according to their miserable beliefs.

I accepted the bottle that the Architect Adaza offered me. I sat beside the fire, between two layabouts who moved up for me. I checked out the scene, examining each face one by one. They looked as happy, but just as weary, as if they had come here after surviving a sinking ship. They had no past, they owed this moment to wine; they believed in fire, in city walls, and in the stars.

Adaza sat beside me and placed his staff on the ground. As he gazed into the fire, tears welled up in his eyes. A couple of times he toppled forward. He became engrossed in the dancing flames that changed from yellow to blue, before suddenly disappearing. Like castaways who regret surviving a shipwreck, he was ready to return to the dark, to be buried at sea. There was no branch left in this world for him to cling to, and he was seeking no treasure. If he had the strength he would take the final step, or if someone were to push him gently from behind he would fall into the sea and lie still beneath the waves.

Those who realized he had fallen silent shouted out, "Where's the poem? Where is it?"

One man who noticed that Adaza was not replying raised the bottle in his hand and said, "I'll recite you a poem." He was blind in one eye, the other eye burned with fire.

"Go on," they said.

"I want there to be women in it."

"And stars."

"That'll depend on the luck of the draw."

The one-eyed man took a swig of wine and said, "Before your carmine lips / I didn't know what misery was."

He stopped and looked at his friends, to ensure they were listening to him. There was the sound of a dog barking in the distance. The man continued with his poem.

"While your hair is splayed in the wind / Songs flow skyward / Your cool legs in the stream / Shimmered like silver fish / The day dawned, the sun set / You gathered up your hair / And left with the migrant birds / Behind you night's door remains open and / You have abandoned me on the banks of the stream / Before your carmine lips / I didn't know what misery was."

"Is that it?"

"Was that about women?"

"Or stars?"

"Like you know anything about poetry!"

The dogs' barking grew louder, everyone turned and looked at where it was coming from. Several dogs were approaching from the gaps between the broken stones in the city wall, just one white dog remained aloof. The dogs ran, their shadows merging into one in the moonlight. They approached and nuzzled the drunks' arms. They rolled around on the floor and roamed around. They sniffed out the bones the drunks had saved for them. The white dog waited in the distance.

The one-eyed man took no notice of the dogs. He took a swig from the bottle in his hand, then rose to his feet. "I'll just go and have a pee, then I'll come back and recite you another poem," he said. No one paid any attention to him.

After taking a sip of wine, I too rose to my feet. I followed the one-eyed man who had stood up to go to the toilet. The city walls extended toward infinity in the moonlight. There was nothing on this side of the city save the city walls, the stars, and the fire. As the sky grew bigger and bigger, one of the drunks launched into a song with his shrill voice. "As the evening sun was sinking into the horizon / You went away and left me my beloved."

The one eyed man approached an alcove in the city walls and stopped. He was unsteady on his feet and struggled to undo his zipper. I caught up with him in a few steps. I pushed him into the alcove and put my hand over his mouth. My steel knife was at the ready; I waved it in the air several times before holding it against his throat. He couldn't understand what was going on. He opened his eye wide and it glinted in the light of the full moon. There was more bafflement than fear on his face. Was this really happening, or was he asleep? He racked his brain, trying to recall first me, then where he was, then himself. If it weren't for the barely audible song in the distance he would have imagined he had died long ago and woken up in his grave. He was short to start with and he shrank considerably. I crushed him under my weight and flung him against the wall. I brandished the knife in the air again. "Don't scream, I'm going to ask you something," I said. I withdrew my face and shifted the weight of my body from his. I removed my hand from his mouth but pointed the knife in my other hand at his eye. "I beg you, please don't kill me, you can have all the stolen goods," he said. He stank of wine and mold. I could hear his heart beating. "I'm going to ask you a question and you're going to tell me the truth," I said. He nodded. "I swear," he said. Instead of asking him why he still insisted on living, why he didn't dig a grave in this rubbish dump and climb into it with his one eye and his filthy stench, I said, "Where did you learn that poem you just recited?" His eye lit up and then grew dull. "Did I do something wrong?" he stammered. "You did wrong by being born," I said. "Answer me, where did you hear that poem?"

He would have given a simple answer to that simple question, but the sharp edge of the knife pointing at his eye was tampering with his reason.

"That was our primary school teacher's poem," he said.

That was the extent of his life's mystery, he had told me what I needed to know.

"Where did you go to school, at Black Fountain Village?"

His face lit up. "Yes, I'm from Black Fountain. Our teacher who came from Istanbul . . ."

I didn't give him a chance to finish his sentence. I grabbed him by the throat and pushed him against the wall. "Don't you dare utter a single word about him," I said. "Don't talk about your teacher, talk about your village."

He held my wrist with his skinny fingers and looked at me imploringly. What had he got himself into, what had he done wrong? His veins were dilated, his brow was covered in sweat. Spit drooled from the edge of his mouth. Just as he was on the point of suffocation I loosened my grip and released his throat. I spoke for him. "The way to your village is through the mountains, via a steep road. There are always clouds hanging over it. You don't grow trees in your fields, you breed livestock. You build your houses out of black stones. Your village is called Black Fountain, but you have no fountain, you draw your water from wells."

I held his chin and forced it up, I stared into his eye and continued.

"The walls of your village are more dependable than you are. They don't change, regardless of whether the sun is shining or whether it's dark. And they remain standing for at least a hundred years. As for you, you smile at people during the day and hang severed chicken legs outside their doors at night. No one has ever known you to admit your faults, and you don't know how to apologize. You rape your own relatives, then commit murder in the name of honor. The name of God is constantly on your lips. You're first class at crying. You listen to laments and dream of the old days. The whole world could end and you couldn't care less, as long as you don't lose a single stone from the walls of your houses. You believe evil comes from elsewhere. The source of evil is either your neighbor or the strangers that come to the village. You can't see that you harbor snakes in your own heart."

"You're right," he said, in a listless voice. "Look at what they did to me. The people from my own village, my relatives, gouged my eye out and threw me out of the village."

"Silence, I don't want to hear about you. You have no story of your own, you only have a collective story. This is just one story and each of you is living a part of it."

He searched all over his body and took out the money hidden in the secret pockets of his torn clothing. He offered me the fistful of notes in his hand. "Take this, I'll bring you money every day," he said. I flung the knife, making blood squirt from his palm; the money scattered all over the floor. "Ahhh!" he sighed, pulling his hand away.

"You're cowards, you're sly, and, whenever you can get away with it, you're cruel. That was the way you finished off the teacher as well. While you were still sleeping he would get up and light the stove in the school's only classroom. He would draw pictures on the blackboard. He would tell you about mountains that looked nothing like yours, and describe animals you'd never heard of. You didn't care about the world being round, or about the sea occupying more of the earth than land does. But he would still usher you into the school yard in the evenings and show you the Milky Way and the Northern

Star. When you had gone home and the place became the dogs' roaming territory, he would shut himself up in his small study and, in the light of his dim lamp, write the poems he would read to you. He wasn't aware of the dark shadows lurking outside his window. It took time for him to realize what kind of people you were, what kind of lives you led in those houses with the doors locked so securely. Each house, each person, was a dark cave. It was hard for him to believe that. That's why his last poems were full of disillusionment. Your village was Black Fountain, but you had no fountain, you too were a lie, just like your village. It was that lie that the teacher couldn't bear."

He stared as though his one eye were about to pop out of his head. He bit his lips. He clung to my arm. He began to weep. He was like a rat caught in a trap. Who knows when he had last cried like that? It wasn't his wrongdoings he was thinking of, it was my knife. I pushed him against the wall. I grabbed his collar.

"Stop crying or I'll slit your throat," I said. "It's too late for that now. You people are always late for everything. You should have cried years ago and begged the teacher for forgiveness. What did he ever do to you, apart from tell the truth to the old men sitting by the wall? As he spoke, you lost sleep, waking up in the middle of the night covered in sweat. You went out to the door in the dark and looked out into the distance, far into the distance. You smoked all through the night. You didn't want to know the truth. You were content to live with lies, denying your wickedness. How happy you were with that snake in your hearts, you didn't just betray the teacher, you betrayed the very mountain you lived on."

"Who are you, are you from our village?" he asked hesitantly.

"Who are *you* more like, who are all of you?" I was really riled now. "Why didn't you stop and have a look at yourselves even once? The teacher came to your village because he had had enough of Istanbul and wanted to get away from the city's oppressiveness. Otherwise he would have lost his mind. Istanbul swelled up like a corpse and people turned into parasites that fed off that corpse. He had to escape from that nightmare and take refuge in this village. He had to spend his evenings translating French poetry, and find a new vein for his own poetry. But were the villagers any different? Weren't people the same everywhere? The teacher realized too late that he had gone from one nightmare to another. The city was a lie and now the village was also a lie, he was trapped between two lies. Everywhere was rotting, there was nowhere left in the world to escape to."

I moved closer to the man's face, I smelled his greasy hair and prodded his dirty forehead.

"This is the hope he clung to," I said, showing him the dirt on my finger. "That teacher was my father. His last poem cursed humanity. The night he wrote that poem he went outside and gazed up at the sky. The Milky Way was flowing from one horizon to another. The Northern Star was far away. As he couldn't ascend to the north, in other words, to that star, he considered descending to the south, to the depths of the earth. That could be the way to complete his last journey. Wasn't every death a descent? He went to the well in the village square, leaned over and looked down. He stuck his head in. The moss-covered walls smelled lovely. He inhaled the fragrance deeply. He dropped a stone into the water. The stone fell for a long time, eventually sending an echo as it hit the water. Down below it was dark, damp, and mysterious. The heart of the world, the south, was down there."

Noises came from beside the fire. They were concerned because we were taking so long. They called both of our names. "One Eye, where have you got to? Kamo the Barber, where are you?" I stuck my head out and looked. While the drunks continued to drink by the fire, one or two of them were calling out in our direction. They would be here in a moment. The song of the steel knives would start.

When I turned around and saw the white dog I lurched. I stumbled on a stone. The knife fell from my hand. When had the white dog got this close? It had a handsome face and a wide neck. Its long hair covered its silky body, flowing all the way down to its tail. It didn't look like the strays that lurked by the city wall. It wasn't after food. Its teeth shone in the moonlight. Its pointed ears recalled a wolf's ears. Its large feet were not coated in dust. It was staring at me without moving, without letting on what it was about to do. I bent down and picked up the knife. Taking two paces back, I leaned against the wall. I remembered the wish that had brought the knife, myself, and the white dog in pursuit of me to this place.

I heard the rumble of a train. The ground started shaking. The sound of the tracks grew louder, like a hammer beating metal. Clatter clatter clatter clat. The drunks would be here in a moment too. Clatter clatter clatter clat. The song of the steel knives would start. Tonight everyone would have to submit to their fate. I pressed my body hard against the wall. I clenched my fingers. What had the Architect Adaza told them after I had walked away from the fire? "Don't underestimate him for just a simple barber, Kamo has a beautiful wife." The dark was lustful. Trains liked tracks. The drunks were handing round a bottle of wine. The wine bottle was the body of a woman with fiery lips and sweat running down her belly. Trains liked tracks and children liked wells. Clatter clatter clatter clat. My father liked wells too. He watched the stars in Black Fountain Village, measured the speed of the wind and kept a rain calendar. My father liked wells too. Clatter clatter

clatter clat. If only the well in Black Fountain Village had spun like a whirlpool and swallowed up foolish children, deceitful old men and coldhearted women. If only it had swallowed up houses with closed doors and chickens with severed legs. Clatter clatter clatter clat. Would the well still have swallowed up my father?

The night's lust suddenly abated. Lust was like armies of ants that marched in secret alleyways; once it had permeated the entire area, it halted. I felt a ringing in my ears. As the sound of the train grew distant in the darkness, I raised my head from where I lay. Was I on the ground? When had I laid down on the concrete? The lies and the drunks had worn me out. My head ached. I somehow managed to sit up. Leaning against the wall, I stretched out my legs. My neck, my back, my chest, were soaked in sweat. I drank from the plastic water bottle. What time was it? I turned my head and looked at the grille. The light from the corridor stung my eyes. I drank some more. What day of the month was it today? I had lost track of the days. They hadn't brought the Doctor or the others back. It was a good job I had been alone when I had had my epileptic fit. I didn't need anyone's help.

I looked at the opposite wall. It was covered in scratches, letters, bloodstains. The plaster had cracked and peeled off in several places. There was graffiti written who knows when distributed randomly throughout the cell. "Human honor!" said one message, "One day definitely!" said another, "Why pain?" said yet another. "Why pain?" That was what everyone who came here thought the most. When pain divided the world in the same way as it divided the mind, people thought of this place as the location of pain, while the Istanbul above was the painless location. So here was the age of mirages! The best way of hiding one lie was by telling another. And the way to hide the pain aboveground was by creating pain underground. People who were locked up in the frigid cells here missed the crowds and the streets outside. And those outside were happy because they slept in their warm beds, far away from the cell. Whereas Istanbul was full of people asphyxiated by hopelessness, who slithered to work in the mornings like slugs. While the walls of the houses above grew roots and reclined on the walls of the underground cells, the inhabitants of those houses clung to a false happiness. That was the only way Istanbul could stay on its feet.

"Showtime!" The sound of the guard's shouting resonated throughout the corridor. What was going on? Had the iron gate opened? "Everyone out! Everyone to the cell door!"

I didn't have the faintest idea what they were doing.

They banged on the grilles. They opened the cell doors one by one. They advanced along the corridor until they reached me. They slid the bolt open and light flooded into the cell. My eyes stung and the pain in my head got worse.

"You, stand up! Get your ass to the door!" The guard left me and went to the neighboring cell. The sound of opening doors continued.

I stood up and went outside. Everyone was lined up in the corridor. Men whose hair was tangled up with their beards and women with bruised faces were staring at one another. The guard strolled to the end of the corridor and came back, opening the opposite cell too. As soon as the door opened the girl inside stood up. When had Zinê Sevda returned to her cell? Had they brought her back during my fainting fit? She came outside and stood in front of me. It was obvious she hadn't slept for a long while. Not just her face and her neck, but her fingers too were swollen. A drop of blood oozed from her lower lip. She wiped the blood away with her hand.

"Come on now!" We looked at the interrogators shouting at the top of the corridor. There were a lot of them. They held sticks and chains. They had rolled up the sleeves of their sweaters and smirked as they eyed us up. "Here comes your guru, your guardian angel!" They dragged someone by the feet from the direction of the iron gate. They dumped him at the corridor entrance. He was naked, except for a pair of black underpants. I recognized Uncle Küheylan's huge bulk. He lay like a corpse washed up on the shore. He was covered in blood. His white hair was dyed red. Had they killed him and was this now going to be his graveyard? A murmur traveled down the corridor. We heard fearful voices. Someone whispered, "Bastards." Someone else repeated the whisper. "Bastards." The guard heard and dived into our midst in a rage. "Who said that?" he shouted. He ran up and down, bringing his stick down on several people at random. Broken teeth and spurted blood littered the corridor.

Two interrogators put Uncle Küheylan's arms over their shoulders and tried to lift him. "Come on, you great lout, walk." Uncle Küheylan was alive. His groans echoed through the corridor where we waited without stirring, reaching the furthest prisoners. "Come on, you old codger!" Uncle Küheylan moved one hand, reaching out as though to grope the empty space. There was something bestial about his bowed head, thick neck, and broad shoulders. He emitted the kind of bloodcurdling roar that only a wounded animal would make. Spittle trailed down his mouth. The words he mumbled turned into an incomprehensible rattle. Who was Uncle Küheylan now? What was this groaning creature? He placed one foot on the ground and let the other drag. The interrogators released his arms and left him standing on his one foot. He hesitated for a while. He took deep breaths. He moved the foot from behind him until it was level with his other foot. He raised his head. His face did not look human. His lips were swollen, his tongue drooped. His eyebrows were slit, his blood-filled eyes closed. Pus seeped from the wound on his chest.

"Take a good look!" shouted one of the interrogators. "See our work close up! Who can escape our justice?"

Uncle Küheylan was like those captains who take to the sea in pursuit of white whales, struggle against storms but return to the port defeated. Just as in his father's stories. His ship had been battered, its sails torn to shreds. But just like those captains, with every defeat he fantasized about new voyages. As he advanced on his bloody feet he could hear the sound of the whirlwind ringing in his ears. He mistook the blood running down his nasal passage for salty sea water. This was a never-ending dream. Everyone searched for their white whale in the open seas, whereas Uncle Küheylan searched for his in the Istanbul Sea. Doing so made him drunk with pleasure and he was powerless to resist its allure. He wasn't looking for an island that would harbor him. He had deleted all the islands on his map. He would either conquer the seas or be buried beneath the waves. His back was scored with countless knife slashes. As he was dragging his heavy feet on the concrete, he raised his head as though he had heard a scream in the distance. He tried to ascertain the direction of the wind.

While Uncle Küheylan was making the longest journey of his life, Zinê Sevda, who was standing very rigid in front of me, clenched her fists. She blinked like a child, and slowly moved out of the line. She took two paces toward the center of the corridor. She stood before Uncle Küheylan, as erect as a tree. There were five or six meters between them. As all heads turned toward Zinê Sevda, the interrogators looked at each other. Silence descended on the corridor. The only audible sound was Uncle Küheylan's blood dripping onto the concrete floor.

"What's she doing?"

"Chief, that's the girl they brought from the mountains."

Zinê Sevda wiped her forehead and cheeks with her hand

and smoothed her hair. Under the curious gaze of the onlookers, she crouched down. She knelt before Uncle Küheylan like a marble statue. She held out her two arms. She waited to embrace the wounded body that was advancing toward her. The soles of her feet were a mass of angry welts. Her neck was covered in cigarette burns. She was not a mermaid who had emerged from the waves and was singing on the rocks as the sun set, but a wounded human being. Could Uncle Küheylan see her? Could his bloody eyes make out the girl kneeling before him with her arms open wide?

"Get up, bitch!"

Zinê Sevda ignored the interrogators. This time she wiped the black blood oozing from her lip with her tongue. She opened her arms even wider.

"Get that bitch up!"

One of the interrogators standing at the edge of the corridor arrived, brandishing his stick. He stood in front of Zinê Sevda. He threw the cigarette in his mouth on the floor and crushed it with the ball of his foot. As he slowly rotated his boot on the concrete floor he looked at Zinê Sevda. He smirked, showing his yellow teeth. Stepping back, he landed a kick on her stomach. Zinê Sevda went flying like a log, banging against the cell door. She hesitated for a while. Holding her stomach with her hands, she slowly straightened up. She knelt once again and looked at Uncle Küheylan. There was an insurmountable void separating them.

The interrogator swept the cigarette butt on the floor aside with his foot. He bent down and brought his face close to Zinê Sevda's. When she did not react he withdrew. He was still smirking. He twirled his baton in his hands as though it were a toy, then raised it into the air. He was right in front of me. With one sweep I caught his lifted hand. His baton remained suspended in the void. The interrogator and I came eye to eye. Motherfucker! Did he know me? Did he know the song of the steel knives? My temples throbbed. As everyone stood shivering on the concrete, my face burned like fire. A drill was rotating in my brain. Did he know the song of the steel knives? Motherfucker! He pushed me and tried to release his hand. When he realized he wasn't strong enough, he screamed.

# 4TH DAY

*Told by Uncle Küheylan*

## THE HUNGRY WOLF

"As the hunters were struggling up a steep hill, a storm hit them. The blizzard had soon buried everything in snow; it was impossible to see through the blanket of snowflakes. Night fell early. The lost hunters made out a light in the darkness. Slipping and stumbling in the snow, they headed toward it. Eventually they arrived at a mountain hut inside a garden. They knocked on the door. We're freezing, please let us in, they called out. A woman's voice on the other side asked, who's there? We're three hunters from Istanbul, we've lost our way, we need somewhere to shelter, they said. My husband's not here, said the woman, I can't let you in. The hunters begged her. If you don't open the door we'll die here, if you like we can give you all our weapons, they coaxed. The wind was howling, they could hear an avalanche approaching in the distance. The woman opened the door and invited the hunters to warm themselves beside the stove. She served them food. The hunters took a mirror, a comb, and a pocketknife out of their saddlebags and presented them to the woman. You saved our lives, we're eternally grateful to you, they said. The woman thanked them for the gifts, then retired to her room. The hunters lay down beside the fireplace and went to sleep. Before long they were woken by a whistling sound. Strange noises were coming from the fireplace. The flames changed from one color to another.

A light descended from the chimney and stood before them. A fairy with green wings appeared inside the light. Do not be afraid, said the fairy, I have come to write fate. Our fate? they asked. No, said the fairy, your fate was written before you were born. I have come for the pregnant woman in the other room. I'm going to write the fate of the child she will soon have. Tell us what the child's fate will be, they said. I can tell you, but you won't be able to change it, said the fairy. The hunters insisted. The fairy smiled and gave them what they wanted. The woman would have a son, she said, he would grow up strong and healthy, and when he was twenty years old he would marry the girl he loved. But on his wedding night the boy would be eaten by a wolf. No, said the hunters, we won't let that happen. Don't argue with fate, said the fairy, and sprinkled some dust over the hunters. The hunters fell asleep and, upon awaking the following morning, they told each other what they had dreamt. As they had all had the same dream it must have been real. They placed their hands on their guns and swore to keep the secret and to save the child's life. The woman had no idea of anything. They said you are our sister now, we have something to ask of you. What is it that you wish, asked the woman. We want to come to your child's wedding, you must tell us when it is, they said. The next twenty years passed wearily for the hunters. Each day they prepared themselves for the wedding night. When the time came and news of the wedding reached Istanbul, they strapped their guns to their shoulders. They hastened like lightning back to the mountain hut where they had received hospitality so many years ago. They disclosed the secret that they had kept so faithfully. They put a large chest that they had brought with them in the center of the room and placed the bride and groom inside it. They wrapped seven chains around the chest and put seven padlocks on the lid. There will be no sleep for us, they declared, and, to stop themselves from accidentally falling asleep, they cut their little fingers. They listened to the howling wind until dawn. They opened fire at the slightest movement. At the first light of day they gave whoops of joy and said we did it! First they unlocked the seven padlocks, then they unraveled the seven chains. But when they found the bride alone in the chest, bloodstained, they couldn't believe it. What happened, they said, what happened? The bride stammered, I can't understand it either, no sooner had you closed the lid of the chest than I turned into a wolf and I ate the man I loved. I have no idea why, but I ate him."

The Doctor was listening to me, intrigued, his expression a combination of amusement and fear. The look in his eyes changed several times.

"Did the end of the story surprise you, Doctor?" I said. "Do you know, I've come across people who laugh instead of being surprised that the wolf ate the boy."

"You might find people here who laugh too," said the Doctor, looking at Kamo the Barber, who was sleeping. He leaned slightly toward him and brought his ear closer, as though trying to hear Kamo's breathing. He waited for a while, then straightened up. "I hadn't heard that story before, Uncle Küheylan. I like the hunters' tale. Did your father tell you that one too?"

"Yes, the first night our radio broke down, my father told us that story to try and distract us from instant boredom."

"Were you bored easily?"

"People were each other's entertainment in the village, we didn't know what boredom was. Radio changed us. Whenever the radio broke down we didn't feel like doing anything, there didn't seem any point in the games we always played. We wondered what city people did when it happened to them."

"How strange," said the Doctor.

"My father came back from one of his trips with a transistor radio. When his trips to Istanbul were short we knew he was with his friends there, but when they were long we realized they were holding him prisoner in the city's cells. This time he had been away for a long time. To stop us from looking at his thin, pale face and worrying, he won us over with small presents that he pulled out of his suitcase. The radio, which we were seeing for the first time, thrilled us more than any of the other presents. That evening we listened to a novel on the radio. A man loved a woman but she rejected him. The woman left Istanbul and went to Paris and returned many years later. Their paths crossed again, and they sat together in a tea garden as the trees shed their golden leaves around them. The man lit the woman's cigarette. Just like couples on picture postcards, said the novel, they contemplated the passing boats, and Topkapı Palace. Eventually the woman turned and gazed into the man's eyes. Ardor drove the love-crazed man into the desert; do you have a desert? she asked. Yes, said the man, this city became a desert while you were away. The woman asked, what would you do if you woke up one morning and found I had turned into an elderly rat? I would show you compassion, said the man, and if you died I would mourn you. The woman lit another cigarette and said, I'm going to tell you a story. She seemed to be testing the man. But the radio presenter announced that that was the end of that day's episode and that the continuation would be at the same time next week. We had to wait a week to find out what story the woman would tell."

Maybe because he had a headache, the Doctor half-closed his eyes. He turned away from the light and tried not to look toward the grille, but he listened to me with interest.

"The next week the radio broke down. No matter how hard he tried, my father couldn't make it work. The bored look he saw on our faces for the first time must have alarmed him because he said, don't worry, I know that novel. Did he really know it? In the village he needed to know it and we needed to believe him. Before our very eyes he unraveled the story that the woman on the radio told the man. He clicked his fingers like a magician and, reflecting the shadow of the pregnant woman and the fairy onto the wall, bit by bit he brought the story of the hunters to life. He showed us the mountain hut and the chest inside the house. That night for the first time ever I craved a different kind of happiness. I dreamed that my father would take me too to Istanbul, with its golden lights. Afterward I asked my father if that story had a question. You tell me, said my father, what were the question and the answer in that story? Why did the woman in the novel tell the man that story?"

"Uncle Küheylan," said the Doctor, "I like riddles. But here we don't even know what the riddle is, let alone the answer."

"My father said we had to work out the question and the answer. He said we had until the next evening."

"And did you?"

"My mother did. She was the riddle expert in our house."

"Give me time, I'll also try and work out the answer by tomorrow."

"No problem, Doctor, what's more plentiful in here than time?"

Demirtay, who was sleeping with his head on his knees, sat up. He rubbed his eyes. It was obvious he was cold, he wrapped his two arms hard around his chest. Glancing at Kamo the Barber, who was sleeping, he said, "He can still sleep despite the cold, I envy him. I think I'm the one who feels the cold the most in here."

"Couldn't you sleep?" I said.

"No I couldn't, Uncle Küheylan, I listened to your story. It was like watching a film. The scenes came to life before my eyes, the stormy night, the snow swirling in the wind, the hut with the light shining in the window. I think the question became clear at the end of the story. I mean, was there any way they could change the child's destiny, despite everything?"

"If the question is that simple the answer should be simple too. Do you know the answer?" asked the Doctor.

"Yes I do, Doctor, I think they couldn't change his destiny."

"Why not? If they had put the boy into the chest by himself wouldn't he have been saved?"

"In that case one of the hunters would have turned into a wolf, he would have torn the other two to pieces and then got inside the chest."

The Doctor objected. "That way the other hunters would have had a chance to kill the wolf. The hunters didn't just want to save the child, they wanted to meet the wolf head-on too. They cut their fingers, they shed their blood. They wanted to lure the wolf to the smell of blood, they wanted it to challenge them."

Demirtay pondered as if he were solving a problem in an exam. "Give me some time too to come up with a better answer," he said.

The Doctor turned to face me. "Uncle Küheylan, what was your mother's answer? Did she also say you can't change fate?"

"No, she thought something else."

"I have an answer, do you want to hear it?"

"What's the rush, Doctor? You asked me to give you until tomorrow."

"While you were talking to Demirtay I was thinking. There wasn't a question in the hunters' story. And it wasn't going to come from within the story, but from outside it. The woman in the novel was going to ask a question about herself. That's the reason why she told the story, isn't it?"

"You're doing well, carry on."

"The woman wanted to discover to what extent the man was prepared to sacrifice himself. She was going to ask him if he would get into the chest with her if he were the boy in the story. She didn't want to solve the problem, she wanted to know if the man was strong enough to face up to it."

"You have spoken like my mother, Doctor. Do you know the novel?"

"No, I don't."

"The novel had a happy ending," I said. "According to my father, some love takes time to blossom. And that was the fate of this novel too."

"The novel's fate," said the Doctor, as though to himself. He scratched a vertical line on the wall with his nail. "Is fate a line like this? Does it change or not? I'm going to ask Kamo when he wakes up. Uncle Küheylan, you should sleep too and rest a bit more."

"I'm not sleepy. Kamo's fast asleep. He might not have any cuts or scars on his face, but the interrogators pounded his head yesterday, they pushed him onto the floor and kicked him."

When they had dragged Kamo the Barber into the cell yesterday, thumping and beating him, we were both half-dead. We were in too much pain to sleep. I was more concerned about Zinê Sevda in the opposite cell than about Kamo. I wondered why she had stepped forward and let them batter her. She had knelt in the middle of the corridor and held out her arms to me. She had stayed there despite the beating, not backing down. When Kamo the Barber had tried to defend her by grabbing the interrogator's hand, Zinê Sevda had been as surprised as everyone else.

"No," said Kamo, "I didn't grab the interrogator's hand, he attacked me because I accidentally touched him."

I remember it clearly. I was bleeding all over. Although

I could barely move my legs, which felt like lead, I could still make out the prisoners lined up on either side of the corridor. I could still hear. Zinê Sevda was kneeling opposite me, holding out her arms to me. Kamo the Barber had grabbed the torturer's wrist and flung him against the wall. The air had turned blue with screams and swearing. They had beaten Zinê Sevda and attacked Kamo. I couldn't move my tongue. Wheezing sounds came from my throat.

"You're mistaken, Uncle Küheylan, I didn't help the girl. What would that have changed? Everyone has to deal with their own pain. I have my own problems, I can't go poking my nose in anyone else's pain. No one can ease anyone else's pain in this world. I know that. I didn't attack the torturer, and I didn't defend that girl. Think what you want, I don't care."

Did he regret his compassion? Did caring about others make him uneasy? Some people shied away from loneliness, while others shied toward it. And Kamo the Barber was looking for somewhere in this tiny cell where he could take refuge. He barely spoke, kept his head bowed, and studied the ends of his feet. His gaze wandered like an ant on the floor, climbed up the walls, looked for a hole to crawl into, a crack to hide in, then finally alighted on the ends of his feet again. "Time's a bitch!" he mumbled to himself. As he bowed his head to sleep he repeated the same words, like a mantra. "Time's a bitch!"

Our movements slowed down in this cell buried so far underground, our bodies became more and more heavy. Our minds, which had grown used to the pace in the world aboveground, faltered as they tried to adapt to the conditions here. Our own voices sounded alien to us. The tiniest sound made our ears ring. Our wasted fingers twitched in the dark, as though they didn't belong to us. The most difficult thing for us wasn't being able to recognize others, but being able to recognize ourselves. What was this nightmare we were living?

Whose was this body that was submitting to pain, and how much more could it take? Time, stretching before us with its putrid stench, was our worst enemy here; it buried itself in our flesh like a plow that works the fields, drawing blood, and then more blood.

Did Kamo the Barber mean the time outside, instead of the time in here? Was time the bitch in the world above, which was accessible by an invisible ladder? In that place there were no train stations, crowded ferries, or boulevards where everyone bumped into each other as they walked. There were no lampposts, bridges, or towers either. Everything consisted of a great meaning. One part of that meaning was haste, the other part was agitation. Every tiny thing was a reflection of that greater meaning. Drawn curtains, leaving the workplace at the end of the working day, and the squares where lovers arranged to meet, were all reflections of it. If it rained, and washed and cleansed the city's dirt for days, it would still be that meaning that emerged with the first ray of sunshine. Time that ticked on in maternity hospitals, in back streets and in late night bars, toyed with the city's pace. People forgot the sun, the moon, and the stars and lived only with times. Time for work, time for school, time for an appointment, time to eat, time to go out. When it was finally time to sleep, people had no more strength or desire left to think about the world. They let themselves go in the darkness. They were dragged along by a single meaning, a meaning that was hidden in every single thing. What was that meaning and where was it taking us? People created small pleasures for themselves to stop their minds from clouding over with such questions, and chased after them relentlessly. They ran away from life's hardships, slept peacefully, and thus lightened their minds' burden. And their hearts'. They believed that. Until a wall inside them came crashing down and their hearts were crushed. When they realized that the thing beating under the rubble was not their heart, but time, they grew afraid. They were left with no choice. Whether one denied it or not, that bitch time came and seeped into a person's skin, and the city's veins.

Was that the kind of time that Kamo the Barber believed in? Was that why he bowed his head forward? He sighed and cursed. Underground, he still fell victim to the anxiety that existed aboveground. He was searching for a secluded place where he could be by himself. Young though he was, he believed he had reached the end of his life and looked not at the future but at the past. The torturers knew that too. "Old man!" they would say to me, "Do you have as many secrets as your cellmate, is your memory as deep as Kamo the Barber's?"

As I bore pain, I too was curious about my memory's limit. I didn't think of what I knew but of what I didn't know. The more I wanted to forget, the harder my memory tried to remember. Sometimes I shouted, sometimes I was silent. This is the furthest pain can go, I told myself each time. Then the pain intensified and I reached a new limit. What a strange feeling discovery was. People discovered pain too. As my flesh was being ripped and my bones crushed I would constantly make the acquaintance of new pain. The interrogators would mock me. "Who d'you think you are? Jesus on the cross?" My arms were stretched out on either side of me, I was tied to a heavy beam. I was suspended in the air. Under my feet was emptiness, above my arms infinity. I was the fixed point in the sky, the world and the stars revolved around me. I tried to get to know myself in the throes of pain. The interrogators would laugh. "We've spilt the blood of so many like you and fed it to the dogs. And we were the ones who crucified Christ and tortured Mansur Al-Hallaj to death. Our history is more glorious than yours. Do you know the anarchist Edward Jorris? He came to Istanbul to kill Sultan Abdülhamit. Abdülhamit always went to Yıldız Mosque for the Friday prayers and when he came out it always took him one minute and forty-two seconds to walk to his carriage. The anarchist Jorris calculated the time and prepared a bomb. But that Friday, Abdülhamit stopped to chat to Şeyhülislam on the way out of the mosque and missed being killed by the bomb. Twenty-six people died. They caught the anarchist. Do you know what we did? We hammered nails into his bones, we pulled his fingernails out one by one. We made him our slave. Who did anarchists think they were, when even Christ gave in to pain? Didn't Christ reproach God in his last breath, crying out Father, why have you forgotten me? Everyone's on their own when they're suffering. You'll squeal too."

Blindfolded on the cross, I became oblivious. My ears would ring, I would forget where I was. I could hear the cry of a wolf in the distance. How many days, no, how many weeks ago was that? One night, as I was stumbling through knee-deep snow, I saw a wolf. The clouds hanging over Haymana Mountain had cleared and the stars had appeared one by one. There was a full moon. The wolf was standing high up, on the forest side, watching me. It was alone. In its eyes I could read the hunger suffered by all the wolves in the forest. Was I the only thing it had managed to find in the darkness? Hadn't it been able to sniff out a deer or a rabbit? I took out my Browning from my coat pocket and clutched its cold hilt. I loaded it. I know, that place was the wolf's home, the wolf's mountain. I was just a passing traveler. I had to get to the village behind the mountain before daybreak.

I had learned that a young boy I knew was wounded and that he was recovering in a shepherd's house in the village. I mustn't delay, I had to get that boy out of the village before dawn. The snow was denser in some parts, making it more difficult to walk. My pace slowed down and I stumbled. I felt like I was carrying rocks on my back. Even my own body felt heavy, sweat ran down my neck.

I stopped when I reached a new plain. I tightened and retied my loose bootlaces. I brushed the snow off my coat. The wolf that was following me waited too. Its tail was covered in snow. It had a piercing stare. It stood on the slope without moving. Did it also find it difficult to walk in the snow? Judging from its wasted body, the winter would be a harsh one. It neither came closer nor moved away. There was a bullet shot's distance between us. But I wasn't going to harm it. I picked up the gun I had left on the snow while I was tying my bootlaces and put it in my pocket. I raised my empty hands in the air, showing them to the wolf.

The wolf turned its head toward the sky and started howling. It was ready to defeat every enemy or to die alone. The only thing it feared was hunger. The sound of the echo reached far and wide, resounding through the forest and the sky. There on top of the hill it looked like a rock that had been there for years, defying the harsh winds. There was no wolf stronger than this one, and no breath hungrier than that wolf's. Everyone should know that, and bow their head to it. Its howl went on and on, reverberating in the snow, the forest and the night, and reaching the stars.

When the wolf had finished its howling, I started mine. Raising my head just like it had done, I screamed. My voice echoed and rippled. I held out my hands toward the stars. I too was here, under the same sky. I was ready to defeat every enemy or to die alone. I shouted until I was worn out. Then I stopped to catch my breath. As I rubbed a handful of snow into my hands I wondered whether I was a person who had come face to face with a wolf, or a wolf following a person. Which of us had just howled and put its seal on the night? My breath smelled of hunger. My neck was cold. Was this forest my home, or was I just a passing traveler?

I looked up at the sky. My father used to say that we had another life in the sky. Our world had a reflection, like a mirror. And each of us had a double living in the world in the sky. The people there slept during the day and woke up at night. They felt cold in the heat and got hot in the cold. They couldn't see when it was light but could make out the furthest object in the dark. The men in this world were women there, while the women were men. They didn't take life seriously, but attached great importance to dreams. They liked hugging strangers. They weren't ashamed of being poor, but of being rich. For them laughing was crying, while crying was laughing. When someone died they sang songs and danced. When I was a child I often stared at the sky to try and catch a glimpse of my other self. I wondered what I was like in that other life. Now, as I contemplated the forest in the darkness, I wondered whether we had another world in the forest too. Who knows, maybe our lives had reflected onto the forest as well. That was why our voices echoed. That echo was the response from our other life. Each person also had an animal equivalent among the trees. Some were gazelles, some were snakes. Maybe I was a wolf. A savage, lonely, gaunt wolf. And now, exhausted by hunger, I was following an old man on a snowy night.

The dry frost had made the sky as clear as glass, the forest was bathed in navy blue light. I looked at the wolf on the top of the hill. Like me, it too had stopped to rest. Its breathing was more regular now. We mustn't waste time, we needed to keep going. We started walking again. Leaving deep footprints in the snow, we focused our gaze on the horizon. We knew another slope would appear behind every slope and that on each slope there would be a new wind blowing. We were used to solitude. Like the shooting stars in the sky, we were here today, gone tomorrow. That was why we enjoyed walking side by side with a stranger. Our shadows in the moonlight were all we needed to trust one another. Would we walk together on the return journey too? Would we walk together under the same sky again? When I got to the shepherd's house I would take some meat and place it before the wolf on the way back. That was another reason why I was hurrying.

I passed Haymana Mountain without once stopping for a rest, the sweat pouring down my back, and reached the village before daybreak. When I saw the shepherd's house at the village entrance I stopped and glanced around me. The village was sound asleep. Smoke floated out of the chimneys in thin streaks. The roofs were blanketed with snow. But there were too many footprints on the ground. In the snow the footprints of oxen, dogs, and the villagers were all mixed together. A dim light was burning in the shepherd's window. He had left the gas lamp on. That was our signal. If the light wasn't lit I would know that something had gone wrong. I turned and looked behind me. The wolf had stopped some way back and was watching me. Once it had picked up the dogs' scent it hadn't come any closer. It was waiting on the border of its own world. But the dogs were nowhere to be seen. They weren't at the gate of the courtyard either. Either the cold had driven them into the barn, or they had gone down to the village. Examining the footprints in the snow carefully, I approached the house. I had a good look around, in case there were any footprints that looked like soldiers' boots among the footprints of rubber soles. I didn't see anything suspicious. I paused and sniffed the air. I scanned the opposite slope. How could I have known that the soldiers were lying in wait for me? How could I have guessed that they had been waiting to ambush me since last night? The only clue was the absence of the dogs. That didn't arouse my suspicions. I trusted the light in the window. I had abandoned my mind to that light. I wanted to take the wounded boy away as soon as possible and be far away from there before daybreak. But no sooner had I entered the courtyard than I was at the end of my journey. When the soldiers hiding behind the wall pounced on me I didn't have a chance to reach for the gun in my pocket. They flung me to the ground and beat me on the head with the butts of their rifles. They tied my hands and dragged me into the house.

I spat out the blood in my mouth and screamed. Tears of rage pricked my eyes. I couldn't believe that I had fallen into the trap so easily and been snared like a rabbit. I struggled, knocking over the kettle on the ground with my legs. Then I looked around to try and see who had informed on me. There was no shepherd and no sign of any wounded boy. The soldiers brought in a tall young man from the next room. Pointing at me they asked, "Is this him?" "Yes," said the young man. I thought for a moment, and then remembered. I had picked him up from this house last year and taken him to the group he was to meet in the mountains. He also nodded to the question, "Was he the one who brought the materials from Istanbul?" "He knows Istanbul like the back of his hand," he said, referring to me.

Istanbul? Where did he get that from? On the night we had met last year the young man and I had chatted on the way to the meeting place in the mountains. As usual I had raised the subject of Istanbul and tried to learn new things and see the city through someone else's eyes. As he described the Golden Horn I added the bridges over it, as he talked about the shop windows in the wide streets, I mentioned the squares at the end of them. So he assumed I was the one who had made contact with our friends in Istanbul, or else when they forced him to give someone's name, mine had been the first to enter his head. "Lies!" I cried, but the soldiers didn't believe me. They beat me and made me bleed. For two weeks they demanded the names and addresses of my connections and spread out a map of Istanbul before me so I could show them neighborhoods and street names. They demanded to know my secrets in the city. I told them the ones I knew. I talked about Istanbul's quays with their wooden buildings, its skyscrapers plated in glass, its gardens with judas trees. The best places to watch the sun set, I showed them the fast disappearing parks where, despite the crowds, you can still sit down at the end of the working day. I described the lights that flicker like fireflies in the distance at night. "The people from Istanbul are losing their faith in the city," I said, "but I believe in Istanbul."

Every city desired a conquest and every era created its own conqueror. I was a conqueror of fantasies. I believed in Istanbul and lived by fantasizing about her. As hopelessness spread like the plague, I knew they needed me there. They were waiting for me. I was ready to sacrifice my body so I could give life to Istanbul. Pain was the mirror of my love. When Christ raised the dead he did not give life to a corpse, he reminded a man who had forgotten that he was immortal of his immortality. I too had to remind an immortal city of her immortality. If necessary I would be crucified like Christ and gather all the world's suffering on my body. Istanbul, whose beauty was being ravaged a little more each day, needed me.

The wolf that had accompanied me on the night I had walked in the snow, had combined its time with mine. My father, who told me stories at night, had joined his time with mine. I couldn't forget either my father's stories or the wolf. With these things in mind, I had a strong desire to come to Istanbul, and thus took the final step of my life. I told the soldiers, "If you take me to Istanbul I'll show you the places you want to see and tell you the secrets you want to hear." If I was going to suffer I wanted to suffer in Istanbul, if I was going to die I wanted to die in Istanbul.

This Istanbul cell where I had ended up did not seem alien to me. I felt at home here. The cell seemed endless to me. Beyond the walls were the sea and the streets, and then new walls. It was impossible to tell one from the other. Each wall led to a street, and each street led to a sea. One behind the other, they stretched out endlessly. Pain on one side became happiness on the other, tears on one side turned into laughter on the other. Sorrow, apprehension, and joy were as closely entwined as sleeping kittens, sometimes it was difficult to tell their names apart. Just as you were thinking death was near, living suddenly sprang to life. Infinity was as fleeting as an instant. Right now I was at that limit. I could sense the sea behind the wall I was leaning on, I knew the streets winding ahead of me. I listened to the voice inside me. Like everyone else, I was more attached to what I hadn't seen than to what I had seen.

When Kamo the Barber started to cough I tore my gaze away from beyond the wall and forced it back inside. I realized I was cold. I looked at the Doctor and the Student. Their faces were shaded by darkness. Their breath smelled rank. They were as cold as I was. They hunched their shoulders and hid their hands in the hollow of their underarms.

Kamo the Barber, who had stopped coughing, raised his head from his knees. He examined us like a child who has woken up in the wrong room.

"Are you all right?" asked the Doctor.

Kamo didn't answer. He leaned over and picked up the plastic water bottle by the door. He drank. He wiped his mouth with the back of his hand.

I repeated the Doctor's question "Are you all right, Kamo?"

If he was in pain he would never admit it. He stopped frowning and his features relaxed.

"Uncle Küheylan," he said, "do you like wolves?"

Had he dreamt it? Was he asking about the wolf that had accompanied me on that snowy night, or the wolf that had eaten the young man in the hunters' story?

"Yes," I said.

He turned to face the light. Without blinking he focused on one spot. His face cheerful for once, he said, "If I were a wolf I would eat all of you."

Were we supposed to laugh or shudder?

"You're hungry. We have a bit of bread left. Shall I give it to you?"

"I'd still eat you."

He was talking without looking away from the light. Whatever he had dreamt, he was determined to eat us.

"Why?" I asked.

"Does there have to be a reason for everything, Uncle Küheylan? If it makes you feel better, I'll tell you why. You tell stories set in the cold. You make it snow, you have the hunters get caught in a storm. You make this drafty cell even more drafty, you turn the concrete we sit on into ice. When I'm really cold you give me no choice but to be a wolf. I want to rip you to pieces and eat you."

Could he smell the blood that clung to every inch of our body, which had dried on our hair, our faces, our necks? As his fangs itched, did he crave our battered flesh? I smiled to myself. Turning toward the light, I focused my gaze on one spot, like him. If everyone has a dark abyss inside them, Kamo was waiting at the edge of his. He stared into an infinite void, seeing only darkness, even in the light. That was why he was so disparaging of pain. The world and living seemed frivolous to him. He ate little bread and drank little water. He hoarded words in his memory, preferring to stay silent most of the time. He liked the dark and sleeping. He would close his eyes and withdraw into himself, as though abandoning himself to a buzzing inside his head. When he looked at our faces he would immediately notice the light clinging to our skin and pity us. Our condition made him sad. Maybe he asked himself the same questions all the time: Was fate like a line etched onto a wall? Could it never be removed, couldn't fate ever change?

"Uncle Küheylan, are you okay?" asked the Doctor, touching my arm. "You drifted off . . ."

Did I? I didn't know what was going through my head either.

"Ah, I was thinking about Istanbul. The Istanbul up above."

"Istanbul?"

Whenever I forgot what I had been thinking about, or whenever I wanted to change the subject, Istanbul was the first word that came into my head.

"When I get out of here," I said, "the first thing I'm going to do is go for a stroll on Galata Bridge. I'm going to stand next to the people fishing and watch the Bosphorus. Then I'm going to look for the person who's my double and who leads a different life here."

"Your double?" said the Doctor.

"What do you mean, a different life?" added the Student Demirtay.

"If I had been born in the city what kind of life would I have had?" I said. "There's an answer to that question because my double lives here. You say you always tell stories that you already know. This is a story that you don't know."

They eyed me with interest.

"What don't we know?" they asked.

"You know me as well as you know Istanbul, as well as you know pain. There are gaps in all three."

"Then tell us, we want to know it all."

"I'll tell you," I said. "In our tiny village my father used to

show us the sky at night, he would tell us that we lived a life
there. There was a mirror-like reflection of our life up there.
A double of every one of us lived there. I used to get out of
bed in the middle of the night and gaze out of my window
at the sky. I used to wonder what the child who was my
double was doing. I would observe the sky more whenever
my father left us to go to the city. I used to think that the
Istanbul stories he told us when he came back belonged to
our other life. Maybe Istanbul was the city in the sky where
the people who were our reflections lived. My father would
go there to see our doubles. He loved a child who looked
like me and told her stories about the village. The child in
Istanbul lived as though she were me, and because she did
the things I dreamed about doing, this is what occurred to
me one day: If I had a reflection in Istanbul, then I must be
her village equivalent. She wanted to know about me too.
Once I realized that, I started living for that child too. I tried
to do the things that she couldn't do in the city, I caught fish
in the river, I picked sloes in the mountains. I bandaged the
wounds of injured animals and carried heavy bags for old
ladies. Thinking that everyone lives for someone else as well,
I was twice as responsible. I remembered that when I laughed
a lot she was crying, that when I cried she was laughing. We
completed each other. I was a boy and she was a girl. Now I'll
tell you that girl's story. Would you like that?"

"Yes, tell us."

"Let's have a cup of tea first, we're parched."

I bent over. I raised my hand as though holding a teapot,
and filled our invisible tea glasses. Holding the glasses with
my fingertips, like I would if they were very hot, I handed one
to each of them. Then I passed them the sugar. The tea was
strong and fragrant. I stirred it slowly. They did the same.
When the Student Demirtay stirred his a bit too quickly I

signaled to him to slow down. The clinking of the spoon against the glass might travel down the corridor and reach the guards. Demirtay smiled. Life had discovered that smile, that tea, and these stories in here.

# 5TH DAY

*Told by the Student Demirtay*

## THE NIGHT LIGHTS

"It was during the war. War stories are long but I'll be brief. A military unit was weak with exhaustion after a series of conflicts that had gone on for days. They had run out of supplies and lost contact with the hinterland. They searched for a place where they could retreat; after walking for hours in the darkness they eventually arrived at a plateau. They drank water from a pool and gathered blackberries from the bushes. They couldn't risk shooting a deer, the sound of the gunshots would give away their hideout. After a short nap they climbed up a steep hill. They traveled by night and slept in the shelter of the rocks by day. They lit no fires, they ate any snakes or lizards they managed to hunt raw. If he could have been certain they wouldn't kill him, there was more than one amongst them who would have surrendered to the enemy for the sake of one meal a day. Had their entire army been routed? Who could they make contact with, and how? They couldn't find any signals, they couldn't enter into any villages and ask. The entire area was under enemy command. It's actually a long story, but I'll be brief. Growing fewer in number by the day, three days later they reached the top of a new mountain and lay down exhausted in the sunshine, and slept. When evening came and they found water and washed, they started to feel a bit more like their old selves, and tried to work out where they were. One soldier with a gold tooth pointed to the valley down below and said his native village was there. They stood in the darkness like lost children, gulping as they looked at where he was pointing. The lights in the village flickered like fireflies. The soldier with the gold tooth said he could go to his village and return with food. The commander objected. He might get caught and killed by the enemy. The soldier with the gold tooth said, we're on the point of death anyway. If I succeed I won't just come back with food, I can bring news of our boys, as well as information about the enemy. Everyone supported him. The soldier took his leave of his comrades, descended into the valley and vanished in the darkness. The sky changed color three times, going from dark blue to flaming red. Toward daybreak the soldier with the gold tooth appeared from between the rocks, with two holdalls on his back. In answer to his comrades' eager questions he said sit down, I've got things to tell you. He unloaded the holdalls from his back. The village is teeming with the enemy, he began. They don't know my village as well as I do, I managed to slip past without anyone seeing me and made it to my house. I knocked on the door. My wife opened the door; at the sight of me she would have shrieked, but I covered her mouth and calmed her down. Okay, so what happened next? The soldier with the gold tooth who asked this question delved into his holdall and took out a slab of cheese. Okay, he said, whoever guesses what happened next will get this cheese. The soldiers, whose breath stank from days of hunger, answered eagerly. You asked about enemy numbers, said one. You asked where our soldiers are, said another. Just as it started to look as if the questions would go on forever, a soldier from Istanbul sitting at the back raised his hand, you shagged your wife on the spot, he said. Laughing, the soldier with the gold tooth tossed him the cheese. The soldiers exclaimed in surprise and laughed out loud. The soldier with the gold tooth took a pie out of the holdall. I'll give this to whoever guesses what happened after that, he said. This time you really did ask about our soldiers, said one. You asked after your children, said another. The soldier from Istanbul sitting at the back raised his hand again. That type always sat at the back, whether it was in the army or at school. You shagged your wife again, he said. Laughing, the soldier with the gold tooth gave him the pie as well. He took a fried chicken out of the holdall and waved it in the air. I'll give this chicken to whoever guesses what I did after that, he said. You shagged her again! called out all the soldiers in unison, as though it was their early morning drill. The soldier with the gold tooth couldn't stop laughing. No, he said, after that I took my boots off."

I repeated the last sentence. "No, I took my boots off."

Covering my mouth, I started laughing fitfully. The Doctor and Uncle Küheylan laughed too, while their shoulders went up and down. We laughed soundlessly, but the walls shook with the impact of our convulsing bodies. We were like naughty children hiding in a secret nook and laughing where the grownups couldn't see them. Our mouths spread wide, we looked on happily. Knowing what would make someone laugh was one way of knowing them. We knew Kamo the Barber, on the other hand, by what wouldn't make him laugh. His face was dour. He gazed at us blankly, oblivious to what we found so funny.

Once we had settled down a bit I said, "We've laughed so much, I wonder if something terrible is about to happen to us."

"Something terrible?" said the Doctor. "Something terrible happen to us, here?"

We started laughing again. Only when people were either drunk or laughing did they forget about the future and shrug their shoulders at life. Just as time comes to a standstill when a person is suffering, it also comes to a standstill when he laughs. The past and the present are wiped away, only the infinity known as that instant remains.

Tired by our laughter, we slowed down. We wiped tears from our eyes.

"I knew that story about the soldiers," said Uncle Küheylan, "but there wasn't anyone from Istanbul in the story I knew, it was set in Russia."

The Doctor replied for me. "All stories become the property of Istanbul in here," he said.

"You don't just stop at telling stories you already know, you change them and mold them into whatever shape you want."

"Didn't your father do the same thing, Uncle Küheylan? Didn't he fling the Istanbul sailors into the oceans in pursuit of white whales, didn't he bring the hunters in the wolf story all the way to Istanbul?"

The Doctor and Uncle Küheylan became engrossed in discussing soldiers, hunters, and sailors. They talked about the coastal road that had meant the end of the old fishing village in Kumkapı, about the ever-decreasing number of judas trees along the shoreline of the Bosphorus, about how the Architect Sinan's four-hundred-year-old work, the Ilyaszade Mosque, was demolished so a petrol station could be built in its place, and about how an earthquake a thousand years ago had caused the nearest island to the shore to sink into a sea like Atlantis, and asked, "Is Istanbul an island too?"

Istanbul was an island that was growing fat on the sins that would one day lead to her downfall, according to the Doctor. Sins here did not stay the same, but changed all the time. That's why the city was not a known place, but somewhere people learned about day by day. Her mystery whipped her craving for change, fanned her yearning to attach herself to the future. When today grows vague, the truth grows vague too, ceding its place to symbols. Buildings replaced mountains, and balconies with flowers replaced the shore. And love too would turn into an insatiable, hairy, damp animal, constantly in search of new experiences.

Uncle Küheylan protested, arguing with the Doctor that symbols were more real than truths. In this world, where they did not come of their own free will, people were not liable for discovering their own existence, but for bringing it into being. Mountains were mountains before we existed, just as trees were also trees before we came along. But was the city that way, were steel, electricity, and telephones thus? People who created music out of noise, and mathematics out of numbers, created a new universe along with the city. The more distant they grew from external nature, the closer they got to their own nature. Instead of mountain peaks, they believed in roofs sprouting up one beside the other, instead of rivers they believed in crowded streets, and instead of the stars, they believed in lights that shone everywhere.

Which did I believe in, the stars or the city lights? I pondered that last month, while looking out of the window of the house in Hisarüstü where I was hiding, trying to work out where the stars ended and where the city lights began. When I took a break from reading I became lost in the Milky Way and my fantasies, then wondered whether the shimmering forms I was looking at really were the Milky Way.

For the first few days I was not alone in the house in Hisarüstü, Yasemin Abla was there with me. I didn't know her real name, and she too knew me by another name, Yusuf. We had met in Gezi Park in Taksim; because we had never met before, according to our brief, I had recognized her by the green scarf around her neck and she had recognized me by the sports magazine I was holding. She looked about five or six years older than me.

"Yusuf," she had said when we arrived at the house, "we'll be staying here for a few days. The neighbors know me, if anyone asks we'll say we're brother and sister. But try not to let anyone see you."

It was a one room gecekondu. There was a small bathroom by the entrance. The kitchen consisted of a stove in the room we were in.

When it was time for bed we took it in turns to get changed in the bathroom. We slept on two separate couches. When the smell of a burning match woke me up not long afterward, I half-opened my eyes. I saw Yasemin Abla sitting by the window, cigarette in hand, contemplating the view outside.

"Couldn't you sleep?" I said.

"We can't get in touch with one of our friends. He missed two appointments yesterday. I was thinking about him."

"Does he know this house?" The question was out of my mouth before I knew it.

"There's only one address he could give if he got caught and we evacuated it last night. He doesn't know this house."

"I just asked."

"I don't blame you for worrying, Yusuf."

I got out of bed and joined her, sitting down on the chair on the other side of the table. I also lit a cigarette.

"Yasemin Abla," I said, trying not to let my anxiety show, "have you ever been arrested?"

"No, and you?"

"No, me neither."

The house was on a slope. Rickety gecekondus sprawled all the way down the hill. The streetlights that stretched down to the sea mingled with the lights of the ships and the boats sailing on the Bosphorus. This was one of Istanbul's most beautiful shorelines. Instead of the opulent villas and skyscrapers, she lavished her hospitality on the tiny gecekondus.

We brewed tea and sat up until dawn. We didn't talk about politics, but about books and our dreams. I was envious of Yasemin Abla's repertoire of poems, of her ability to recite a couplet containing any word I said. When I said "sea," she murmured the couplet, "O free man! Thou shalt always cherish the sea." When I said "clock," she replied, "Clock! Menacing, horrific, stone faced god!" She laughed like a grade A student. We had turned off the light and her face shone radiant in the light of the streetlamp. At the end of the night, when mist was draping itself over the red of dawn, we got back into our beds. We slept, heedless of the cries of the seagulls and sparrows.

At around midday Yasemin Abla went out. After it had grown dark she returned, carrying a bag full of food.

"There's still no word from our missing friend, Yusuf. I'm traveling out of the city tomorrow, I'll be back in three days at the latest."

"What should I do?"

"I've brought you food. If I'm not back by the evening of the third night, empty the house. Don't leave anything here that might give a clue to your identity."

Yasemin Abla heated water on the stove, she went into the bathroom and washed. When she came out she was wearing her pajamas.

When she saw me sitting at the table trying to sew the tear in my jacket she asked, "Can you sew?"

"No," I said.

"Give it to me then, I'll sew it for you. The hook has come off my earring, you can put it back on for me."

I took the amber earrings from her and compared them, to work out how to repair the one without its hook. I moved my pocket knife slowly, so as not to damage the amber.

As Yasemin Abla was sewing the tear on the shoulder of

my jacket, she raised her head. "Do you like handicrafts?" she asked.

"Not really. How about you?"

"I used to be a seamstress. I love touching fabric, and cutting it. I made my pajamas and my dress myself."

I looked at her dress hanging on the wall. It was low cut, knee-length, with a belt. The flowers on the print of the dress matched her earrings.

"Stand up and try your jacket on," she said.

I put on the jacket and moved my arms forward and sideways.

"You've done a great job," I said.

Yasemin Abla came closer and straightened the jacket's creased collar.

"Well, you'll have plenty of time on your hands. Iron your jacket before I get back."

"At your command," I said, smiling.

"It's not a command, it's a wish."

Her hair was wet, she smelled of roses. She had the freshness of someone recently bathed. She stepped back slowly. She picked up the teapot from the stove and filled the tea glasses.

She liked talking. She told me about the impoverished house where she had grown up, and the world she had looked out on from the small window of that house. Once again, she recited couplets containing each word I spoke. She watered the geraniums on the windowsill. The geraniums in one of the two pots were blossoming, while the flowers in the other were withering. She said that when she returned she would water the flowers in the garden too. There were four-o'clock flowers, oleanders, and roses in the garden. As we talked, the night nestling between our words and the flowers seeped out and flowed away, like water from a cracked bottle. We did not notice that the sky had grown light and that the stars had retired.

When I awoke not long afterward to the sound of rain, she was not in her bed. She had crept out silently.

I sat by the window and lit a cigarette.

A storm was brewing outside. An unruly wind was howling. The Istanbul Sea was uncanny. It had raged suddenly, turning day into night. The clouds had grown black, like in oil paintings. In the Bosphorus the waves were tossing a ship about, flinging it toward the shore. The ship, flailing in all directions, had sounded its SOS siren. It might sink and be engulfed by the waters at any moment. The siren's piercing shriek mingled with the sounds of the rain, the wind, and the waves. As the ship's entire crew looked up at the sky and supplicated God, perhaps the drunks, beggars, and those on the brink of suicide on the shore begged for the ship to come and pick them up from the rocks first, and then sink, if that was its intention. Sinking with a ship was the best way to go. The sea cracked its whip again and again, foaming with wrath. The waves reared like untamable wild horses. Yasemin Abla had picked the perfect weather to go out in. Either that, or the storm had waited for her to go out and for the ship below to arrive at the Bosphorus. As the wind scattered the last petals of the four-o'clock flowers, the oleanders, and the roses in the garden, the streets were empty. Dogs and the homeless were sheltering in the ruins of crumbling buildings. Istanbul, dizzy with destitution and extravagance, waited with her arms spread wide, while the ship's crew, alternately begging and cursing the storm god, could not envisage any grave other than the sea. When every avenue was closed, was it better to accept one's fate, or to curse? The storm inspired such debates. And yet one fuchsia geranium on the windowsill faded, whilst another bloomed, in the same air, and with the same water.

It was only then that I noticed the amber earring. It was sitting between two plant pots, untouched by the rain and wind outside. It was the earring I had repaired the previous night. Where was the other? I searched everywhere, on the couch, by the front door. I glanced in front of the mirror in the bathroom. Had Yasemin Abla forgotten the other earring there as she was packing her things? Had she left in that much of a hurry?

I sat on the couch and, holding the earring with my fingertips, raised it in the air. It was a golden translucent grape, swinging from a silver hook. Lights and curls swirled inside its ancient depths. Orange and brown waves undulated gently inside it. I stared at this amber earring that had hung from women's ears, and been displayed in shop windows, for so many years, as though I had never seen one before. How did the selection process of our minds work? When did someone become aware of an object's existence?

Just like the earrings I hadn't noticed before, perhaps I had walked in the same street as Yasemin Abla without noticing her either. Maybe it had been another rainy day. People huddled under umbrellas, scuttling alongside the magnificent tall buildings, brushed past young girls busking in passage entrances. Some reminisced about the lover who had abandoned them, while others despaired over their unruly children. Everyone spoke the same language, but no one understood one other. Each mind had other minds living inside it. When it rained, Istanbul became a forest densely populated with bare trees. Everyone grew flustered, and every house, every street, and every face looked the same. I was walking past Yasemin Abla, rushing to get to her appointment on time, her hair wet. Pulling the hood of my duffle coat down over my forehead, I hurried on. If she had dropped one of her earrings and carried on walking without realizing, if I had picked up the amber earring at my feet out of the puddle, if I had stopped for an instant and examined my wet hand and the gray crowd that had swallowed Yasemin Abla, would Istanbul have changed for me? Would that earring have filled my heart with a joy I had never known before?

The odd thing about Istanbul was the way she preferred questions to answers. She could turn happiness into a nightmare, or the other way round, make a joyous morning dawn after a night devoid of all hope. She gained strength from uncertainty. They called this the city's destiny. The heaven in one street and the hell in another could suddenly change places. Just as in the tale of the king and the pauper: A king desired a bit of entertainment. He ordered a pauper dozing in the street to be brought to the palace. When the pauper woke up, everyone revered him as a king and served him. Once the pauper had got over his amazement he believed he genuinely was the king. He thought his other life of penury had been a dream. At the end of the day, when night descended and he fell into a happy sleep, they carried him outside again. When he opened his eyes he found himself back in the street, amongst the rubbish. He couldn't work out what was real and what had been a dream. For several nights they played the same game. When the pauper first woke up he was in the palace, and when he next woke up he was in the street. Each time he believed his other life had been a dream. Who could say that stories were growing stale and weren't allowed into the city? Weren't that king and that pauper both from Istanbul? One got pleasure from toying with people's destiny, while the other tried to live by swinging between one end of the scale of truth and the other. Did the people hurrying in the rain now know in what state they would wake up tomorrow morning?

In the same way that Istanbul was not Istanbul, neither was the amber earring an amber earring. It had its history.

Yasemin Abla had bought that earring because she liked it and thought it suited her. Then she had given it to me to repair, and added me to its history. Inside this amber earring with its yellowish tinges was a story and a beautiful person's dream.

I returned to the window and took another look outside. The sea had settled and the waves were now calm. Where was the ship struggling against the storm a moment before, sounding its SOS? Had it continued on its way, or was it buried at the bottom of the sea? It had stopped raining. The dogs had gone out into the street. A man was strolling absently along the rows of houses. He wasn't wearing a coat or carrying an umbrella. He took no notice of the puddles he stepped into. He paused for a moment and turned his head toward the house. I couldn't make out his face in the darkness, but it wasn't difficult to imagine that he was weary and hungry. He decided against continuing on, and turned around. He quickened his pace, as though he had forgotten something and was hurrying to retrieve it.

I brewed a pot of tea. I had breakfast, although it was late. I looked at the row of books lined up on the only shelf on the wall. I chose two books. One was *An Anthology of World Poetry*, the other was the novel *Memed, My Hawk*, by Yaşar Kemal. I lay down on the couch. After reading several poems I started on the novel.

The clamor of the children and the street vendors resonated in the sunshine after the rain. How vigorous and cheerful the sun was; just as it withdrew into itself during the storm, its presence pervaded everything afterward. I wanted to open the window, but knew that I mustn't let anyone see that the house was occupied. I peered out into the street from behind the curtain. I opened the window a tiny crack, imperceptible from outside. I inhaled the cool, fresh air.

I passed the days reading, lying on the couch, and sleeping a lot. At night I contemplated the lights in the neighborhood and the boats sailing on the Bosphorus. The sky changed every night. The colors flowed in turn from one end of the sky to the other, the wind scattered the lights in the distance in all different directions. I waited until the evening of the third day with a calm heart and my fingers entwined around the amber earring. I finished the novel and read certain poems over and over again.

Yasemin Abla had said "the evening of the third day." I started to think of the worst case scenario, I imagined she had been caught. I got ready as the sun was setting. I tidied up. I packed my toothbrush and my razor. As I was tying the dustbin liner containing our cigarette butts I heard footsteps outside the door.

There was a knock at the door, but it wasn't the agreed-upon knock.

I waited.

A child's voice said, "Is nobody in?"

It must be the child of one of the neighbors. I didn't budge.

The same voice came in a whisper this time, "Ağbi, will you open the door?" Ağbi? How did she know me? If they had seen me arrive with Yasemin Abla, why was she calling me and not Yasemin? I didn't get it. I went to the door without switching on the light and slowly opened the door a tiny crack. A little girl was staring at me, wide-eyed.

"Ağbi, I have homework to do for tomorrow, will you help me? My grandmother told me to call you."

"Your grandmother? Who is your grandmother?"

"We live in the house behind yours. Yasemin Abla helps me with my homework too."

"Yasemin Abla's out. I'll tell her you dropped by when she gets back, and she'll come and see you."

"My grandmother asked for you. She said go and call you, Yusuf Ağbi."

A hundred questions flashed through my mind in an instant. How did she know that Yasemin Abla wasn't back? How did she find out my name? My curiosity wouldn't allow me not to go. And waiting at the neighbor's house was a better option than staying at home.

"I'll just get my jacket," I said.

I picked up my rucksack on the way out. I wouldn't be coming back here. I threw the bin liner onto the pile of rubbish behind the low garden wall.

"What's your name?"

"Serpil."

Serpil walked up the narrow alleyway beside the house. She knew her way around in the dark. I followed her in silence. Once at the back we climbed over broken fences. We walked through another alleyway I would never have found by myself, and climbed up a dilapidated stone stairway. When we were in front of the houses I stopped and looked. We were above the gecekondu where I had been staying.

Serpil walked through the open door first.

"Come inside, Ağbi," she said.

It was a one-room house, just like ours. A woman sat on the couch by the window. She was knitting.

"Are you here, Yusuf?" said the woman.

"Good evening," I said.

"Come and sit next to me, my boy."

It was only then that I noticed the woman was blind. I sat opposite her and looked not at her face but at her fingers busily knitting. Knit two, purl two she counted, as her knitting grew longer. She stopped, as if she were aware that I was looking at her fingers.

"Come closer," she said, putting down her needles.

She held out her hands and touched my face. She felt my cheeks, my chin, and my forehead. She put one hand on my neck and moved the other along my nose and eyebrows.

"You have regular features and a handsome face," she said, as though she were talking about her knitting. "Yasemin told us about you. Help the child with her homework. I can't always get my head around school problems."

I didn't think I had ever seen a house so stricken by poverty. There were no curtains on the window. The pane was broken and they had covered the gap in the top corner where the glass was missing with a plastic bag. There was a camping cylinder by the opposite wall and next to it a cardboard box containing a few plates and glasses. They were boiling water for tea on the weak flame of the camping cylinder. The rug on the floor was faded and in tatters. The plaster was peeling off the walls. There were no table or chairs. There were two quilts folded one on top of the other at the top end of the couch. It was clear that at night the grandmother slept at one end of the couch and Serpil at the other.

Serpil picked up her schoolbag from the floor and came and sat beside me. She opened her bag, which was discolored and splitting at the seams, and took out her text and exercise books.

"Our teacher set us three questions."

"Let's start then," I said, "read them out one by one."

Serpil looked first at her grandmother, then at me, and started reading.

"Unit questions. Question one: Why do the seasons change? Why isn't it always summer or always winter?"

"How am I supposed to know that?" said the grandmother.

Serpil and I looked at each other and smiled.

"Write, Serpil dear," I said, "There are two reasons: The first is that the world revolves around the sun. The second is that the earth's axis is not straight. Because the sun's rays hit the earth from different angles throughout the year, the temperature also changes. That's how come we have seasons."

"I knew it," said the grandmother.

"Why didn't you tell me if you knew?" said Serpil.

"Not the question, my lovely, I mean I knew that all Yasemin's friends were clever."

I coughed abruptly and tried to correct her. "I'm not Yasemin's friend, I'm her brother," I said.

"Brother, friend, what difference does it make, you're all the same."

All three of us chatted as we completed Serpil's homework. We discussed why the snow on the mountain peaks didn't melt even though the seasons changed, and why there was only one season in the poles, although there were four where we were.

"We're like the poles," said the grandmother. "We stay poor all the time. I wish the rich and the poor could change places, like the four seasons. That wouldn't be bad justice at all."

It was clear from the autumn draft that blew in from the gap in the window that they would soon be needing that justice. What were they going to do once Istanbul's cold and snow and the damp that seeped into one's bones came? Would they light a heater? Serpil's toes peeped out of the holes in her socks. Maybe her grandmother was knitting her a pair of socks and then planned to knit her a thick sweater. They were both thin. Their fingers were bony and their faces pale. I could tell that it was just the two of them in the house because they had no furniture except the couch and no covers except the two quilts.

"I'd better go," I said.

The grandmother held my arm. "I won't hear of it, you haven't had any tea yet, or anything to eat. Serpil darling, if you've finished your homework pour us some tea. And bring your Yusuf Ağbi some food."

"I've just got one last thing to do, Grandma. I have to memorize a poem."

"Which poem?"

"A poem about our Heavenly Homeland."

"Heavenly?" laughed the grandmother. "Some heaven!"

I sat up. "Let Serpil study, I'll pour the tea," I said.

"I don't want to put you to any trouble, my boy. There's some bread and olives there too. You can have them with your tea."

"Thank you, I'm full. I ate before I came."

Serpil sat beside the quilts and opened her textbook in preparation for memorizing the poem.

I poured the tea. I added sugar to the glasses and stirred.

The grandmother put her knitting on her lap and held the hot glass between her two palms.

"I started to knit when I was Serpil's age," she said. "I could see then. Our village was on the other side of the world. We had two seasons there. In the summer I worked in the fields, in the winter I knitted. There I was thinking I would spend my whole life in the fields, and now I make my living by selling the sweaters I knit. The neighbors act as go betweens, they tell their friends about me. And some days I go down to the beach and sell them on the street. But how far can we make the money we get from the sweaters stretch? This child needs more than that."

"Not just the child, you too."

The grandmother put the tea glass she was holding on the windowsill. Leaning toward me she said, "If I ask you a question will you be able to answer it?"

"What is it about?"

"It's about Serpil."

I stared at her blankly.

"It's a simple question," she said. "Serpil is my daughter's daughter and my husband's sister. How can that be?"

More than the question itself, I pondered how little sense

it made. "That sounds like a riddle," I said.

"I ask Yasemin similar questions, and give her until her next visit to answer them. I want her to have another reason for coming back. Will you be able to work out the answer to the question?"

"I doubt it, it looks complicated."

"I'm very happy to hear it. I'm going to give you time too. Wherever it is you're going, look after yourself, and come back safely. I want the answer to the riddle."

"Don't worry, I'll come back with the answer," I said, trying to sound cheerful.

The grandmother sat back. She wiped her eyes with her fingertips. "Do you know, Yusuf," she said, "I miss the dreams I had before I lost my eyesight. When I looked at the young girls at weddings in the village I thought they were mountain nymphs. They had long necks and bare cleavages, birds fluttered on their breath. I used to dream that I would be like those girls when I grew up, that I would cast light on mirrors, but before I reached adolescence my life had changed. For an entire summer, winds smelling of mildew blew in the village, the crops rotted. Shepherds found deer drowned in the river, and corpses of wolves that had fallen over the precipice. Majestic winged eagles that flew as though they were the sultans of the heavens fell out of the sky one by one. The disease that was blinding them soon spread to the children. Many of my friends died in a single night, complaining of pain in their eyes. The women mourners arrived and started up their lament. I was lucky, I lost my sight but stayed alive. I cried hard, the women mourners lamented even harder. They said the village had been cursed for setting traps for baby deer and for shooting baby wolves. Do you know that story, Yusuf? There was a city inhabited by blind people, everyone there was born blind. One day a child regained his sight and started to see the things around him. The villagers were terrified of this disease and killed that child to stop it spreading to all the other children. They burned his body. I'm thinking of Istanbul. What does this city, which commits such terrible sins, deserve? What kind of a curse should smite her? Or has she already been smitten and are we suffering the consequences? Here they lynch anyone who regains their sight. You have dreams, my boy, and they lynch you too." The grandmother slowed down, as though she were growing sleepy, her voice grew fainter. She murmured to herself. "They'll lynch Yasemin, with her long neck, her bare cleavage, and the birds fluttering on her breath too."

I looked outside. The garden entrance to our gecekondu was visible from the window. It was possible to observe who went in and out from here. But who was going to do it, the blind grandmother? It had grown dark, Yasemin Abla had not returned, nor would she after this time.

The sounds of ships' horns and seagulls' cries came from the distance. The stars flowed onto the city, like a dust cloud from the east. The sky looked wet, as though it were overlaid with water. Perhaps there were more stars beyond the horizon and they were waiting because there was no more room in the sky. The sky was both infinite and compact enough to fit into a bell jar. It was difficult to tell where the stars ended and where the city lights began.

The grandmother leaned forward and held my hand. She placed a folded piece of paper in my palm.

I opened it with great curiosity and read the short note: "the house is being watched . . . gray point . . . tomorrow . . . 15 . . . ps: forget the earrings . . ."

The earrings?

The grandmother delved into her cleavage and extracted an earring from her bra. It was the other amber earring completing the pair.

"Has Yasemin Abla been here?" I asked excitedly.

"I'm blind, I couldn't say," she said, enigmatically. "There's an alleyway that backs onto the rear exit. Serpil will show you. You can leave that way without anyone seeing you."

I reread the note in my hand. We had our own precautions. We named our meeting places after different colors. The gray point was the bus stop in front of the University of Istanbul Library. And the meetings were always an hour before the stated time; we were going to meet at 1400 hours. Sending the other earring was Yasemin Abla's strategy for ensuring I believed the note was from her. Her warning to "forget the earrings!" was as clear as a nail driven into the wall. I mustn't leave a single trace behind me, I mustn't carry anything on me that was in any way linked to anyone else.

I kissed the grandmother's hand.

"There are some geraniums in our house. If I leave you the key will you water them?" I asked.

"Don't worry, my boy, we have your key," said the grandmother. She picked up her knitting, wrapped the wool around her finger and started knitting again, raising and lowering the needles like a bird's wings. As I was leaving she called out behind me. "Don't forget my question, I want the answer."

Outside, the biting wind licked my face. I wrapped my scarf tightly around my neck. Following Serpil, I plunged into the darkness. The alleyway twisted and curved into infinity, forking in places. There was brush everywhere. Someone who didn't know where they were going would get lost before they knew it. It was like a secret labyrinth. The light was growing dimmer, the sound of dogs barking from below grew fainter. Once we had passed the hill and the brush we came out at a vegetable garden. We paused at the point from where I had to continue my journey alone.

I took out the money I had in my pocket and gave half of it to Serpil. I told her to study hard and to take good care of her grandmother. I leaned down and kissed the top of her head. It was then that it struck me that her face, with its glowing radiance, was perfect for the amber earrings. It was candid, delicate, and charming. She looked like a mountain nymph. All that was missing was the yellow amber. I moved her two plaits away with my hand, and raised her chin. I put one amber earring in one of her ears and the other in her other ear. "These are yours now," I said. She blinked in disbelief and raised her hands to her face. She touched the earrings dangling like two drops of water. Her face had the most beautiful expression in the world. If I let her she would grow wings and fly off into the star-studded sky.

As I entered the vegetable garden and slowly started walking, the verses I had learned from Yasemin Abla sprang to my mind. "O free man! Thou shalt always cherish the sea."

At that moment someone called out my real name. I stopped in the darkness and looked around me. I couldn't work out where the voice was coming from. My heart pounded in my breast. A cold sweat ran down my neck. When I heard the same voice again I half-opened my eyes.

"Demirtay," said the Doctor, "you're talking in your sleep."

"I must have dozed off," I said, staring at the dark walls of the cell. Sleeping and losing myself in thought was healing. I dreamed that I was out of here and regressed to my old life in the days before they captured me. Afterward it was always awful. When I opened my eyes in the cell again, hopelessness and regret clawed at me. I saw a pus-colored wall before me. Why did I get caught, why hadn't I run faster, I berated myself. I wanted another chance. A chance that would radically change my life, I said. Then I would writhe in pain from the injuries covering my body.

"Uncle Küheylan," I said, "shall I ask you a riddle?"

"Lord bless us, are you going to get your own back and put me to the test now after my riddle yesterday?"

"My riddle's harder. Listen. A woman has a little girl with her. I ask if it's her granddaughter. This is what she says: This is my daughter's daughter and my husband's sister. How can that be?"

"Did you dream that?"

"No," I said. I didn't mention the grandmother and Serpil.

"My daughter's daughter, my husband's sister," repeated Uncle Küheylan to himself. "It's a good question. Let me think about it and let's see if I can solve it."

Uncle Küheylan and the Doctor pondered the question while wondering why they hadn't taken anyone away to be tortured for the past two days, and why they were leaving all the cells in peace. They hadn't taken anyone yesterday or today. The iron gate had only opened when the guard was changing and when they were bringing our ration.

"The interrogators are people too, they got tired of torturing people for ten, twenty hours a day and they've all taken the day off so they can have a break. They're lying on a beach somewhere warm, maybe on an island in the ocean, letting the sun shrivel up their souls," Uncle Küheylan said, laughing.

"No," said the Doctor, "torture is sweaty work and they went out before their sweat had dried. They caught a chill in the cold and wind and it spread quickly. Now they're all at home taking it easy and drinking lime blossom infusion with lemon and mint."

While the Doctor and Uncle Küheylan were laughing, a small button slid across the concrete floor of the cell, landing by our feet. We couldn't understand where it had come from. It was a yellow, star-shaped button with two holes. Uncle

Küheylan picked it up and held it to the light. "This button comes from a woman's clothing," he said. We all went to the grille and looked out. Zinê Sevda was standing in the opposite cell like a portrait in a gray frame. She had ripped off one of her buttons and thrown it to us from the gap under the door. She smiled when she saw us, or rather when she saw Uncle Küheylan. Her purple-ringed eyes lit up. She traced "How are you?" in the air. Uncle Küheylan replied, writing the letters laboriously, like a schoolboy who has just started classes.

Leaving them alone together, I sat back down. I placed my feet on top of the Doctor's. I contemplated Kamo the Barber's impassiveness as he slept with his head on his knees. He hadn't said a word today, but behaved as though we weren't there. He had withdrawn into his shell and slept all the time.

When Uncle Küheylan, who was standing at the door, leaned down and said, "Kamo, come to the grille, Zinê Sevda wants to thank you," Kamo raised his head. He stared with an even more jaded expression than usual. He examined his surroundings as though trying to remember where he was. Then, waving his hand in the air in a dismissive gesture, he signaled that he wanted to be left alone. He hugged his knees, buried his face in his arms, and retreated into his own world. The most secluded spot he could escape to was his sleep. That was the furthest he could get away from us.

# 6<sup>TH</sup> DAY

*Told by the Doctor*

## THE BIRD OF TIME

"A girl boarded a large ship in the port of Istanbul with great stealth, climbed up the steps, and hid in a large lifeboat. She wrapped herself up in a sail and strained her ears to listen for any sounds coming from outside. Once the ship had set sail she heaved a sigh of relief. Time aboard passed between sleep and wakefulness. She listened to the crew singing. When the ship anchored in a port, she waited until everything had turned quiet and darkness had fallen. She descended the steps unseen by anyone, and started running. She was heading toward a new world. As she ran until dawn she noticed that the full moon was following her, turning wherever she turned. She reached the desert. She lay down on the sand. She rested a while. Far off in the distance she noticed a hovel. In front of the hovel an elderly hermit was facing the sun, praying. The hermit stood up slowly, and stared at the silk-clad beauty coming toward him, as though he were in a dream. He hurried inside his hovel and, kneeling before a holy manuscript, spoke to himself: God is putting me to the test. I must not succumb to the desires of the flesh. Besides, I'm an old man. I'll go outside and give the girl some water. The girl told him she did not want to live in the palace harem, that she had run away from Istanbul and that she wanted to stay with the hermit. That way she could also discover the right way to serve God.

The hermit advised her to keep walking, saying there was another hermit who lived behind the sand dunes who was much better qualified to show her the right way to serve God. The girl walked wearily under the blazing sun. Around noon she reached the second hermit's hovel. Thinking he had seen a mirage, the second hermit rubbed his eyes and stared hard. The creature approaching him was a long-haired, slender-waisted nymph. This was the hardest test the hermit had ever had to endure. As God had subjected him to such a difficult challenge it must mean that he was well on his way to becoming a hallowed saint. Upon this realization, he fell to his knees and held his arms heavenward. Dear God, he prayed. I may be old but I still have desires. My flesh is burning, my blood is boiling, but I will resist. I shall not go the devil's way. Then, seizing the water bowl, he advanced toward the girl. She drank thirstily. Drops of water trickled from her lips, down to her chin, all the way to her neck. The girl looked at him through lowered lashes, take care of me, she implored, let me stay with you, show me the way to serve God. The hermit sighed. Ah my daughter, he said, how I would have loved to show you the way to serve God. There's someone who can do that much better than me. Go over those dunes, go to the hermit who lives in the spot where the sun sets. There you'll find the way to serve God. What was the desert? What was it, other than sand and sun? Grains of sand were all alike, so were sand dunes, and so were hermits. They were all like each other, one repeated the other's words. As long as the sun burned with unabating fire, what was the desert? The girl walked on and on, growing wearier and wearier, her pace getting slower and slower. As the sun was on the verge of setting she went over the final sand dune and spied the hovel below it. Here is the most beautiful part of the desert, she said. In front of the hovel was a hermit who was much younger than the others. Kneeling facing the setting sun, he was rapt in prayer. When the young hermit heard the girl's voice he turned and looked. Before him he beheld a nymph, with budding breasts and bare thighs. It was a gift from God. The hermit held the girl, who had swooned from exhaustion, in his arms, and carried her into the hovel. He dabbed her forehead, neck, and cracked lips with a wet cloth. He waited at her bedside until daybreak. God showed people beauty in many ways. Roses on bushes, water in the desert, and the moon in the sky were beautiful. In addition to all that, the nymph girl was a mirror of heaven. The path to God was that of the quest for this beauty. That was why the hermit was interred in the depths of the desert at such a young age. As the sky outside was beginning to turn light, the girl opened her eyes. She gazed at the hermit. I don't want to go back to the palace, she said, let me stay with you, show me how to serve God. They stepped outside the hovel, knelt before the newly risen sun, and closed their eyes. God was with them. They spent that day gathering leaves and making a bed for the girl. At night they slept side by side. The hermit thought long and hard, he had torrid dreams, and one night he made his decision. Are you prepared to serve God with all your being? he asked the girl. She was. Listen, said the hermit. The Devil is God's archenemy. God banishes him to the fires of hell, but he gets out again. A person's duty is to serve God. Now you do just as I do. The hermit slipped out of his clothing. The girl too removed her silk dress. They were now naked. The sky had turned darker, vaster, and was studded with stars. They knelt on the sand and gazed up at the full moon. While they waited in silence, as though in prayer, physical changes began to take place. The hermit's manhood gradually became resurrected until it was rigid. What's that? asked the girl. That's the Devil, said the hermit. He's causing me pain. Surprised, the girl bent down to take a closer look. She frowned. She pitied the hermit.

Adopting a pious tone of voice, the hermit said, I know why God sent you here. He wants to know whether we will be able to put my Devil into your hell. He is testing us both. We have to help each other. The girl gazed at him loyally. She said she was willing to do whatever it took to get God's blessing. The hermit rose to his feet and led the girl inside the hovel. When they awoke the following morning their faces bore a different expression. They smiled at one another in bed. The Devil really must be God's archenemy, said the girl, he grew violent when he was driven inside me and ran rampant in the fires of hell. I counted, we sent him back to hell six times in total during the night. The hermit told her they needed to keep up the good work. To tread the path to God they would require a great deal of faith. He mounted the girl. Once again he put the Devil back in hell. There is nothing as sweet as serving God, said the girl. I think anyone who thinks of doing anything but serving God is a fool. But all night long I've been thinking: Why didn't God destroy the Devil from the start? If He wants to destroy him but isn't strong enough, that means God is weak. But if He doesn't want to destroy him even though He can, that means He consents to evil. If God is strong enough to destroy the Devil and wants to do it, then why does the Devil still exist? Where does this evil come from? They spent their days in the desert talking, sleeping, and worshipping God. The sun rose and set in the same spots, but each night the moon had a different face. One day as the hermit sat beside the hovel, gazing into the distance, the girl protested. I didn't come here to sit in idleness, she said, I came here to serve God. What have we been waiting for since yesterday, why aren't we putting the Devil back into hell? The hermit smiled. He said they had taught the Devil his lesson and that they would not punish him unless he reared his head with pride. The girl looked dismayed. She placed her hands on her belly. You may well have quenched the rage in your Devil, she said, but the fire in my hell is still burning. Hell wants the Devil. They saw a cloud of dust in the distance. The sand in the desert flowed skyward. A group of men on horseback came over the dunes and stood beside them. We've come for the princess, they said. They mounted the girl on a horse. Turning back the way they came, they disappeared in the same cloud of dust. Back in the Istanbul Palace, they entrusted the girl to the care of the doctors and ladies in waiting. They bathed her in rosewater and sat her down before a mirror. They wove beads into her hair, anointed her skin with perfumed oils and lined her eyes with kohl. Once they had prepared her, they took her for an audience with the court's older women. The older women asked her what had befallen her and what she had done in the desert. I worshipped God, said the girl, my life was nothing but virtue. I opened my legs and the hermit put the Devil into hell. I learned how happy worshipping makes people. If only I could have continued serving God. For a moment the older women were silent, then they burst out laughing. Don't worry, they said, anyone who wants to put the Devil into hell and serve God can do it here too."

I laughed as though I were in the Istanbul Palace with those older women, instead of in the cell. Leaning forward, I tried to repeat the last sentence, but I was laughing too much.

Uncle Küheylan and Demirtay laughed even harder than I did. It was good for them to either sleep or laugh in the time left over from suffering. It brought the vigor back to their faces, and revived their voices that had been broken by torture. Like the courtiers, the more they looked at each other the more they laughed, forgetting where they were. Either that, or they laughed that heartily because they didn't forget the cell for an instant.

For the first few days no one could perceive what it was

like here. No matter how hard he strained, he couldn't make a connection between the cell and himself. Then he would start to think about time. Was the life we led in the city above us a few weeks, or a few hundred years ago? Was there a time difference between our lives and the lives led in the Istanbul Palace? The more we spoke the more we realized that we hadn't landed here out of a void, but that we had come from some external time. But which time? We tried to find out by telling each other stories, by following the scent of the present moment.

After one last guffaw, the student Demirtay fell silent. "Up until the last scene in the story everything came to life before my eyes, like a film. The ship sailing through the waves, the girl walking in the desert, the stars above the hovel, the cloud of dust in the distance . . . and then the film snapped. Once I started laughing I came out of the time in the story and returned to the time in the cell. The images in my mind vanished along with the last sentence."

"You said the same thing the other day about Uncle Küheylan's wolf story. You bring everything you hear to life, like a film. Are you planning to become a filmmaker?"

"I'd love to, so I could film these stories. If no one's done it already . . ."

Uncle Küheylan, who had been listening intently, joined in. "Is that a well known story?" he asked.

"Hadn't you heard it before?" I said.

"No, I hadn't."

"Uncle Küheylan, this is the first time any of us has told you a story you didn't already know. We should be congratulated."

"Doctor," he said, "I may know Istanbul well, but there are still plenty of stories about her that I haven't heard. My father said he heard new names and incidents every time he went, he was always so excited when he told us his new stories. He said the streets and buildings of Istanbul grow by creating a sensation of infinity. Like a desert. In between the points where the sun rose and set there were a great many worlds, all of them different. In Istanbul, on the one hand people had the impression that they were holding the entire universe in the palm of their hand, and on the other, that they were disappearing here, their perception of themselves changed every day, along with their perception of the city. One evening my father met an old man on the shore of the Golden Horn. The man was holding a round pocket mirror. He kept looking first at the mirror, then at the opposite shore. My father sat beside him. He greeted him and waited for a while. I'm observing my unsightliness in the mirror, said the old man. I didn't look like this when I was young, I was handsome. I fell in love with a girl and married her. We had children. We spent forty happy years together. When my wife died last week we buried her in a graveyard close to Pier Loti, on that hillside opposite us. Once my wife's gaze was gone, my good looks too became a thing of the past. The years have slipped by so quickly. Now, whenever I look in the mirror, I notice how old and ugly I've become."

Uncle Küheylan bent his knees, leaned against the wall and, sitting up very straight, continued.

"After my father had told us that story he said the number of people who used to think they were good looking but now find themselves ugly, and who regard Istanbul in the same light, is growing bigger all the time. Raising his hand toward the light, he said, I'll show you those people's time. He made a reflection on the wall that looked like a bird with broad wings. Look, he said, this is the bird of time. In the past it flies and flies and flies. When it reaches the present day its wings come to a halt. It remains suspended in the wind. Time in Istanbul is the same. It flaps its wings in the past. When it reaches the present day its wings come to a halt, and it glides slowly in emptiness."

Uncle Küheylan looked at his large hands. He stretched out his fingers as though they were large feathers.

"Although I believed in the bird of time when I was a child," he went on, "I found it hard to grasp the concept of the Istanbul my father talked about. It's only now in the cell that I understand it. Every time I open my eyes I see a black winged bird above me. The bird of time circles above us without ever flapping its wings."

We raised our heads and looked at the ceiling. It was dark. It was deep. We became absorbed in it, as though this were the first time we had ever beheld such intense darkness, as though it would swallow us up in its vortex. Prior to us, who had crossed this darkness? Who had managed to stay alive, and who had taken their last breath here? It was as though we had been born underground instead of above it, with each passing day we became a bit more oblivious of the outside world. If the opposite of cold was hot we knew the word hot, but couldn't remember what sort of thing it was. Like worms in the earth, we had grown accustomed to the darkness and damp. If they didn't torture us, we would live forever. Bread, water, and a bit of sleep were all we needed. If we stood up and stretched out our hand, would we be able to reach the darkness above?

"Uncle Küheylan," I said, "one day we'll get out of here. We'll explore Istanbul together. Then we'll sit on the balcony of my apartment that overlooks the sea. You'll tell stories and I'll listen."

"Why will I tell them and not you?"

"You know more stories than there are in the *Decameron*, Uncle Küheylan. Do you like rakı? We'll accompany our stories with rakı."

"That sounds perfect. Why don't we prepare a rakı banquet

this evening, Doctor?

"Good idea. I'll cook the food. I'll make fish. But how will we know it's evening?"

"Given that we don't know about time, then we're its masters. Here it's evening when we want it to be, and the sun rises when we want it to."

The student Demirtay sat up like a mischievous child. "Are you going to invite me, too? You won't exclude me from the rakı just because I'm young, will you?" he said.

Uncle Küheylan and I looked at each other. We donned doubtful expressions.

"Uncle Küheylan," continued Demirtay. "If you like I'll go down to the beach where the fishermongers are. I know where they sell the best fish. I'll get salad from the greengrocer's on the way back, and a big bottle of rakı from the corner shop."

"It's still early."

"What are you talking about? What if it's almost evening, what if the sun has descended onto the rooftops? What if the streets are full of screaming schoolchildren on their way home from school?"

"There's no need to rush, we need to think about it."

"Uncle Küheylan, if you invite me to your dinner I'll tell you the answer to yesterday's riddle."

"The riddle?"

"Then, if you like, I'll ask you another riddle . . ."

Uncle Küheylan paused, then spoke slowly. "You'll go down to the beach. You'll select the choicest fish. And on the way back you'll get salad and rakı. Is that right?"

"There's no need for you to go out and get tired. You can sit and chat on the balcony overlooking the sea and tell your stories. I'll do the shopping and be back before the evening crowds. And in the meantime I'll eavesdrop on the people talking in the street and the fish market and on the bus, I'll find out who rigged the latest horse races, where the latest fire broke out and who is the latest singer to get divorced. I'll get a newspaper as well."

"Don't forget to buy lemons," I added. "I'll lay the table. I'll pour the rakı. As the city lights go on one by one, I'll put the stereo on and play you my favorite songs."

"Yes, let's listen to songs," said Uncle Küheylan, "But if I try and sing when I'm drunk, don't let me. Some people are famous for their beautiful voices. I'm known for how badly I sing. The villagers who heard me sing changed their minds and went in the opposite direction."

Uncle Küheylan laughed heartily.

"I've got a terrible voice too," I said. "When I'm drinking rakı I only listen to my wife. There aren't many voices as beautiful as hers."

"Does she like rakı too?"

"She did. She died a long time ago. When her disease started to spread, she secretly recorded her voice onto cassettes. She knew that was the best way for her to sit at the same table with me for the rest of my life. In the evenings, after I put on the stereo, I sit at the table and fill my glass. I become engrossed in contemplating Istanbul. The lights on either side of the sea look like the magical lands in fairy tales. The walls and towers of Topkapı Palace rise up like the palace of the fairy king. The hazy lights are a fine veil that gently envelops the walls. On the left the lights of the Maiden's Tower, the Selimiye Barracks, and, if I'm lucky and it's a clear day, the Princes' Islands in the distance, twinkle. I can't work out when I drained my second glass and started on my third. My wife's voice singing a classical Turkish song crackles out of the stereo. She's singing about separation city. Separation is a city far removed from hope. Not a single bird, nor piece of news, nor greeting reaches us from there. There are only hopeless cries, futile waiting, and a mournful rather than comforting evening. The rakı in the bottle decreases, while the stars in the sky increase. Just then my wife starts a new song. Everywhere there are flowers blooming. The evening sways, like a crystal chandelier. There are ferries' horns in the distance, and seagulls drawing lines in the sky with their wings . . ."

I raised my head and looked up. Was the bird of time circulating above us, was it marking the way for us in the darkness? Would we ever be able to leave here and go to a balcony, would we really be able to chat looking out at the sea, engrossed in contemplating Istanbul?

"Uncle Küheylan, nowadays I'm like the man your father met at the Golden Horn," I said, continuing, "When I remember my wife I think I also get carried away by the thought that the happiness of the past belongs only to the past."

Demirtay looked at me quizically. "This is the first time I've ever seen you sad, Doctor," he said.

"Sad? I don't know about that. I try to think nice thoughts in here, and when it comes to sorrows, I prefer to drown them at the rakı banquet."

"I'm invited to your banquet too, aren't I? I can tell from the way you're talking."

I didn't reply. I waited for Uncle Küheylan to speak.

Once he had scrutinized Demirtay a bit harder, Uncle Küheylan told him what he wanted to hear. "You're a bright kid. Come and join us tonight. We can all drink rakı together."

Instead of being happy, Demirtay leaned forward looking irritated. "Uncle Küheylan, could you stop calling me a kid? I'm obviously not a kid if I'm going to your rakı banquet."

"It's just habit, Demirtay. You're a fine young man."

Satisfied, Demirtay withdrew and leaned against the wall. "Are you going to invite Zinê Sevda too?" he asked.

"Good idea. I'll ask her along too."

A sea breeze blew in under the cell door. All three of us fixed our gaze on the door. The breeze that had brushed against the concrete and flowed inside, brought the smell of the sea with it and deposited it on our bare feet. It was the harbinger of news from a salty, seaweedy world. We felt the cold rising up from our ankles. It was a momentary sensation. Sometimes we would catch the scent of the sea, sometimes of pine, sometimes of orange peel, and we would do our best to cling to that sensation that slipped away in an instant. Before it abandoned us in the cell and returned to where it belonged in the Bosphorus, we would inhale it eagerly, drawing the scent into our lungs. We were never satisfied, we always craved more. Perhaps we would also be able to hear the howling of the storm, if we had just a little more faith in our fantasies and abandoned ourselves just a little bit more to our longing, we would be able to hear the sound of the waves swelling in the north wind, and the engines of the fishing boats.

"Doctor," said Uncle Küheylan, like an elderly fisherman calling out through the waves, but whose voice broke up in the storm, "what was that book you were talking about just now, the book with all those stories?"

"Do you mean the *Decameron*?"

"Yes, that's the one. I couldn't remember it because it has such a strange title."

"The book itself is strange too," I said. "A group of men and women flee the city to escape from a plague epidemic, and take refuge in a cottage. They wait for the epidemic to pass. If the route to escaping death was to flee the city, the route to passing time was to converse. For ten days they sat by the fire every evening and told stories. *Decameron* means 'ten days' in the language of the ancient Istanbul dwellers, that's where the book gets its title. They told erotic stories, romantic stories, and scandalous stories, and they laughed a lot. They diluted their fear of the plague with stories that didn't take life too seriously. The story of the princess who ran away to the desert was one of them."

"I knew about the stories that were told over a thousand and one nights, but I'd never heard of the stories that were told over ten days. I wonder why my father never mentioned them. Perhaps he had too many other stories to tell."

"Maybe he did tell them, but just didn't say where they came from."

"Who knows?" said Uncle Küheylan, pausing as though trying to remember all the stories stored in his memory, then he asked, "Was Istanbul the city in the *Decameron* where the plague broke out?"

"Uncle Küheylan, you know that every city is Istanbul for us. If a child stays out after dark and loses his way in the narrow streets, that place is Istanbul. The city of the young man who ventures out to find his lifelong sweetheart, that of the hunter who sets out in search of the fleece of the black fox, that of the ship dragged through the storm, of the prince who wants to hold the whole world in the palm of his hand, like a diamond, of the last rebel who has sworn he will never come to heel, of the young girl who runs away from home to pursue her dream of becoming a singer, the city where millionaires, thieves, and poets go is Istanbul. Every story is about here."

"You talk like my father, Doctor. He used to say that in Istanbul it's the same underground as it is aboveground, in both of them the bird of time glides like a dark shadow, without flapping its wings. My father knew the secret of this place, but he demonstrated it with stories instead of revealing it openly. Istanbul wasn't a part of something, it was the whole where all the parts came together. That's what he tried to tell us. Maybe he discovered that secret in a place like this, somewhere underground."

"Now we're discovering the things your father found out too."

"But the people in the *Decameron* are better off than us. They fled the city and escaped death. Whereas we are in the depths of the city, tossed into the darkness. What wouldn't we give to be with the people telling stories in the *Decameron* instead of in here, isn't that right? They went there of their own free will, but we were brought us here against ours. Even worse, they got further away from death, but we're getting closer. If our Istanbul is the same city as the one in the *Decameron*, I think each story's fate flows in a different direction, don't you agree?"

"You're right, Uncle Küheylan," I said.

Before I could continue we heard the grating of the iron gate. We tensed automatically. We looked at each other, then turned our eyes toward the grille. We strained to hear what they were saying outside. We waited for their voices to reach the corridor. We knew that the feeling we had had for the past two days every time they had opened the iron gate, wondering whether they had come to take one of us away or to bring us food, was not curiosity, but anxiety. They had brought today's ration a few hours ago. Now they would either change guards, or collect a file and go back. I racked my brain to try and think of another possibility that wouldn't affect us, or destroy our peace of mind in the cell. We were content with the way things were here. As long as we weren't taken away to be tortured, we were happy to sit huddled together, to chat, and to drift off into a light sleep, like rabbits. We didn't measure our happiness against that of the world aboveground. The world up above was a distant, old memory. In the cell the only measurement we could go by was pain. For us the absence of pain meant happiness. We would settle for that. If they would only let us be, we would live happily like this.

Uncle Küheylan said, "This will pass too." He was speaking to Demirtay, not to me.

The student Demirtay had turned visibly pale and had focused his attention outside, straining to understand the voices in the corridor. What we heard was not the guards' everyday conversation, but the voices of a big group all talking at once. Sometimes they spoke in whispers, sometimes they burst out laughing. Our two-day holiday was clearly over. Where would they start with us, with the opposite cells, or with the rear corridor?

"It will pass, won't it?" said Demirtay, his voice feeble.

"Of course it will," said Uncle Küheylan. "Hasn't it always? Why should this time be any different?"

"Every time they took me away to be tortured I felt prepared. But during this two-day break my flesh has relaxed, I've grown used to being left in peace. Now it's going to hurt even more."

"Demirtay, the pain doesn't change. It's exactly the same as it was in the beginning. They've taken us time and again. We'll go again, and again we'll come back sure of ourselves."

Fear always crept into our ribcages, gnawing at our hearts with its small rats' teeth. We doubted ourselves all the time. Would we be able to withstand the vertiginous fire of pain, that horror that was just on the threshold of madness? As the electric shocks shot through our flesh we lost the ability to think, but yet a sense we could not explain held us by the hand, keeping our will to live intact. Was there a world outside of here? Was there a future for us? As our bodies grew heavier we felt all of existence giving way to anxiety, we felt the Moon revolving around the Earth and the Earth revolving around the Sun in great agitation, accelerating as they revolved. The pain, which would become unstoppable, bent both time and our minds.

"Perhaps," I said, "they won't take anyone, maybe they'll turn around and leave just as they came."

I too had grown accustomed to the relaxation to which Demirtay had succumbed, I almost believed that I would never be taken away from here again. Perhaps they had forgotten about us, or else it was too much effort for them to descend so deep into the entrails of the city. We were animals who were occasionally thrown food, then left to their own devices. We fingered the damp on the walls, sniffed the air and snuggled up to one another. When they said come we came, when they said go we went. We strained our ears, listening to the sound of the footsteps echoing through the corridor and gradually getting closer as though hearing them for the first time.

"When we get back I'll give you the answer to the question you asked me," said Uncle Küheylan.

"Which question?" asked Demirtay, all curiosity.

"Have you forgotten your own riddle? Didn't an old woman say the child beside her was her daughter's daughter and her husband's sister? I thought it over long and hard and I've worked out the answer. We'll discuss it over the rakı banquet when we get back."

Demirtay's face lit up like that of a child eager to be fooled by lies. "All right. You work out that question, then I have another one for you. We won't leave the rakı table until daybreak. Okay?"

"Of course, Demirtay. It's an honor to drink with you."

The door opened. Light streamed in, like a southern wave striking the shore. We raised our hands to protect our faces, blinking our dazzled eyes.

"All you morons, on your feet!"

Slowly, we stood up on the bare concrete.

With one sweep of the hand they grabbed first Demirtay,

then Uncle Küheylan by the arm. "You stay here," they barked at me.

Was I staying? I was torn between feeling elated and grieving for my departed companions. I looked at the Student Demirtay's thin shoulders and Uncle Küheylan's confident stride. They were heading toward pain I would not endure. Alongside the grief that caused me was the relief of knowing that my own body would not be crushed, that my face would not be turned into a bloody mess. Pain was inescapable, but this time it had bypassed me and taken others. I knew our instincts led us to think of ourselves first, to look out for our own injuries. We had learned that in the first year of university. But there were other sides to people too. We endured pain for the sake of those we loved, and braved the torture in here.

"You get up as well, asshole!"

They were talking to Kamo the Barber. Kamo, who had been inconspicuously slumped against the wall for the past two days, sleeping continually like an aged tortoise, raised his head, grunting. He eyed the interrogators in the doorway. Making no attempt to get up, he fixed his gaze on them.

"I'm talking to you, dickhead!" The interrogator's voice was menacing.

Kamo the Barber stayed where he was, as though he were an inseparable part of the wall. His back was glued to the tiles, his feet nailed to the ground. He couldn't remember how long he had been sitting there. He sighed, looking irritated. He twitched. He held onto the wall with one hand. Believing now that they would take him away too, he stood up, looking neither anxious nor relaxed, but with an air of total indifference. He had dreamt countless times that they had taken him away to be tortured, but each time had opened his eyes in the cell. Why had he waited while everyone else was suffering, why had he slept in the cell while everyone else went through the iron gate? He questioned himself, and because his body was not lacerated with pain, he flew into a rage. He was hoping that physical pain would ease the pain in his heart. For days he had been waiting with that hope.

Kamo walked to the door, passed between the interrogators and strode out into the corridor. No one had to drag him. This was an invitation he had been eagerly awaiting for days. He didn't care what lay at the end of the corridor he was headed toward, behind the iron gate he would cross, at the core of the fate that was about to befall him.

The interrogators did not depart immediately. Referring to someone waiting in the corridor, they said, "Bring that motherfucker and throw him in with the doctor." They dragged a blood-spattered man by his hair and sent him reeling inside with a thump on his back. He landed on top of me and we both fell down together. I banged my head on the wall. I thought my arm that was trapped underneath us was broken. Once the door was closed and it was dark again, I came to my senses. I sat up. I looked at the man lying slumped beside me. He was groaning.

"Are you all right?" I said.

I helped him straighten up. He sat up with difficulty and leaned against the wall.

"My wound hurts," he said.

"Where are you wounded?"

His hair, face, and neck were all caked in blood, but he clutched his left calf.

"On my leg. It's a bullet wound."

"A bullet wound?"

"Yes, they caught me two days ago in a clash. They removed the bullet in hospital then brought me here. They've been torturing me since the morning."

When I stretched out my hand to touch his leg his face

tensed, his body turned rigid. Patients didn't like their wounds to be touched. While trying to make sense of this reaction that I had found strange during my first few years in the profession, I realized that it wasn't just patients, but ordinary Istanbul dwellers too that winced at being touched. In the past, when there were contagious diseases like the plague or cholera, people still lived at close quarters with one another's bodies. Times have changed, now, while diseases like cancer, diabetes, and heart trouble, that people have to endure all alone were taking the place of contagious diseases, people were withdrawing into their shells, living contactless lives. Saying "I'm human" was a message that translated as, I'm moving away from others, putting a distance between myself and them. In these times when not just strangers, but even friends avoided one another's bodies, I was aware that those who came to my consulting room felt like caged cats. That kind of anxiety couldn't be attributed to fear of the disease alone. I thought the only thing that would make the population desert Istanbul would not be an outbreak of plague, but an outbreak of touching, that the inhabitants would fly into a panic at the prospect of being touched and look for somewhere to flee.

"Let me see to your wound, I'm a doctor."

His trousers were torn and their seams ripped. I could see the wound on his calf. Someone had put a dressing on it and it was covered up with a bandage. I gently lifted the tape that was securing it. I turned his leg toward the light seeping in through the grille so I could get a look at the wound.

"It's not bleeding. They haven't taken the stitches out yet."

As I replaced the dressing I noticed that the man now seemed more at ease, that he was watching my movements with a calm expression.

"I'm cold," he said.

I touched his forehead. "You have a fever. That's normal

with a recent wound. Don't worry, it'll pass."

"I hope so."

I picked up the piece of bread and cheese beside the water bottle and passed them to him.

He paused, as though he had beheld something completely alien. He hesitated. After staring for a long time at the bread I placed in his palm, he bit it, and devoured it in two mouthfuls. His chest was heaving. He took the water bottle and drank greedily.

"My name's Ali," he said, "everyone knows me as Ali the Lighter."

I remembered that name. In fact, it was fixed in my memory like a driven nail. I drew closer to his face to get a better look at him. I looked at his knit eyebrows and his furrowed forehead. I doubted he was even thirty years old, he looked older than my son.

"You can call me Doctor, that's how everyone knows me," I said.

"Don't tell me you're the doctor from Cerrahpaşa."

"The very same."

We knew each other's names but had never met. The meeting we were supposed to have had a few weeks ago in one of Istanbul's picturesque streets, or in a café on the beach had ended up being in this cell. Our right to life was not yet spent, we had not yet reached the end of the road then. He too eyed me with interest.

"I imagined you'd be a young student from the Cerrahpaşa Medicine Faculty," he said.

Should I tell him the truth?

When my wife got pancreatic cancer she wanted to die straight away, rather than prolong her suffering. "Give me an injection and set me free. You be the one to take my last breath," she had said. In the early days of our courtship, when we were two unpracticed lovers exploring Istanbul, according to the fashion of the time we made a wish on every quay and plucked the petals of a flower in every park. As we neared the end of the number of petals we wondered whether we would have an odd or even number of children. At that age people are so curious about the future. Where would we be living in ten years, what would we be doing in twenty years? We couldn't even contemplate fifty years into the future, we only hoped that when we reached that age we would have had our fill of life. My wife reached the border of that country known as death early, and she wanted to cross to the other side without suffering. "My darling wife, if you'll agree to us dying side by side I'll inject us both with the same needle," I said. She tried hard to smile as she responded. "You've got to live. You have to raise our son, watch his children grow up, and only then can you come and join me. Not before."

When my son grew up and turned into a young man I wanted him to get married as soon as possible, partly to fulfill his mother's dream. But he left home, neglected the final year of his studies at the Medicine Faculty, joined one of the many revolutionary groups that were all over the city, and carved a different path for himself. There was constant news of clashes and deaths. I followed events in the newspapers. Whenever I saw names that were similar to his, or photos of faces that looked like his, my heart leapt to my mouth. Sometimes as I was boarding a ferry, or walking under a dark bridge, or strolling on the beach late at night when I hadn't been able to get to sleep, my son would suddenly appear beside me and hug me tightly. He had his mother's smell. I would touch his fingers, look at his face that was getting thinner all the time, and try to capture the light in his sunken eyes. "Don't worry about me father, I'm well. These days will pass." But they didn't pass. Time stretched endlessly ahead, and my anxiety and my longing increased at the same pace.

On a rainy autumn morning I had left the house early again and was on my way to my consulting room, which was a fifteen-minute walk away. My son came under my umbrella and linked arms with me. "Don't stop, let's keep walking," he said. He was soaked, like a stray dog. He was shivering and coughing, covering his mouth with a handkerchief. He had not gone very far before his knees gave way; as he fell to the ground he tried to hold on to me. I hailed a cab and took him to the hospital. My son had tuberculosis. In a city where contagious diseases were on the decrease and people avoided touching one another, my son had fallen victim to tuberculosis, he was paying the price for his beliefs with his own body. My son, who would say during our discussions, "Father, good is contagious as well as evil," was now a victim of a contagious disease, as though that were his just desert. The old city was dead and the new city was somehow refusing to be born. Howling sounds came from beneath the earth. There was a stench that even the rain could not wash away. Young children built a thousand dreams, they raced ahead like ships headed for the misty borders of the ocean, and finished washed up on the shore, their sails in tatters. When did this city ever love her children? To whom did she ever show compassion? One day when I was talking in this vein my son said, "Father, our mission is not to beg for love but to create it. That's what we're fighting for."

My son, who gave his father lessons on life, was now lying shaking, delirious and beside himself in a sickbed. The sweat pouring from his forehead soaked his pillow. I sat beside him all day, listening to his breathing, checking his temperature. That night, when the hospital corridors had become deserted and only the distant sounds of the nurses' footsteps remained, my son opened his eyes and whispered, "I have to get up, I have an appointment tomorrow." Even if I had allowed it, he was talking about doing the impossible. "Father, it's really important. My friends' lives depend on it. I have to meet someone tomorrow." As well as tuberculosis he had kidney and stomach problems. He was beyond the point where he could neglect his health. It was out of the question for him to get out of bed for a long time yet. "My son, don't worry, if it's that important I'll go in your place," I said. Unable to reply, he closed his eyes and fell into a deep sleep. He had the same innocent expression as he had when he was a baby. No matter how much he grew up, that baby face that I would sneak into his room at night to watch by lamplight returned infallibly when he was asleep. I wanted him to wake up with that same expression, but when he opened his eyes at daybreak he gazed at me sorrowfully. He raised his bony fingers. "Father," he rasped. "My son," I said. I was ready to give up for him the life that my wife hadn't wanted. I stroked his hair ravaged by tuberculosis, I held his hands ravaged by tuberculosis. Wheezing sounds came from his chest. "Father," he said, "if it wasn't important I would never let you go. You have to go to Ragıp Paşa Library in Laleli. There you'll meet a girl. She's the go between. Then you have to go to the real meeting place that she'll indicate and meet someone called Ali the Lighter. Be vigilant of the time. Your meeting with Ali the Lighter is an hour before the time the girl will say. I've never met either of them. They'll think you're me. I'm known as the Doctor because I study in the Faculty of Medicine. So it won't be all that different for you. If anything goes wrong and you get mixed up with the police, just tell them who you really are."

When was a man completed? My wife said that after she had given birth she had felt things that she could never have imagined. "I feel complete, it's as though all the loose pieces inside me have fallen into place," she had said. An air of serenity I had never witnessed before settled on her face. I had looked at her with envy, wondering about her satisfaction with the world. What kind of a completeness was it? How could I attain that feeling? Was it enough to perform acts of kindness for others, or to pass for my son? Would taking my son's suffering on my own shoulders join up all the pieces inside me, elevate me to satiety? I asked myself the question that I often thought as I sat alone facing the Istanbul Sea, as I lay my head on my pillow at night, and as I wended my weary way to work in the mornings: When was a man completed?

One day my son too would ask himself the same question.

"My son," I said, "I have admitted you here under another patient's name. No one knows your real identity. You're safe."

# 7TH DAY

*Told by the Student Demirtay*

## THE POCKET WATCH

"When the director of Beyazıt Library, Şerafat Bey, arrived at work that morning, he realized that there was no one waiting at the door. Every morning there were always a couple of bibliophiles there, but this morning he was alone. Walking toward the lateral wall of the building that had been converted from a mosque stable into a library, he opened the parcel of liver he was carrying. He crouched down and placed the finely chopped pieces of liver onto the cobblestones. He watched the cats gather, then turned his attention to the pigeons under the plane tree. He took a paper bag filled with wheat out of his briefcase and scattered a handful around the tree. Here the cats and the pigeons got on well together, they didn't bother one another. As the director stood up and was walking toward the door he saw the two early-bird bibliophiles approaching. He wished them good morning and reminded them that they were ten minutes late that day. The two bibliophiles consulted their wristwatches and said they were on time. The director took his pocket watch out of his waistcoat pocket. He compared it with that of the bibliophiles. Theirs was slow. The director gave them an indulgent smile, but when, throughout the day, he saw that they were not the only ones, that everyone's watches, inside and outside the library, were ten minutes out, he realized that there was something going on. Time's gracious hand was changing in Istanbul. School bells, cinema performances, and boat trips were all ten minutes out, and no one was aware of the discrepancy. The children selling newspapers in the mornings at the tops of their voices announced no such news. Every day the director opened the library according to his own watch, and asked himself the same question: Why were all the clocks suddenly slow? It's actually a long story but I'll be brief. In one part of the world a war was ending, while in another a new one was brewing. Despite the smell of spring, the air in Istanbul was oppressive. Mariners set out to sea with a serene expression, women forgot their washing on the line for days. The director, Şerafat Bey, couldn't bear the fact that everyone's watches were slow and that his regulars were arriving late, and resolved that he had to do something. Once he had fed the cats and the pigeons in the mornings and worked in the library until midday, he started to delegate tasks to his assistants and spend the rest of the day visiting the other libraries in the city. Whispers circulated around the reading rooms. The presenter on the state radio read the news and the muezzin in the mosque called the faithful to prayer ten minutes late. While the time in Istanbul was undergoing a complete change, now the only watch that appeared to be wrong was his. He didn't know that he was in danger, that he was being watched by men with black rosettes. He couldn't even begin to estimate the consequences of the tardy radio and calls to prayer. I should at least save the libraries, he thought. He told the librarians the correct time and the truth that only he seemed able to perceive. He also told them that the cats and pigeons that had lived side by side in Beyazıt for years had changed, that the cats had grown peevish and that the pigeons flapped their wings nervously. We must appropriate time, and remind future generations of the truth, he said. As long as his pocket watch continued to work nonstop, as long as someone wound it up every day and made it go, time was on their side. He believed that sincerely. One morning, completely by chance, Şerafat Bey dodged a car that was coming straight for him; at lunchtime at the last moment he returned the poisoned sherbet that a street vendor held out to him on the grounds that the glass was dirty, but when he arrived home in the evening and was entering the garden, he could not evade the knife that someone aimed at his back in the darkness. The neighbors rushed over upon hearing his wife's screams, they called a doctor. Realizing he had reached the end of the road, Şerafat Bey took his watch out of his pocket and handed it to his wife for safekeeping. His wife looked at the pocket watch with the red ruby encrusted cover and said sadly: What can be the meaning of yours being the only watch that's right when everyone else's is wrong? Şerafat Bey gazed at his wife tenderly and motioned to her to draw near. As she bent over, under the curious scrutiny of the neighbors, he whispered something in her ear, then he closed his eyes, never to open them again. The next day they washed his slight body and, following the funeral prayers, performed ten minutes late, bore him to the graveyard. They covered him with damp earth. The neighbors shed tears, raised their voices in lament and, in between wails, they sidled up to Şerafat Bey's wife and asked what her husband had whispered to her before he died. His wife replied tearfully, shaking her head from side to side. I didn't hear my husband's words, she said, I'm a bit deaf, you see."

Uncle Küheylan repeated the last sentence for me. "I'm a bit deaf, you see."

We all laughed together.

We were not subjected to pain in the cell, but we

were suspended on the border of pain. Wasn't it the same aboveground? There, in the midst of the skyscrapers, the suburbs, the blaring car horns, and the unemployment epidemic, any misfortune could have befallen us, we were prone to fall prey to any affliction. While this vast city was draping our bodies in artificial furs and keeping us warm, she was liable to suddenly push us away and flush us down the toilet, like an unwanted fetus. This risk whipped our appetite into action, making us live each day with intensified desire. We believed we had almost reached heaven, and that hell was beneath our feet. That's why pleasure in the city was abundant, while fear was continuous. We got carried away by the fervor of our laughter. Every emotion came larger than life, we lived it purely for our own ends, and then it was consumed, leaving a cloying stench on our skin. The more we saw of this, the more ardently we yearned to change Istanbul.

After days of resistance, now my watch too was slow, like that of the Istanbul dwellers in the story; during interrogation I asked myself more questions than the interrogators did. I was a man, not a machine, and my flesh and bones had almost reached their endurance limit. Would it hurt anyone if I talked, I wondered, desperately searching for a way to evade pain. What would happen if I provided a couple of details to make the interrogators stop? What would be the harm in giving them a name, or an address? The person I would name would have long since gone into hiding, the address I would show them would have been evacuated from day one. I would weigh all this up and try to persuade myself. I could just give them trivial information, I wouldn't put anyone in danger. I would fool the interrogators and spare myself a lot of pain. Was that impossible? As these thoughts gnawed at me, I didn't know how the words had got into my mind. The electric shocks that shot through my body turned first into pain, then desperation, and finally, into innocent words that roamed around my brain. I was approaching a borderline and I had no idea what lay on the other side of it.

What should I do, what should I cling to? I wanted to consult the Doctor, but, apart from giving me hope, there wasn't much he could do. He couldn't cure my weakness, he couldn't resolve the doubts in my mind. A bloody wall was rising right under my nose. I could see nothing else. I was as lonely as the librarian Şerafat Bey, who, despite what every other clock said, believed his was the only watch in Istanbul with the right time. The expression "great dreams lead to great disappointment" sprang to my mind. I felt sad that I was accepting defeat for the first time in my life, I was grieved because I hadn't been able to withstand the torment inflicted by the city.

"You told me that story before, but the ending was different," said the Doctor.

"Just as you can't bathe in the same river twice," I said, "neither can you tell the same story twice in Istanbul."

Life was short and stories were long. We too wanted to become a story, to blend into the river known as life and flow with it. Telling stories was a way of manifesting that desire.

Uncle Küheylan joined in, saying, "That pocket watch is one of the things about Istanbul that fascinates me. According to my father, the rubies on its cover shone like stars in the dark. Anyone who looked at it once searched the sky for nights on end, and only believed the pocket watch was right once they had found the stars that looked like the rubies."

"There was a library I used to go to when I was a child, the clock was always ten minutes fast," said the Doctor. "In those days there were a lot of stories about the ruby encrusted watch, but they all ended differently. Just like Demirtay changes all his stories, the watch stories changed too. I didn't give it much thought when I was a child, but now I'm beginning to wonder about that pocket watch too."

"As though we've got nothing else to worry about in this cell . . ." I mumbled to myself.

Uncle Küheylan, who was sitting next to me, turned and looked at me. "Do we have other worries, Demirtay?" he asked. He was as serious as if he wasn't sitting on bloodied concrete, but all snug in front of a fire in his local coffeehouse.

I wanted to laugh at his self-assuredness. Instead I told them about the dead woman I had seen in the interrogation room yesterday. At one point the interrogators untied my hands and feet, made me get off the table they had strapped me to and removed my blindfold. There was a woman lying against the wall. She was naked. Her body was covered in knife slashes. It was obvious that she was dead, her lips and chest made no movement to indicate that she was breathing. One of the interrogators walked up to her and landed a kick on her stomach. Then another. And another. Then he stood on her fingers and began to crush them. As he crushed her fingers the interrogator looked at me, wanting to see me shudder, curious to know what I would say. He amused himself by swaying his head right and left, in time with the crunching sound of the woman's broken fingers. There was a watch beside the woman's hand. Its face was broken. Realizing I was looking at the watch, the interrogator directed his gaze at it too. He became absorbed in it for some time, as though he didn't know what it was for. Then, with his bloody, mud-caked boots, he stood on the watch. Slowly he moved his heel. He crushed the hour and minute hand, the springs and the wheels. His body rocked backward and forward, as his head moved around in circles. A drunken expression settled on his face. It wasn't just an ordinary watch, he had the past and the present, yesterday and tomorrow under his feet. Who could stop him? This transcended the pleasure of driving fast cars, drinking in garish nightclubs, and sleeping in hotel rooms with a lingering scent of women. He was destroying time, holding death in the palm of his hand. Blood, flesh, and bones were on his side. There was no stopping him. As the hour and minute hands crunched under his feet, beads of sweat sprouted on his forehead, the veins on his temples bulged. Like the mighty pharaohs, he thought he was more on the level of the gods than of people. For him there were no sins, nor punishments. He ruled over the suffering of others, and over their last breath.

"They showed me that woman too," said Uncle Küheylan. "I think it was after your interrogation. The watch on the floor was smashed to pieces, there were bits of metal everywhere."

"That's the second dead body I've seen since I've been here," I said.

Was there any point in that woman's watch being right once she was dead? That's what I wanted to ask. Or, what was the point of our suffering in here while aboveground everyone was going about their life unaware of our existence? When the first humans set out to build the Tower of Babel, God confused their languages so they were unable to understand each other and stopped them building the tower. What good did it do? Enraged, humans conquered not just the earth but the sky as well. They built not one but a thousand towers, boring through the sky repeatedly. As their buildings grew taller, humans realized God had been annihilated, and no longer sought Him. By building cities more intricate than ants' trails, they brought every language and every race together in the same place. They lived as though they would never die. If there was a need for a new God, humans were the only candidate for the post. The mightier they grew, the longer their shadow got, and, as they gazed upon their shadow, they forgot what kindness was. They knew not what they did. They replaced kindness with right, and right with gain or loss calculations. They erased the first fire, the first word, and the first kiss from their memory. All that remained to remind humans of kindness was pain. And they tried to relieve that with drugs. We thought more about kindness here because we endured pain, that was the scale by which we measured our worth. But I wondered, as long as everyone aboveground in the city was indifferent to us, what was the point of our suffering underground?

"Demirtay," said the Doctor, "let's not talk about death, let's talk about how people up there are living life to the full. Istanbul remains splendid, despite our absence, she's still lively and buzzing. Isn't that nice to know?"

I didn't reply.

Uncle Küheylan scrutinized both of us. When he realized we were waiting for him, he spoke, his voice serene.

"In our house we used to have a wall rug with a picture of a deer on it. I'll tell you about it. One day my father pointed at it and asked: Could you love a real deer as much as you love the one on this rug? I found it odd that he should pronounce the words real and deer together. I was sitting by the window. It was night. Outside there were stars, beneath the stars were mountains, and behind the mountains were deer. My father looked at me as though he could see the stars, the mountains, and the deer in my face and told us the story of a melancholy young man in Istanbul. This melancholy young man saw a picture of a woman and fell in love, fantasizing about it night and day. One day he happened to meet the woman in the picture, but, after a single glance he turned away, not deigning to cast her a second look. I love the woman in the picture, he said, I don't feel anything for the real woman. It wasn't the woman's existence that stoked the young man's heart, but his fantasies of her. Was it love that was strange, or people? My father said that Istanbul dwellers lived with this mentality too. Istanbul dwellers liked the paintings of Istanbul that they hung on their walls much more than the streets they walked in every day, the rainy rooftops, and the teahouses on the beach. They would drink rakı, recount legends, recite poetry, then they would gaze at the paintings on their walls and sigh. They thought they lived in a different city. Outside, the waters of the Bosphorus flowed in between breaking on the shores, ships set sail on the waves, seagulls spread their wings from the Asian to the European side. Under bridges children built fires and bet each other that they could tell the make of a car by the sound of its engine, night workers listened to reproachful Arabesque songs. In houses, coffeehouses, and workplaces, Istanbul's visible face beamed out of the front of the paintings on the walls, while its invisible face remained on the back. Everyone stared at the paintings as though bewitched, and then wended their way sorrowfully to bed. They divided time in two, just as they divided sleep and wakefulness."

Uncle Küheylan carried so many words around in his head that he had more stories than there were streets in the city.

"This is how the Istanbul dwellers divided time," he said, holding out his hands on either side of him. "They thought the real Istanbul was a city of the past. This tired city had been bursting with energy in the past, had had a glorious sultanate, but had now drifted off to sleep. And perhaps she would never again awake from that deep sleep. Like magnificent mansions, magnificent stories were also buried under the rubble. Istanbul dwellers who believed that worshipped the past and read novels that spoke of old times. Was there any other time but today's? Wasn't this the city where time from all eras convened? Or was that resource beyond our reach? They preferred to forget questions like those that crossed their minds. They did not look near, they looked far. They endured grief for the sake of forgetting, but didn't realize that they were also forgetting the present. Living and dying was the same thing for them, whereas the past was infinite. They were hopelessly in love with bygone eras, but they scorned the city where they opened their eyes every morning. They heaped concrete upon concrete and built domes that mimicked one another. They demolished, they smashed, then, when they returned home exhausted, they went to sleep with a pretty painting of Istanbul above their heads."

Uncle Küheylan faced me as he continued. "Are you listening, Demirtay?" he said. "I loved the deer on the mountains as well as the deer on the wall rug. I grew attached to the old stories about Istanbul but I'm attached to Istanbul as she is now too. I've realized that even though people may have loved Istanbul in her present state, they felt no affection for her. Love without affection made them selfish. Like lovers who oppress the one they love, they couldn't see what was lacking in themselves. Convinced the age of happiness had abandoned them, they didn't believe in Istanbul."

"Is that why you wanted to come here?" I asked. "To see what Istanbul was really like?"

"I wanted to know if I could make my dream come true before I died. I made it here at the final turning of my life. Did the price for coming here have to be the pain I endured? Why wasn't I brave enough to come before, why did I choose to come only once death was staring me in the face? I don't torment myself with all these questions. When I got caught I told the interrogators I would tell them all my secrets if they took me to Istanbul. Now, like machines, they ask me the same questions every day. I describe Istanbul to them, they don't get it. I show her to them, they don't see her. They want me to give in to pain, to give up my love. They want me to stop believing in myself and in Istanbul, and to be like them. They torment me in every imaginable way. They tear my body apart to try and make my soul look like theirs. They don't realize that my faith in this city is only getting stronger."

"Uncle Küheylan, so what if our faith gets stronger?" I said, my voice irritated. "No one sees us suffering here. People don't know we exist."

"The people who torture us see that we're suffering."

I knew that our suffering here was imposed by both the city and time. Time and the city were the same, that's why God's rule had been overthrown here. There was no one watching over us. Those who said God invented good, and evil came from people, were wrong. If God had wanted to, He would have made good boundless. What was stopping Him? I think He invented evil, and it was left up to people to invent good. Did the people living aboveground realize that? Was there anyone who thought about us, who gave a damn about everything we were going through?

"The best witnesses of pain are the ones who inflict it. We're as big a part of their lives as they are of ours," insisted Uncle Küheylan.

"You're talking about time and watches," said the Doctor. "Ali the Lighter had a thing about them too. He kept asking what time it was."

The Doctor had chatted to Ali the Lighter when they had brought him into the cell yesterday. He had examined his injuries and, noticing how cold he was, removed his jacket and put it on Ali's shoulders. Ali the Lighter had wanted to know about time in here and had complained about there not being a clock. Like all new arrivals, he too was curious about time's direction. Whilst outside, time was in the rays of the morning sun, at night it was in the darkness of the sky. In the workplace, it was found in office hours. At school in the bell signaling break time, in the car in the speedometer. In the streets aboveground, every sound, every object, stated where time was located. But where was it here? Was it in the gray wall, on the dark ceiling, or in the iron gate? Was it in the scream that echoed like wolves' howling in the distance, in the blood that seeped into the wall, in the final look of those led out of the cell who would never return? That had preyed on Ali the Lighter's mind too; when they had come to take him and he had limped slowly out of the cell with his injured leg, the first thing he had done was ask the guards what time it was. "You're at the end of time," they had told him, "there is no time for you anymore."

On the day he was captured Ali the Lighter had been in Belgrade Forest with his friends. They had decided to meet there because it was cold and snowing and they assumed it would be deserted. There were twenty of them. It was the first time they had met in such a large group. They had worked on their plan for the secret torture building three floors underground known as the Interrogation Center, and discussed their strategy for raiding it. They had signaled the entrances, the guards' locations, and all the different routes they could take. They had designated tasks and decided who would prioritize what. They had smoked a large number of cigarettes and talked about their friends who went missing after being detained, and about the young people who had recently joined them. Despite the bleak news they still managed to joke and tease each other. Though they had no faith in today, they did believe in tomorrow.

As they sat shoulder to shoulder, huddled in their parkas and scarves, their ears suddenly pricked up at the sound of the warning whistle of the guards on duty. One of them stood up and walked toward the guards; very soon he was back. We're being surrounded, prepare for a clash, he said. They divided into groups of four, scattering in all directions of the forest before the circle closed in on them. They had no intention of being hunted. They tried to work out the whereabouts in the woods of the real concentration. They scanned the area with their sharp eyes. It wasn't long before they heard the first gunshot. One of the groups had had a close encounter. The sounds reverberated. The circle led by Ali the Lighter was trying to cross another area. If they could carve a passage in the west it would be easy for them to reach the residential areas. The branches trembled under the roar of the helicopter above them. Sparrows, starlings, and crows hastily took wing. Under the shelter of the trees' wide branches, the group managed to move through the forest without the helicopter spotting them. They kept close to one another. When the sound of gunshots increased shortly afterward they realized that other groups had also joined in the clash. It was going to be difficult to get out of there before darkness descended.

As Ali the Lighter and the rest of his group were passing a hillside, the sound of nearby gunshots made them dive to the ground. When they saw there was no one in their field of vision, they realized the shots were not aimed at them. It was one of the other groups fighting. They were on the other side of the slope. They decided to cross over to help out. They could surprise the attackers and clear a path for their friends. They moved in silence, but things did not go according to plan. As they were passing through one circle they found themselves trapped in another. With bullets whizzing past them and bombs exploding, they lost their way. Who was firing, who was attacking, who was retreating? It was impossible to know. As branches snapped, sending snow flying in all directions, they lost track of each other's voices. They fired until the helicopter above them had left to go elsewhere. Then the gunshots ceased. Ali the Lighter realized he had lost his friends, he was by himself. He looked all around him, but saw no one. He followed the footprints in the snow and searched behind the bushes. His friends had either been shot or changed direction.

He moved around constantly. Rather than seek an exit by himself he chose to follow the sound of gunshots and go to the aid of the other groups. He succeeded in eluding the small circles every time. When he loaded his final ammunition clip amongst the dense trees, he was panting and exhausted. He fell to his knees and lay on the ground, abandoning himself to the snow. He wanted his sweat to dry. While pondering which direction to take, he looked at the branches above his head. It was then that he realized that night was falling. The clouds were being erased, the sky was clearing. Darkness was extending rapidly, like ink spreading through water. The trees were growing taller. It was a moonless night. When Ali the Lighter heard someone next to him calling out his hand automatically went to his weapon.

"Ali."

He walked toward the shadow under a red tree. When he saw it was Mine Bade from his group he fell to his knees.

Mine Bade was sitting on the ground, leaning against a tree trunk. Her breathing was labored.

"I've lost a lot of blood," she said.

"Where did they shoot you?"

"In the chest."

"I'm getting you out of here."

"Don't even try. I know I'm near the end."

"No, we're going."

"I hope the others made it."

"Well, the gunshots have stopped . . ."

"They must have got away."

"I can carry you. It will be easy to go out of the forest in the dark."

"Ali the Lighter, I know you never leave anything unfinished. But forget about me, go and carry out the plan we talked about today."

"You mean the raid?"

"Yes. You have to go and attack the Interrogation Center and save the people they're torturing there."

"We'll do it together."

"I would have loved to. The man I love is there too. I'd give anything to save him, to run into his arms . . ."

Mine Bade closed her eyes before she could finish speaking. Alarmed, Ali the Lighter felt her face.

They heard an elderly owl hooting in the distance.

Mine Bade opened her eyes again.

"I'm so thirsty," she said.

Ali the Lighter grabbed a handful of snow and held it out to her.

"Melt this in your mouth."

"Do you know who I love, Ali?"

"Yes."

"I never told him. I was too timid."

"Don't worry. He loves you too."

"Really? Do you mean it?"

"We all talked about you two. Everyone knew you loved each other. I think the only ones who didn't know it were you two."

Mine Bade took a deep breath. She rested her head against the tree trunk. She looked up at the stars. The sight of two consecutive shooting stars thrilled her as much as when she had been a child.

"Did you see the shooting stars?"

"Yes."

"I made a wish."

"Don't worry, when you wish on a star it always comes true."

"My face feels as though it's on fire."

"When did they shoot you?"

"An hour ago. I walked aimlessly until I eventually collapsed against this tree trunk."

"They might follow the trail of blood and find you."

"They won't follow any trails until morning. And besides, I won't see the morning."

"They could come in the dark too. Let's not stay here. There are houses where we can hide in the neighborhood just outside the forest."

"Ali, I'm not afraid anymore. Do you think it's because you've told me that the man I love loves me too?"

"It's good that you're not afraid anymore."

"So I didn't need to tell him I loved him. All I had to do was take him in my arms."

"Perhaps he was more afraid of declaring himself than you were."

"Is that why he looked at me like that?"

"How?"

"He had this way of looking . . . right now . . . in the torture chamber . . . do you suppose he's in a great deal of pain?"

"We're going to rescue them."

"Don't waste your time with me, Ali. Go and find our friends. Go and rescue the people who are suffering."

They heard the elderly owl hooting again in the distance. The branches rustled. The sound of a gunshot rang out nearby.

Ali the Lighter lay Mine Bade on the ground. He lay down beside her. He surveyed the surrounding area, inspecting the trees and the bushes. He couldn't see anyone. It was dark. The stars did not provide enough light to see very far on that moonless night. He held his breath. He listened to the forest. When he heard the sound of birds taking flight a short way ahead he said, "Wait here but don't move, I'm going to check that area over there and I'll be back."

He walked slowly and silently. He searched behind the trees. He raised his head and looked up at the branches. Seeing no one, he concluded he must have gone the wrong way. Just as he was turning back the sound of a gunshot beside him sent him reeling to the ground. The searing pain in his leg made him writhe. He clutched his wounded leg with one hand and groped in the snow for his gun with the other. They didn't give him a chance. They surrounded him. They stamped on his back and his head. They handcuffed him.

"Let me go!" he screamed, again and again. "Let me go!"

Their suspicions aroused by Ali the Lighter's behavior, the men examined the footprints in the snow and headed toward where Mine Bade lay. When they reached the red tree, they shone their torch on the area around it. They looked at the bloodstains. They saw no one.

"Who was here? Who were you shouting out a warning to?" they demanded.

"I didn't warn anyone," said Ali the Lighter.

"Your footprints lead here too. Tell us, whose blood is this?"

"What blood? All I can see is snow."

As Ali the Lighter collapsed under the blows raining down on him, he thought of Mine Bade. He was happy she had got away despite her injury. He had reached the end of the road. They would either kill him there or allow him to live a few more days. He was prepared. He tried to curse but his mouth was so full of blood that the only sound he could emit was a groan. As he faded out of consciousness he saw the light of the helicopter hovering above them and heard the sound of gunshots resounding in all four corners of the forest.

Would Mine Bade's wish come true? Would she manage to escape from the forest, and would the wound on her chest heal?

"That's not what she wished for," I remonstrated with the Doctor, who was describing that night as though he had lived it personally. "I think Mine Bade wished for a raid on this Interrogation Center, and for everyone suffering here to be rescued. Her wish will come true, they may well come and rescue us."

"You might be right, Demirtay. Maybe her wish did concern us."

"And it wasn't just one shooting star, but two. Even if one misses, the other will hit the target."

"I hope it won't miss."

"Who does Mine Bade love? Did Ali the Lighter tell you?"

"No."

"He's here, in the same slaughterhouse too, apparently."

"It's packed with cells underground," said the Doctor thoughtfully. "Who knows which one he's in?"

"The part of the story I liked best was when Mine Bade was happy to discover her man loved her. I would have wished for the same thing, I would have wished to find out here and now that I was loved."

"But this isn't a story, Demirtay, it's real."

"Doesn't everything that's happened in the past and that we tell in words become a story, Doctor? Here there's no such thing as the past. Haven't we discovered that over these last days?"

We were like ordinary Istanbul dwellers. We either idealized yesterday, or fantasized about tomorrow. We tried to feign that today didn't exist. On the one hand we told the story of the past and on the other we told the story of the future. And we thought of the present as the bridge between the past and the future. We were terrified of that bridge collapsing, of plummeting into the void below. We ruminated incessantly over this question that we couldn't get out of our minds: Who possessed today, to whom did today belong?

A loud noise came from the other side of the iron gate. We strained our ears to listen. When we heard the same sound repeatedly we realized it was gunshots. The interrogators were either testing their guns, or venting their rage by killing someone.

"That's a Beretta," said Uncle Küheylan, showing us that he was as knowledgeable about guns as he was about people. We waited for a repetition of the distant sound. The passages beyond the iron gate were long, labyrinthine, with a lot of walls. It was impossible to tell how far away the sounds were. When we heard the same explosions again Uncle Küheylan said, "That one was a Browning."

Then the noises stopped. The walls returned to their previous silence.

"Time is getting on, there's no one around," said Uncle Küheylan. "The sun's going down, it will be evening soon. We were going to throw a rakı banquet yesterday but it didn't happen. Shall we have it today instead?"

We were going to drink on the Doctor's balcony. That was our fantasy. As the lights in the neighborhoods on the other side of the Bosphorus came on one by one, we would select one charming feature of each. We would count Üsküdar, Kuzguncuk, Altunizade, Salacak, Harem, Kadıköy, Kınalıada, Sultanahmet, Beyazıt, and identify mosques from the length of their minarets, and distinguish where the traffic jams were from the sound of the car horns. For centuries people had been doing everything in their power to ravage this city. They had smashed and demolished and jammed buildings on top of each other. We would wonder at how Istanbul had managed to withstand such devastation, marvel at how well she had retained her beauty, and be swept away by her relentless allure.

We played out the scene before us: the Doctor spread a

white tablecloth over the table. He fetched cheese, melon, fresh borlotti bean salad, hummus, and haydari yogurt dip. He added toasted bread, salad, and cacık. He then made room for dishes of rice-stuffed vine leaves and spicy ezme salad. Finally, he placed a vase of yellow roses in the center. There wasn't space on the table for another thing. As he poured rakı into the glasses he checked to see he had put the same amount in each. He added water to the rakı. He went inside and switched on the stereo. A romantic song started playing.

"Dinner is served."

We raised our empty hands as though drinking a toast.

"Cheers."

"Cheers."

"May our worst day be like this one."

For a moment our hands remained suspended in the air.

Uncle Küheylan repeated his words: "May our worst day be like this one."

We all burst out laughing.

It was a good job we were on the Doctor's balcony and not in a bar, otherwise our racket might have disturbed the people at the other tables.

Below us the sound of car horns mingled with the cry of seagulls; heedless of us, Istanbul went about her habitual ebb and flow. A group of young friends was drinking beer in a pavement terrace opposite us. One of them was playing the guitar, the others sang along with him, their voices too far away for us to hear. A woman on the top floor of the next building was talking on the telephone as she looked out of the window, straightening her hair with one hand. The curtains in most of the houses were not drawn. Children played around an old man as he sat in his armchair watching television. The sea grew darker as the sun set. The Eminönü–Üsküdar ferry was lit up and was setting sail with a thousand types of happiness and hope aboard.

"Zinê Sevda will be here soon," said Uncle Küheylan. "She said she'd be late, she had some errands to do."

We raised our glasses to her health.

"To Zinê Sevda, the mountain maiden."

"To Zinê Sevda, the mountain maiden."

The Maiden's Tower was also lit up. It sparkled and swayed, like a mother-of-pearl necklace around Istanbul's neck. It was close enough for us to reach out and touch. While we gazed at the Maiden's Tower, each of us became engrossed in our own memories and succumbed to the melody of the song drifting gently out of the stereo.

"It's obvious now," said the Doctor, "why they haven't tortured us, or taken anyone out of their cell for the past two days. It coincides with the clash in Belgrade Forest. It was a big one, covering a large area, and it lasted a long time. Our interrogators must have gone too. And left us in peace."

Uncle Küheylan smiled. "While our suffering here is getting easier," he said, "people somewhere else are dying. What a strange world! Now, as our suffering is about to begin again, let's hope that those elsewhere are well."

We raised our glasses.

"To others' wellbeing."

"To others' wellbeing."

We were drinking quite fast. We'd missed the taste of rakı.

Now I wanted to be as cheerful as the young friends on the opposite terrace, as happy as the woman at the window and as serene as the man in the armchair watching television. If I could leave this balcony and go downstairs, I'd go under the bridge, minding my own business. I would treat myself to a balık-ekmek sandwich. I would watch the boats on the Golden Horn. Then I would take a leisurely stroll up Yüksek Kaldırım to Beyoğlu and go into a cinema. Sometimes I chose cinemas instead of films. I would select them according to the building, the carvings, and the memories they evoked. No matter what film was showing, if it was in a cinema that touched my heart, I would enjoy it.

"Uncle Küheylan," I said, "isn't it time to answer my riddle? What do you say?"

"You're right."

I repeated the question the grandmother had asked me in the tiny gecekondu. "An old woman has a little girl with her. The old woman says, this is my daughter's daughter and my husband's sister. Tell me, how can that be?"

Uncle Küheylan helped himself to a piece of toasted bread and dipped it in the dish of hummus in front of him. He chewed slowly. He wiped his moustache with the back of his hand.

When he noticed me waiting eagerly, he said, "Be patient, Demirtay, I'll tell you in good time. In our village there was a dark-skinned woman of about forty, who lived alone with her blonde daughter. Their neighbor was a strapping young man of twenty. The dark-skinned woman got intimate with the strapping young neighbor, they had many trysts in the hayloft and then they got married. Around that time the young neighbor's father returned to the village. He had gone to Istanbul to work years before, and disappeared without a trace. Everyone thought he was either dead or had forgotten the village. The father was also around forty. And lonely. He got together with the neighbor's young blonde daughter and started a new life with her. Before long they had a baby daughter. The dark-skinned woman, now a grandmother, was delighted, and spent all her time with her grandchild. As she sat in front of her house playing with her granddaughter, she cheerfully recited this rhyme to every passerby: My daughter's daughter, my husband's sis, there's no other case quite like this. And even though people looked at her without knowing what she was talking about, she was telling the truth, wasn't she?"

"That's not fair," I said, amazed that he had got it so quickly.

"Why? Isn't that the right answer?"

"I hate to say you've got it right, but it's not fair. You guessed right first time."

Uncle Küheylan and the Doctor laughed like old men who have been together all their lives. They clinked glasses and took a sip from their rakı.

"I didn't get it right first time. I've been thinking about it for two days, it was only after I had gone over forty different possibilities that I came up with the answer."

"Is that story you told true, or did you make it up?"

"What kind of a question is that, Demirtay? Weren't you the one who just said that everything that happened in the past and that we tell in words becomes a story? Well the reverse is also true. Every story we tell here occurred in the past and is totally true."

He was right. There was a truth about my riddle that was keeping it rooted in reality: In the house in Hisarüstü, the grandmother was looking out for my return, waiting for me to bring her the answer to the riddle. I had promised her. I was going to return safe and sound. I was not going to get swept away in the Istanbul current. I would help the needy, walk alone in the crowd, and I would not get carried away by the head-spinning allure of bright lights on billboards. I might meet Yasemin Abla at a secret meeting point. I might sit beside her one auspicious night and listen to her reciting poems. I would believe the words in those eternal poems. Outside the moon would rise, the sky would glow, and the stars would bloom yellow, pink, and red.

"Demirtay, what was the other question?"

"Which question?"

"Remember you said yesterday that if we guessed this riddle you'd ask us another one."

I was hopeful when I had left grandmother's gecekondu. I intended to solve her riddle and then ask her one of my own when I went to see her. I wanted to answer her questions with other questions, stay in touch with her, and go and visit her often. But I didn't run fast enough, I fell victim to fate and they threw me into this cell. Instead of in the gecekondu looking out on Istanbul from the top of a hill, I was going to ask the riddle I had saved for grandmother in this cell.

"There's a young girl with a man," I said. "When people asked who she was he said, she's my wife and my daughter and my sister. How is that possible?"

"This looks like a tough one."

"Did you think I would ask you something easy?"

"You say his wife, and his daughter, and his sister, is that right?"

"Yes."

"I can see you're out to make me sweat."

"Dig deep in your memory, you never know, those people might well be from your village."

"Let me think," said Uncle Küheylan, laughing. "If I can't work it out I'll ask the Doctor for help. What do you say, Doctor, will you help me?"

"Of course."

"It's up to you," I said, "you can ask whoever you like to help you. I don't care if it's the Doctor, or Kamo the Barber . . ."

All three of us stopped and looked at each other and we all raised our rakı glasses in unison.

"To Kamo the Barber."

"To Kamo the Barber."

"To his safe return."

While for the first few days we hoped to get out of here and blend into the Istanbul current aboveground that swallowed up people, as time passed our expectations turned inward and shrank, until eventually they fit into this cell. Now the best we hoped for was that those who were taken away to be tortured would return in one piece, without losing their minds or their souls. That's how we were awaiting Kamo the Barber, whom they had taken away yesterday. We told stories, drank rakı, and listened to songs. We turned our heads and gazed at the undulating lights on the sea. We strove to forget about our wounds. When we heard a noise that sounded like the entrance door of the floor below was opening, we stopped and looked at one another. That was the cursed sound of the iron gate. It was close. The grating of the gate reminded us that we were not on the Doctor's balcony, but in this underground cell.

# 8ᵀᴴ DAY

*Told by the Doctor*

## THE KNIFELIKE SKYSCRAPERS

"When a power cut prevented a plane from landing in Istanbul Airport and it was lost on the dark sea along with its four crew members and thirty-seven passengers, the Istanbul dwellers awoke the next morning feeling anxious. During the crossing to the European side on the seven-thirty ferry from Kadıköy, they still read their newspapers and sipped their tea, occasionally peering over at their neighbor's newspaper in case theirs contained different news. Passengers with a window seat wiped condensation from the glass as though they might spot someone crying out for help in the waves, and sat with their noses glued to the window. Traversing the tunnel of time in which Haydarpaşa Station, Selimiye Barracks, and the Maiden's Tower flowed on one side, and Sultanahmet Mosque, Hagia Sophia Church, and Topkapı Palace on the other, they arrived on the shore of concrete buildings and knifelike skyscrapers. Each day they went back and forth from one side to the other, feeling animated and hopeful. Different as their mood might be at home, on the ferry, train, and bus they made sure to don an expression appropriate to the day. On the third morning, as they sipped their tea and read their newspapers with the same solemnity, a long-haired youth played the guitar and sang a new style of rock song in tribute to the victims of the plane crash. The victims would have liked it. Just then

167

they heard shouting on the deck. When they rushed out and all looked over to the other side at the same time, they saw a woman lying unconscious on the Sarayburnu rocks, where the cold waves had tossed her. She was the only survivor of the plane that had crashed into the sea. According to one of the next day's newspapers, the woman's legs were broken. According to all the other newspapers, she had a burst eardrum, or had lost her tongue, or had gone blind in one eye. The same photograph of the woman was splashed across the front pages of all the newspapers. She was lying in hospital surrounded by wires and drip bottles, and sitting beside her was a man in a suit and a felt hat. The headline under the photograph read, I'm over the moon that my wife was saved. In another newspaper the same man rejoiced to be reunited with his daughter. Yet another one said the good Lord has spared my sister. The ferry passengers shared the news they had read and discussed which might be the right version. Each passenger argued that their paper's version was the right one, continuing the debate the next day. The only detail that all the papers coincided on was the woman and man's names: Filiz Hanım and Jean Bey. Like a photo romance, the rest of the story was reported in daily installments, and the details were no longer on the level of mere national news but were now considered worthy of the nimble pens of the culture-literature writers. Each day new photographs were added to this ever longer and more convoluted saga, the lives of Filiz Hanım and Jean Bey were paraded before the public eye for all to see. Jean Bey, who was born and bred in some European country—France, according to some, and Switzerland according to others—came to Istanbul for a holiday in his youth, had a brief love affair with an—according to some, French, and, according to others, Swiss—singer who performed in a nightclub in Beyoğlu, visited all the sights, and returned to his country unaware that he had left behind a woman with child. He graduated from university, started work as a lecturer—he taught sociology, or biology, or physics—and married someone who taught in the same department. He was happy, hard working, and held in high esteem. When, five years—ten according to some—later, he divorced his wife for an undisclosed reason, he vowed he would never marry again. For years he lived alone and, until he fell in love with one of his students, remained true to his word. His student was Filiz Hanım, from Istanbul. They resolved to marry and invited Filiz Hanım's mother to the wedding. When Filiz Hanım's mother reached the wedding at the last moment, owing to the delayed departure of the planes from Istanbul, and walked into the hall where all the guests were gathered, Jean Bey almost expired with shock. The woman before him was the nightclub singer he had enjoyed a brief affair with years ago when he had visited Istanbul. They recognized each other, but behaved as though they hadn't. The ferry passengers who read that Filiz Hanım was both Jean Bey's wife and his daughter stared at one another in disbelief. They had not heard of such ill fate for many a year. The following day they learned in the latest installment of the saga that the story didn't end there. When Jean Bey was still a tiny baby his mother had abandoned the family home, leaving him and his father to fend for themselves. Jean Bey's father, who was seated at the top table in the wedding hall, couldn't believe his eyes when he saw his daughter-in-law's mother. It was his wife, the very same one who had walked out on them all those years ago. They too recognized one another, but behaved as though they had not. Filiz Hanım was not only Jean Bey's wife and daughter, she was his sister too. As the ferry passengers read each word one by one, gulping at the end of every sentence, they exclaimed, well I never! Having grown up on a diet of black and white dramas, they believed everything they read.

Although the newspaper reports were somewhat inconsistent, they found the truth in incoherence rather than coherence. One of the passengers raised his newspaper in the air, and spoke. It doesn't just end there, he said. Okay, so Filiz Hanım is Jean Bey's wife and daughter and sister, but my newspaper has added another bit of information. Filiz Hanım is Jean Bey's aunt too. The ferry passengers protested, saying that was just too much. But, in the hope that they would be wrong and would hear still more amazing facts, they asked to hear the latest snippet of the story. Like everyone who loves gossip, they tried to appear both interested and detached, stirring their tea and looking nonchalantly out of the window. The ferry sailed through a hazy sea known as time, heading slowly toward the era of the knifelike skyscrapers on the far shore of the sea."

I paused. I squinted, like a traveler looking out into the distance. I looked around me. "The ferry sailed through a hazy sea known as time ..."

The Student Demirtay, waiting eagerly to see how I would tie up the ends of the story, smiled.

"Doctor," he said. "You've come to Uncle Küheylan's aid. You've solved the riddle for him."

It was clearly an effort for Demirtay to laugh. His pain was increasing progressively. He was semiconscious when they brought him back from interrogation today. He was mumbling incoherently and groaning. He couldn't move his arms. His head hung down limply. When he stretched out on the concrete as though getting into bed, he took a deep breath and drifted off instantly. I removed my jacket and, instead of putting it under his head so he would sleep more comfortably, I covered him with it, to warm him up a bit. I smoothed his hair. I wiped the blood from his forehead and neck.

When, shortly afterward, they brought Uncle Küheylan in too, I felt as though I was on duty in accident and emergency.

I had a steady stream of injured patients. Uncle Küheylan's eyebrows were split. Once again his shirt and trousers were drenched in blood. The soles of his feet were a bloody mess. I made him lie down beside Demirtay. "May you wake up to a good morning," I said, putting him to bed too. I spread my jacket across both their chests. I listened to their labored breathing. I observed the lines on their faces. I guarded over them until it was our cell's turn to go to the toilet. I helped them go to the toilet at the top of the corridor. Although he made slow progress, Demirtay managed to walk, but Uncle Küheylan couldn't stand on one of his legs. He could only walk by leaning on me.

"What's wrong with that, Demirtay?" asked Uncle Küheylan. "Yesterday you asked both of us. The Doctor answered for me."

"Was it too difficult for you?"

"When I had thought long and hard but still couldn't come up with the answer, I asked the Doctor for help."

"So, the answer to this riddle is in Istanbul, not in your village."

"Yes, it's here. Besides, you tell me, when it comes to riddles that convert lies into truths, which village can compete with Istanbul . . ."

"Was Istanbul like this in the old days too, Uncle Küheylan?" Demirtay seemed to be asking a rhetorical question. "Has this city always been insincere and deceitful?"

Nature did not lie. Day and night, birth and death, earthquakes and storms were all true. Istanbul learned the truth from nature, but lies she created herself. Hoodwinking, duplicity, and playing tricks with the memory were all her inventions. She made everyone worship her and invented drunks who believed they would find their old lovers in their arms when they woke up in the morning. She invented paupers who believed the wealthy had earned their money by honest means. She scattered hope far and wide. Naturally the brokenhearted would have their moment of glory. And the unemployed too would return home one day with bread and meat. To mask loneliness she created brightly lit shop windows. She created minds that, instead of settling for God's absence, wanted to be God themselves. Istanbul, who intensified the scent of bodies, was like a lover who constantly made promises, yet stayed away. The best lies were hers. She created women and men who were desperate to believe her.

"Demirtay, you're getting more and more like my father, you ask difficult questions just like he did," said Uncle Küheylan.

"It's too late, Uncle Küheylan."

"Why?"

"It's too late," repeated Demirtay, shrugging.

Had Demirtay been the same in the outside world? Was he assailed by pessimism as he wandered amongst billboards, coffeehouses, and beggars? As everything in the street underwent continuous metamorphoses and forms all became confused, perhaps his inner world too was confused. He was cheerful and pessimistic at the same time. He grew melancholy whilst laughing, he stopped in the middle of an animated conversation and lapsed into silence. "It's too late." Did he know what it was too late for?

"Demirtay," I interrupted, "as you have not rejected my answer, I presume you accept that I've solved the riddle."

"To tell you the truth, Doctor, I'm more interested in the plane crash than the riddle."

"Do you know about that plane crash?"

"Yes, a friend of my mother's was on that plane. They were supposed to be meeting the next day. My mother was going to give her a novel she had just read. She couldn't believe it when she heard about the accident. She waited for days, hoping for good news."

"What did your mother do with the book?"

Demirtay bowed his head and stared at his feet for a while. It was clear that he felt the cold more with each passing day. Whichever way he turned, his body ached. His movements were slowing down, the light in his large eyes was growing dimmer. Neither talking nor staying silent did any good.

"I don't know," he said, without raising his head. "She must have left it in the bookcase. I never asked her."

"If I were you I would have wanted to know about that book."

"Doctor, it's not the book I'm thinking about right now, it's the passengers. I thought everyone on the plane had died, I didn't realize there was a survivor."

He was curious about the woman who had survived the plane crash, but couldn't bring himself to ask if that part of the story was true. In here people understood concepts, but couldn't be sure what they referred to. They thought they had seen light, water, and a wall for the first time. Every sound meant something different. Someone whose mind was overflowing with questions eyed even his own hands with suspicion. He couldn't understand why stories that were left open at one end were closed at the other. Wasn't Istanbul the same too, living as she did, both above and underground? Demirtay, who had had to endure pain in order to discover that, could not ask, "What is the truth?"

"I wish my mother knew that," he said. "One person's surviving a crash where everyone was presumed dead would have given her a shred of optimism to cling to. It would have helped her deal with her grief better than all those cigarettes she smoked on the nights when it recurred. Raising me by herself was already a big enough burden for her. She worked as a tea lady in a firm. She wanted me to study and have a life that was different from hers. She would go to bed after me and leave at the same time as me in the mornings. At the bus stop, as she gazed at the billboard that changed weekly, in some adverts she would see her dream holiday resort, and in others the beautiful home that would one day be ours. She gushed excitedly about the life we would lead in the future. At weekends she would go and clean houses in distant neighborhoods so she could save money. Everyone had their own neighborhood. The rich and the poor, east and west supporters, those with strong and weak accents had all convened in different neighborhoods. Those who used to feel uneasy about going to bed with a full stomach when their neighbor was hungry had found the solution, they moved to another neighborhood. There were smaller Istanbuls within Istanbul, the hungry and the well-fed were a long way away from each other. As the day was ending on one side of the city, the other side was preparing for the fun to start. As one side was waking up to go to work, the other side had just gone to bed. Everyone was in their own Istanbul, living with people just like themselves. The view they saw when they looked out at the sea was different too. As my mother rushed from one job to the other, dreaming of moving out of our house and our neighborhood and regularly updating our television and fridge, she believed that my future would be different from hers. She didn't know that I didn't believe it. Doctor, did I ever tell you that story? They asked Cinderella why she had fallen in love with the prince. That was the only destiny the tale offered me, she replied. The life in our neighborhood didn't offer us any other destiny either. Every family dreamed of the same thing, but they all ran up against the same dead end and got stuck. Nobody asked why. Neither did I, until I read the books given to me by the older boys we used to play football with on the empty plot."

Demirtay leaned across and picked up the plastic water bottle. He took two sips and carried on.

"In Istanbul bread and freedom were two desires that demanded that one be the slave of the other. You either sacrificed your freedom for bread, or you renounced bread for the sake of freedom. It was impossible to earn both at the same time. The young people in the neighborhood wanted to change that destiny; standing in the shadow of the brightly lit billboards, they dreamed of a new future. As I read the books they gave me I thought: How can a new future be possible when the whole of Istanbul is infested with sores? Streets were packed with cars and plots were packed with buildings. Cranes and metal piers were replacing melancholy trees. Like the number of beggars, the number of birds that struggled to find food was increasing. I read incessantly, trying to make sense of this city that my mother, my teachers, and my friends were so attached to."

Demirtay's voice, which had sounded hoarse when he had woken up, was growing softer. "My mother couldn't keep up with the flow of the city, she was exhausted from overwork. When she spoke of her childhood she said that life didn't use to change so quickly in the past. In those days, she used to say, innovation came gradually. We incorporated it into our lives little by little. Innovation used to excite but not confuse us. We knew what we would encounter the next day. Is that the way it is now? Innovations come quickly and go just as quickly. They're wiped out of our lives without any possibility of getting old. They leave no traces nor memories behind them. Before we have had a chance to adapt to one innovation a new one has already taken its place. But people have a limit. We walk faster than tortoises and run slower than hares. Our minds and feelings have a limit too. We march ahead of tradition and fall behind innovation. This discrepancy that puts a strain on the balance is what breaks the scale inside us. New is not the continuation of old, because there is no old. Everything becomes waste. Permanence is forgotten. Forming ties is losing credibility. Like refuse tips, hearts too are filled with waste. This pace exhausted my mother. She would go to sleep at night with sadness and fill her days with dreams. What else could she do? She was at a loss as to how to make a life all by herself in the midst of all the chaos in Istanbul, what else could she hold on to but dreams?"

Demirtay didn't like being alone. He was afraid of staying in the cell by himself, and was happy when there were more of us. He missed train stations, dilapidated ferries, and bustling avenues where everyone bumped into everyone else as they walked. The beauty of the city lay in its crowds: Everywhere was filled with people, noise, and lights. An existence that was rendered calm in one street roared into life in another. Metal was blended into concrete, steel was plated with glass. Istanbul's people resembled her too. She was born of earth, fire, water, and breath. She was as hard as steel and as fragile as glass. In the city people breathed life into the alchemy to which so many adventurers of the past had devoted their lives. Not prepared to settle for what already existed, they went off in pursuit of mindblowing innovations. They joined together fire and water, love and hate. Finding nature repulsive, they added evil to good in order to change it. They bought lies with money, decorated their houses with plastic flowers, injected their skin with silicone. They awoke every morning with the hope of seeing a more appealing face in the mirror. In Istanbul, alchemy started with oneself.

Demirtay's mother was strong and weak, fast and slow, hopeful and pessimistic. She didn't know how she managed to carry all that baggage at once. She tried to keep up with the sunset, adverts, and car horns. She was afraid of memories.

Memories reminded her that the good times were in the past. The city was devastated. Life was sterile. People were degenerate. Each day was worse than the day before. Like everyone submerged in loneliness, she too liked novels with happy endings. In novels she found the integrity that didn't exist at home, at work, and in the street. She tied together the conflicting ends of her soul. One side of her soul was steel, another glass, one side was tears, another rage.

"My mother believed in books," said Demirtay. He looked at us as though trying to work out whether we believed in them too. "Some nights when she became engrossed in a novel and forgot all about me, or when she smoked more cigarettes than usual, I wondered whether there might be a new wound in her heart. I didn't ask, and she didn't tell me. She was like a child struggling underwater, fighting to come up to the surface for air. She didn't drown, but neither was she able to come up to the surface for air. She rebuked this city that was built on calculations instead of on dreams. She thought Istanbul looked like a fancy book cover. The decorations and patterns on the outside deceived people, distancing them from the truth that was inside. Sometimes, I would ask childishly: Mommy, why do you work so much? Demirtay, she would say, I want to buy a house so that in the future you can live in comfort. I can't give you a good life now, but I'm striving to make sure you'll be happy in years to come. Don't think the future is a long way away, actually it's around the corner. When you read about the lives in books you'll understand it better. Whenever my mother spoke that way I would listen faithfully. It was from her that I learned to believe in books."

"Does your mother know they've caught you?" I asked.

"No. I haven't seen her for months. I haven't been back to my neighborhood because they're looking for me."

"Why, Demirtay?" I asked. "You could have seen her

after work, in the busiest part of the street, without anyone noticing."

"I thought about it, Doctor. I was tempted to try it a few times but I always changed my mind at the last moment. They might have been following her."

My son used to come and see me in secret. Sometimes in the thick of a crowd, sometimes he would sneak into a dark street corner and touch my arm. He would adapt his pace to match mine and walk with me. As I listened to Demirtay I felt fortunate. When I thought about those who had been waiting a long time for their sons and daughters, or even those who had received news of their deaths, I realized I belonged to the happy minority. I had found my son and had him admitted into the hospital. I had delivered him into safe hands.

"Demirtay," I said, "I used to have a colleague with whom I worked for many years. His adolescent daughter left home and joined a group of revolutionaries. One day he heard that his daughter had been shot, and that her friends had buried her in secret. He found out where her grave was. He had a marble gravestone made. He had a picture of a ship engraved on it. It was the picture on the cover of the *Illustrated Book of Istanbul* he had read with his daughter when she was a child. He went every week and spoke to his daughter buried under the earth. He read her sections from the *Illustrated Book of Istanbul*. He told her about domes that sparkled like stars, streets that curved like rivers, buildings that tapered like spears. One day his daughter's friends arrived and said there had been a mistake. A different friend rests here, your daughter is in a graveyard on the other side of Bosphorus, they said. My colleague didn't sleep that night. Nor the next. On the third night he went and lay by the usual grave. He awoke at daybreak. He looked up at Venus. He listened to the wind in the cypress trees. He dug his hand in and took a handful of earth from the grave. He smelled it. He threw it up in the air. He watched the wind scatter the earth and blow it away. I'm the owner of this grave, he said to himself, I've grown fond of it and it of me. He fell to his knees and wept. He believed that if he left that grave, his daughter in a different grave and all the other dead would be left with no one to care about them. My colleague continued to visit that grave regularly. He took the *Illustrated Book of Istanbul* with him, read stories from it and described pictures. Do you know what made me think of that incident? I think your mother did the same thing. She read the book that she was planning to give her friend to the Istanbul Sea, where the plane had crashed, and maybe once she had finished reading it, she let it drift away in the sea."

"Doctor," said Demirtay, looking anxious, "that's the second time you've told a sad story. What's the matter with you? Before you used to advise us not to talk about death and suffering in here."

When I thought about it I realized he was right. "I'm not aware I'm doing it. That means I must lose control sometimes," I said.

Demirtay was trying to warm his hands with his breath; I touched his forehead to check his temperature. I took his pulse. There was no flesh left under his skin, just bone. He shivered constantly. His temperature had risen. I told him to lean back. I raised his feet slowly and placed them on my knees. The skin on the soles of his feet was a mass of cuts and red, pink, and white welts. He was lifeless. I cupped his toes in the palms of my hands, as though swaddling them with cotton wool. I tried to warm him.

He dissolved into giggles.

"What's up?" I said.

"That tickles."

"Good, at least you can laugh."

"Do I have to laugh?"

"Yes, we must laugh. Otherwise we'll be in trouble with Uncle Küheylan for telling sad stories. He's already giving us stern looks."

"In that case I'll tell you a joke."

Had Demirtay thought of a new joke, or was he going to tell us one of his old ones?

"What joke?" I said.

"The polar bear joke."

"What polar bear joke?"

"The baby polar bear."

"Go on, tell us."

Demirtay, who had surrendered his feet to the palms of my hands, started.

"In the land of the north the ground was ice, the mountains were ice, the very air they breathed was ice. The baby polar bear snuggled up to its mother and buried itself in her long, warm fur. Mommy, said the baby polar bear, are you my real mommy? The mother bear was surprised. Of course I am darling, she said. Okay, was your mommy a polar bear too? Yes, my mommy was a polar bear too. What about your daddy? He was a polar bear too. The baby polar bear walked away from its mother and went to its father. This time it snuggled up to his warm fur. Daddy, said the baby polar bear, are you my real daddy? Yes, said its father. The questions went on as before. And was your daddy a polar bear too? Yes. And was your mommy a polar bear too? Yes. It's actually a long story, but I'll be brief. Once the baby polar bear had got the answers it was expecting, it stomped off angrily and stood up on the ice. Why am I always so cold then, it shouted."

We laughed in whispers. If we didn't control our voices they might travel over the walls, all the way to the world aboveground.

"Why am I so cold then," said Demirtay. Demirtay repeated his own words and, like a child who has run all the way back from a long distance, he continued, panting. "I'm always cold as well. It's as though I have blocks of ice inside my flesh instead of bones. Why am I the one who feels the cold the most in this cell?"

On cue, I said, "You're a baby polar bear."

"I must be."

The sound of the iron gate opening wiped the smile off our faces. We strained to hear the voices that spilled out into the corridor.

In the dark, vampires that suck young girls' blood returned to their cave, wolves that devoured children in the woods entered through the iron gate. An overpowering smell assailed our nostrils. It was as though we had fallen down a well in the desert and were waiting for a camel train following the stars to come and rescue us. We dreamed of opening our eyes one morning somewhere far away from here and waking up on warm sand dunes where we couldn't hear the iron gate. We were as helpless as a ship tossed on the waves in a storm. Each of us thought we were the only surviving crew member of a sunken ship, but we were afraid of sharing the fate of the dead seamen.

We waited, completely immobile. We listened to the sounds outside. They opened and closed the door of one of the cells at the top of the corridor. Then they moved on to the rear corridor. They banged noisily on the door of another cell. They hooted with drunken laughter. They sang a song with words we couldn't make out. They turned back in high spirits. They came close to us, their footsteps echoing on the walls. There were a lot of them. Their grunting and their stench were overwhelming. They stopped in front of our cell. Instead of ours they opened the door of the opposite cell. They dumped

Zinê Sevda inside. They swore at her. They insulted her. They slammed the door. They burst out in frenzied laughter, like inmates in a psychiatric hospital.

Demirtay got up and walked slowly to the grille. He glanced over at the opposite cell. Turning to us he said, "Zinê Sevda isn't at the grille."

"She's only just come back. She'll need a few minutes before she can stand up."

Demirtay wasn't aware that he was standing barefoot on the freezing concrete. "I'll wait here," he said.

It wouldn't be the last time.

Life in the cell was repeating itself. As the darkness slowly circled above us, our words described the same person, traversed the same city, clung to the same hope. But we still began each day with enthusiasm, in the hope that today would be different. We stared at each other as though meeting for the first time. When we realized that our dreams, as well as our suffering, renewed themselves, we lapsed into momentary silence. If happiness was limited, could unhappiness have no limit? If laughter was limited, could suffering have no limit? Every day we invented new pretexts for laughing, once we sensed that our laughter too renewed itself, we realized we had reached a new threshold.

We would raise our heads and stare at the ceiling. We tried to recall whether the Istanbul above also renewed herself. Were the market stalls, the mosque pigeons, the cries of children at the end of the school day, the same on both sides? Did the Bosphorus flow the same in all neighborhoods? Were all babies born with the same cry, did all old people expire with the same sigh? We were curious about death. Did death too repeat itself, was each death like all the others?

"Zinê Sevda is at the grille, she's calling you," said Demirtay.

"Both of us?"

"Yes, she wants to talk to you."

I helped Uncle Küheylan get up. We walked two steps to the door. The light from the corridor made us blink. We smiled at Zinê Sevda, as delighted as if we had seen our own daughter.

"Are you all right?" wrote Uncle Küheylan.

"Yes," said Zinê Sevda, and wrote the same question back. "Are you all right?"

"We're fine, my child."

Zinê Sevda's closed left eye was puffed and swollen, the bruises on her face had multiplied. The gash on her lower lip had grown wider. Her neck was black with grime. Her greasy hair was stuck to her head. She looked at me, examining my face as though counting my injuries one by one.

"Doctor, how are you?" she asked.

"I'm fine," I said, "but you've just returned from interrogation, you need to sleep and rest."

Without waiting for me to finish writing, Zinê Sevda raised her finger and wrote quickly, "When you're talking to each other, do you share your secrets?"

"No," I said.

Uncle Küheylan and Demirtay ratified my answer by shaking their heads.

"Are you sure?" said Zinê Sevda.

"What do you mean?"

What did she mean?

We passed the time left over from being tortured sleeping, talking, or being cold. We shared our dreams and built our own heaven here. Just as Istanbul keeps her secrets hidden, we too hid our secrets from each other.

"Doctor," said Zinê Sevda. Her finger remained suspended in the air for some time, she seemed undecided about completing her sentence. "The interrogators know your secret."

My secret?

I swallowed. I shut my dazed eyes tightly, then opened them again.

"How could they know?" I said.

"You told them yourself."

"No, I didn't spill a word while they were torturing me."

"Not under torture, in the cell. They planted one of their men in your cell. You told him."

"What are you talking about, my child?"

What was she talking about?

Zinê Sevda wrote patiently.

"While I lay unconscious in the interrogation room I woke up at one point. The interrogators had left me by the wall and were chatting. I heard what they were saying. Yesterday someone they were interrogating tore off his blindfold and grabbed the gun of one of the interrogators. He fired at random. He ran into corridors where he hadn't been before and fired indiscriminately. He didn't get far. They surrounded him. They shot him without a second thought. That was what the gunshots we were wondering about yesterday were."

Zinê Sevda paused to see whether I was following her.

"I was blindfolded, Doctor," she said. "I couldn't see their faces. They thought I was unconscious. They were stirring their tea and smoking. Then they started talking about you. One of the men told them how he had talked to you and gained your trust. He revealed the information he got from you."

The information he got from me?

"What information did he get from me?"

"You're not the real Doctor . . ."

I stepped back from the grille. I walked away with leaden steps. I continued to the back wall of the cell. I stood motionless, like a child who wants to scream in his sleep but can't get the sound out.

"They know," I murmured to myself, "dear God, they know."

I took tiny steps back to the door.

"One more thing," said Zinê Sevda. "They mentioned someone called Mine Bade. Apparently you're not the man she loves. Mine Bade loves a different doctor."

I had no strength left to walk. I slumped to the ground. I ran my hands over my mouth, my forehead, my hair. My shirt felt tight. I ripped off the buttons one by one. Uncle Küheylan grabbed me by the wrists. He made me lean back against the wall. As I struggled to get free he tightened his grip on my wrists.

What was happening to me?

They said there are three things in life that are irreversible. What were they? Was a spilled secret one of them? I wanted to be able to turn the clocks back. I didn't want to go back to last month or to last year, but all the way back to the earliest era. How lovely to live when human was not yet human, when there was no such thing as cruelty. There was no worry. Existence was not based on suffering. People were satisfied with looking and touching. The number of births was not registered, deaths occurred in the natural order. And there was no need for secrets.

"We are not informers," said Demirtay, holding me by one wrist. His voice was feeble. "We can't tell anyone else your secret because we don't know it. Do we, Uncle Küheylan?"

"You . . ." I said.

"We didn't tell anyone anything."

"What could you tell them?" I said. "They caught me in place of my son. He's the real Doctor. I never told you that. I went to my son's meeting. When I fell into the police's trap I adopted his identity."

My son's meeting was with Ali the Lighter. It was one of

the last hot days of the season. The sun looked beautiful to me. I lavished affection on the Istanbul contained in Ragıp Paşa Library for the last time. I bent down to the ground in that courtyard. I dug a hole in the earth with my hands, plunged underground, tumbled down layer after layer, and, sauntering in the dark like a worm, eventually descended to this cell. I shed my skin and grew a new skin underneath it. In my loneliness I ate my own flesh, when I felt thirsty I drank my own blood. There was a classic love song my wife used to sing. I wrote the lyrics on the wall with my fingernail. Oh flower bud, open, I said, don't imagine the world's pleasures are here to stay. I closed my eyes. I spoke to the darkness. This was where the last judgment would be. All the living were dead, all the dead were living. I listened to the entreaties. One day the door opened. Ali the Lighter entered. He was wounded. His pockets were full of light. When his pain increased the drops of light leaked out and melted. He missed his dead friends, he talked of Mine Bade, he was saddened by my plight. He said Mine Bade loved me. There are two wounds in her chest, Doctor, he said. The bullet caused one, you caused the other. The bullet wound will heal, but what about the one you caused? How can Mine Bade ease her heartache? As Ali the Lighter spoke, the ceiling opened, stars rained down on us. In the distance I could hear the song my wife used to sing. I am the nightingale in your garden of joy, the song went, and you are its rose. My son was free, he loved a girl and the girl had set her heart on him. They would find each other, and before long they would both recover. Ali the Lighter must recover too, and throw off the burden of all that sadness. He must hold on to the light leaking out of his pocket. I wanted to help him. I opened my hand and shared part of my secret with him. Don't worry, I said, that girl doesn't love me, she loves my son. They'll meet and help each other. Don't worry, they'll be better soon.

"Is that all?" asked Uncle Küheylan.

"What do you mean, is that all?"

"Is that all the interrogators know?"

"Yes."

"What's the problem then?"

"They know my son's outside. They'll go after him."

"Do they know where he is?"

"No."

In here I was not myself. I was a father who had taken his son's identity. So Ali the Lighter wasn't Ali the Lighter either. He was a policeman who had been shot in the conflict in Belgrade Forest. He had had treatment, put on a weary face, then come inside with me. He told me things he had found out from files and from the people they had caught as though they were his own secrets. He was wounded, I believed him. He was suffering, I believed him. I gave him water, I shared bread with him. Once he mentioned the girl my son loved, I believed him even more. I thought I would lighten his burden. I wanted to ease his pain. I gave him part of my secret, but I didn't tell him where my son was.

"Are you sure?"

"Yes. I haven't told anyone where my son is."

"Of course you haven't," said Uncle Küheylan, seizing my shoulders. "Because you don't know."

"That's right, I don't know," I said.

"You can't tell them what you don't know, can you?"

"True."

"Because you don't know."

"Because I don't know."

"What are you afraid of then?"

"I couldn't defend my secret, what if I can't defend my resistance either . . ."

Until now I hadn't realized that I had been happy in the cell. Though I endured pain, though I groaned and spat blood, I was happy. I was self sufficient. I loved my secret. Perhaps my veins would bleed dry, perhaps I would take my last breath in here. No one would know what I carried in my heart. As my body became one big wound, my son would recover outside. Even if I died, he would live. People recognized unhappiness, but weren't always aware of happiness. I realized that now.

Uncle Küheylan held my neck up. He gave me water.

"Calm down, everything will be all right," he said.

"It will, won't it?"

"Doctor, don't worry, it will all be fine from now on."

"I might die. That would be good too."

The season had turned to winter. It grew dark early. Feather-light snowflakes rained down on the rooftops. Shop windows glittered, in the Istanbul aboveground, the animated Beyoğlu crowds were spilling outside. Wherever one turned there were cinema posters, the aroma of food, and the sound of music. A tram originating from infinity and bound for infinity passed through the crowd. At the back of the tram a young man held hands with the girl he loved. It was my son. He whispered something I couldn't hear but was itching to know in the girl's ear. His face was ingenious, he smiled just as he had done as a child. The melody of a classical love song drifted in from outside. When my son heard it, he stuck his head out of the window and looked outside. Oh flower bud, open, said the song, open and prolong the pleasure of this fleeting moment. My son examined the crowds as though he were searching for someone he knew, he scrutinized the faces, then held the girl's hand tighter still. A tram from infinity, flowing like light through the Beyoğlu crowds, was transporting my son to a new infinity.

At that moment the iron gate opened. Its grating echoed

through the corridor.

"I might die," I repeated.

"What do you mean, you might die?" said Uncle Küheylan.

"If I die there'll be no one left who knows where my son is."

"But Doctor, you don't know where he is either!"

"It's too late . . ."

"No it's not!"

"It's too late . . ."

Uncle Küheylan stared at me. He slapped me hard across the face. He paused. Then he slapped me again.

# 9TH DAY

*Told by Kamo the Barber*

## THE POEM OF ALL POEMS

"A sleepy passenger just descended from the overnight train met a thin man wearing a cap on the steps leading down to the sea in front of Haydarpaşa Station. The man was looking at a photograph he was holding in his bony fingers, and crying one moment and roaring with laughter the next. As he wept he bowed his head, but when he laughed he was like a madman. The train passenger put his small case down on the ground and went and sat beside the man. He called the simit seller and bought a simit each for himself and the man with the cap. He gazed at the domes aligned with garlands of clouds on the opposite shore. He talked about the fine weather, about how the smell of Istanbul varied according to the season. He read the names on the boats that sailed past in quick succession, endowing each name with a meaning. This was a city where the truth looked obvious, but was not. Steps that led down to the sea, steps that connected trains to boats, steps where people sat to look at photographs carried not one, but many forms of the truth. Everyone clung to a truth in a different part of the city. Was the sun on this side of Istanbul the same as the sun on the other side, there was no way of knowing. Did the wind here blow the same on the other side, no one could be certain. The train passenger and the man with the cap said let's go. They decided to go and contemplate the sun and the wind on the opposite side. They took a ferry from the quay. They admired the ancient palaces, the barracks, and the towers as they drank tea on the rear deck. They thought that rather than being a city that drew history to herself, Istanbul was a city incapable of digging her way out of the entrails of history. It was that history that was sold on color postcards. When they got off the ferry and walked past the street vendors and the blind street singers, they immediately changed their minds. They concluded that postcards sold lies, not history. They jumped onto the commuter train at Sirkeci Station and went all the way to the last stop via neighborhoods inhabited by old people, taverns for early drinkers, and crumbling city walls. They gazed at the Istanbul where there were no more stops, and at the new color of the sky. They watched the dogs at the rubbish dump eating dead birds. They had return tokens. They boarded the same commuter train and the same ferry, traversed the railway tracks and the waves and returned to the steps at Haydarpaşa Station overlooking the sea. The sun was setting. Flocks of birds were flying toward the crimson sun, gliding past minarets and domes. Accepting the cigarette that the train passenger offered him, the man with the cap started talking, as though he had been awaiting this moment all day. Everything happened at around this time, he said. One evening my wife went out and never returned. They said she had run away, or was lost, or dead, but it made no difference to me. I made announcements, put up posters. I started off doing the rounds of police stations and hospitals, but then started frequenting taverns. I pronounced my wife's name whilst drinking. I slept with prostitutes in an attempt to forget her. Like an exile in my own city, I counted the days, months, and seasons. Look, this is my wife's photograph. I carry it everywhere. Her beauty is like drinking water from an emerald encrusted cup that refills itself with the same water each time. It's infinite. It competes with the beauty of Istanbul. When I dream about our old days together I laugh with joy. But when I think about the future I realize I'll never be able to see my wife again. This is the way I am, I've tumbled into a chasm. I laugh at the past in the photograph but cry about the future."

Realizing that I could barely speak as I was nearing the end of my words, Uncle Küheylan helped me sit up. He made me lean against the wall. He reached over and picked up the water bottle that still had a couple of sips of water in it.

"Drink, it will make your throat feel better," he said.

"Uncle Küheylan, I laugh at the past too, just like that thin man with the cap," I said. "But I don't cry about the future, I despise the future."

"Kamo, you're free to laugh at anything you want, and to despise whatever you like. As long as you don't break down in the face of pain," he said.

"I don't care about pain," I said, although my whole body was aching. Every bit of me hurt, from my toes to my groin, from my spine to my neck, from my temples to my chin. When I breathed, I felt as though my ribcage was being ripped apart, lights flickered on and off before my one open eye.

With great difficulty I took a sip of water from the plastic bottle and swallowed, my throat burning.

"Now it's time for this," said Uncle Küheylan, putting a piece of bread in my hand.

"That's going to be hard," I said, looking at the bread that looked rock-hard.

"Can't you chew?"

"My teeth hurt, I've got cuts all over my gums."

"Give it to me then, I'll chew it for you."

Uncle Küheylan took the bread back. He bit a piece off the end.

"How long have you been in here by yourself?" I asked, casting my eye around the cell as though examining a large plaza.

"Just before you came back they took the Doctor and the Student Demirtay away, and left me here by myself."

"What's the student doing? Hasn't he gone mad, hasn't he surrendered yet?"

"No, Kamo, they're both resisting the pain."

"Uncle Küheylan, I wonder how many people are left in these rows of cells who are still resisting. While they were interrogating me they showed me so many prisoners who had squealed, who were on their knees. They were pitiful. They were begging."

"Sometimes the pleading in the cells is so loud it tears me apart. The ones who give in are our brothers too, Kamo. We can't do anything for them except grieve."

"Grieve? Perish the thought! Every time they took off my blindfold I thought they would bring me the Student. So I could see him in all his wretchedness, crying like all the others, begging the red-eyed torturers . . ."

"Stop thinking about all that now and eat this bread."

Using his finger and thumb, Uncle Küheylan picked up the tiny morsels of the bread he had chewed and popped them into my mouth that I had opened wide, like a bird's.

I began the laborious task of eating it. I felt it with my tongue. I placed it in my inside cheek. I swallowed my saliva to lubricate my throat. I picked up the bread with the tip of my tongue and forced it to slide down my throat. It felt like eating thorns. It burned my gullet as it slipped down.

"A bit more . . ." said Uncle Küheylan, holding out a small ball of squashed bread.

"No, I need a rest," I said.

"Okay, get your breath back."

"When did you tie this cloth on me?" I asked, raising my left wrist.

"Does it hurt? I had to tie it tightly."

"It's not the bandage that hurts, it's the wound."

"When they brought you in, your wrist was bleeding. I tore off my shirt sleeve and bandaged your arm. You were semiconscious, don't you remember?"

"The last thing I remember was the nail they hammered into me."

"What nail?"

"They hammered a nail into my wrist."

"Into your wrist?"

"Yes."

"Damn them! It's unbelievable. What kind of people are they?"

"People? They're the real people, Uncle Küheylan. Haven't you realized that yet? When God created nature and the earth and the sky, Satan laid his own claim on people, and fed them with fruit from the tree of knowledge. Once people had acquired knowledge they did what no other living thing had been able to do, they became aware of their existence. And the more aware they became of their existence, the more they admired it. They loved no one but themselves, not even God. The only reason for their attachment to God was their desire for life after death. They measured everything against their own existence. They trampled nature and exterminated living things. When the time came they would kill God too. That's why evil had the upper hand in the world. I told the torturers that too. Satan's bastards! They stuck needles in my ear. They poured some strange substance down it. It was boiling hot. They tried to bore into my brain. I struggled to stop myself from going mad, I tried to break free of my chains. I banged my head on the wall. When they ordered me to beg, I cursed.

Sometimes I groaned, sometimes I roared with laughter. You're people, I said, you're the real people. Bloodcurdling screams I never thought I was capable of came out of my mouth. They stuck my head in water. They kept my mind alert to make sure I felt the pain properly. They worked like surgeons, craftsmen, butchers. They got into my blood vessels and unblocked the channels of pain. They did what being people required of them."

Uncle Küheylan was waiting with the morsel of bread between his finger and thumb.

"Uncle Küheylan," I said, "I didn't join the revolutionaries, because they've got the wrong idea about people. They believe people are inclined to be good, that they can be saved from evil. They think selfishness and cruelty only occur in adverse conditions. They don't see the hell people harbor in their souls, they're not aware that people are clawing to turn the world into hell. Revolutionaries are squandering their lives by looking for truth in the wrong place. People can't recover. People can't be saved. The only way out is to run from people."

Uncle Küheylan eyed me with curiosity and pity. Like everyone else, he took me for an incurable eccentric. He listened to me patiently.

"Is there anywhere left in the world that's out of bounds to people, Uncle Küheylan? They ride in luxury jeeps, police cars, factory workers' buses. They crowd into banks, schools, houses of worship. They invade cities and villages, mountains and forests. The Istanbul you love so much is theirs too. They lie and they assault. Not content with going everywhere, they worm their way inside us too. They usurp our bodies. Even if we manage to run away from people, how can we run away from ourselves? How can we save ourselves from ourselves? Instead of pondering this issue, revolutionaries and politicians, teachers and preachers talk interminably, deceiving themselves and everyone else. That's why I respect the torturers. They don't feel the need to lie. They don't hide the truth. They don't hesitate to embrace evil. I told them they were the most honorable people I knew. At that point they were carving my flesh to pieces, like they were dismembering a live animal in a slaughterhouse. I genuinely respect you, I said, you're the same on the inside as you are on the outside. You are exactly as you seem. My words threw them into a rage, they lost control. They pounded the walls and smashed the windows. They screamed in pain. They slammed the door. They abandoned me chained to the wall, blindfolded, and left the room. Was it day or night? Was life in the outside world flowing at a fast or slow pace? Perhaps they had gone into a side room, perhaps they had grabbed the phone and called their wives, telling them they missed them. I'm so tired, they said. I had another nightmare, they said. I want to get drunk and go to sleep in your arms, they said. Their wives exuded affection. They were good wives, as they had been trained to be from childhood. At times like these they would speak softly, their hearts going out to their husbands. They would tell the man they loved that when he came home they would fling their arms around him, smother him with kisses, snuggle up to him and open their legs for him. They promised their man a body hot with desire. There was nothing else they could do. They didn't know whether it was day or night outside either. Was life flowing at a fast or slow pace? Were the streets crowded or deserted? Once my interrogators had put the phone down, they fell silent. They wiped away their sweat. They crouched by the wall and smoked. They waited for their hearts to stop palpitating. Once their rage had subsided, they opened the door of the room where I was still tied up, and returned to my side with the exact same number of footsteps. They spoke with composure. Kamo, they said, you must tell us about the past. Kamo, they said, you must reveal the secrets of your past. I raised my head and, staring into the darkness under my blindfold, replied. Are you ready to listen to what's beyond the past? While not even God can change the past but leaves us to confront it by ourselves, are you up to hearing more than that? Bastards from hell! Sons of bitches! They removed my chains, untied my blindfold. They made me sit in front of a mirror. They made me look at a face that looked like a corpse. We are the future, they said. Look in the mirror Kamo, you have no future, only a past, and you're going to surrender that past to us, they said.

"Uncle Küheylan, the face I saw in the mirror was crushed, filthy, ravaged. Blood was oozing from one of its ears and pus from the other. One of its eyes was open, the other closed. Its eyebrows were slit. Its lips were split. Spit drooled from its mouth. It didn't look human. We're familiar with the mirror's glass, Uncle Küheylan. We know the wood or metal that the frame is made of, its flowered or glittery carvings. But what about the inside? Can we ever be familiar with the void in the depths of the mirror? Can we ever conceive of the magic contained in its layers? The mirror was like the well I used to lean over and stare into for hours when I was a child. Its sides were visible, but a dark vortex spun in its center. I was trapped in that vortex. My breathing was labored. The pain in my chest oppressed me like a rock. I coughed uncontrollably. My lungs felt as though they were being ripped out. I wondered what I was supposed to do now. Should I smash the mirror beside me, or should I break the neck of one of the interrogators standing next to it? I squealed with childlike delight and burst out laughing. It was as though I were in the hall of mirrors at the fun fair. I ignored the pain in my chest. My laughter became raucous, resonating throughout the room."

As though in an attempt to silence me, Uncle Küheylan

reached over and dropped the morsel of chewed-up bread inside my lower lip.

"Eat that as well," he said, "you need it."

The stench of mold overpowered my nasal cavity. I felt sick. I retched. I took the bread out of my mouth.

"I can't do it, I can't swallow it," I said.

"Okay, let's take a break."

"Then I saw Zinê Sevda there."

"Zinê Sevda? In the interrogation room?"

I knew Uncle Küheylan would brighten up at the sound of her name.

"Yes," I said. "When I picked up the mirror and brought it down on one of the interrogators' faces they all went for me. They vented all their rage on me. All their carefully designed torture techniques went out of the window, they pounded me until I was unconscious. I have no idea how much time passed. They doused me with cold water. When I came to I was shivering on the concrete. My body felt heavy. A smoke screen covered my only good eye, the world looked hazy. I could only distinguish shadows. A table. A chair. Several people standing up. A long wall. Opposite me, at the end of the wall, two thick columns. A body suspended between the two columns. To discern whose body it was I would either have to go closer, or get rid of the smoke in my eye. I rubbed my eye and wiped away the blood around it. I raised my head from the ground and looked in front of me again. A woman was suspended from a metal line between the two columns. Her two outstretched arms were tied to the metal line, while the rest of her body hung down. She could barely move her head. She was naked. Her breasts were bleeding. The cuts that started at her shoulders trickled down her stomach, groin, and legs, leaving a red streak behind them. It was obvious that the interrogators were trying to force me to give in to them, appealing to my sense of compassion by torturing someone in front of me yet again. They took me for someone who gives in to compassion. I rubbed my eye again. I stretched my neck to get a better look. I realized that the person hanging like a crucified saint was Zinê Sevda. She was light. Like a delicate leaf on an autumn tree, she was a long way from the ground and close to the heavens. The ropes on her arms didn't prevent her from falling down, they stopped her from ascending to heaven. Was this the same thin girl who had knelt in front of our cell a few days ago, heedless of all the interrogators in the corridor? Was this woman suspended in the air Zinê Sevda, who had remained motionless despite being kicked and beaten? She recognized me. She raised her head a bit higher. Her one good eye dilated. The edge of her lip twitched. She attempted a smile. It wasn't long before all her strength had gone and her head fell to her chest again. I couldn't tear my gaze away from her. I wasn't embarrassed by her nakedness, or my own. I knew the interrogators were trying to possess our emotions before our bodies. I placed my hands on the floor and, concentrating all my strength on my arms, I straightened up. I knelt. I wiped the sweat from my forehead and the bloodstains that went from my cheek down to my neck. I was as erect as a statue. Immobile. The corridor was silent. The only audible sound was the blood that had run down the length of Zinê Sevda's body and was dripping from her toes onto the floor. I waited there on my knees, just as a statue waits in the sun or the rain or the snow. The interrogators grunted. They cursed irritably. They realized I was reenacting Zinê Sevda's gesture of solidarity when she had knelt in our corridor a few days ago. They leaned over me. They dragged me to the back wall by the hair. They placed my shoulders and my arm on a plank. They took a long, thin nail that glinted like a light and poised it on my left wrist. They drove it in with a heavy hammer. I felt as though they were driving the hammer into my brain, not my wrist. I groaned. Tears gushed from my open and my closed eye. I admire you, I said to the interrogators. You do what no one else can, you make what's inside reflect outside exactly as it is. Before smashing the prisoners' souls, you smash your own open like a pomegranate and scatter them all around. They took their hands off me. They withdrew and exchanged looks. They had no other choice but to continue. They took another nail out of the box. They poised it above my other wrist. They raised the hammer in the air. At that point I could hardly breathe, my eye closed. I blacked out. The last question that crossed my mind before I fainted was this: Did they suspend Zinê Sevda in the air in front of me to make me talk, or were they crucifying me and driving glinting nails into my wrist in her presence as a ploy to make her surrender?"

Uncle Küheylan touched my good wrist, wrapping his fingers around it. He kissed it as though kissing bread. He touched it to his forehead. He closed his eyes. He waited, my wrist still on his forehead. He moaned with the humility of one of the rare people who values suffering. He needn't have. I could deal with my own suffering, he should stick to worrying about his. I tried to yank my wrist away, he wouldn't allow it. I tried again. He gripped my wrist with his large hands, keeping it on his forehead until I coughed. When he realized I had not stopped coughing he raised his head. He placed my wrist on the floor, as gingerly as if it were a baby sparrow. He held my shoulders. He held up my body, which had flopped over to one side, and leaned my back against the wall. He picked up a piece of cloth from the floor and wiped the blood oozing from my mouth. I think it must have been the other sleeve from his shirt. He cleaned my forehead and my neck. He poured the last few drops of water onto the cloth and wet my lips with it.

As my head spun, the beating in my jugular vein was not the sound of my heart but the sound of time. Of time that had returned from the past, crashed against the breakwater of the future and abandoned me there to my fate. I could not keep up with its pace. It would swell and then subside. It revolved between an instant and infinity. It snatched my wife Mahizer away from me, taking her far away, etching her name on my jugular vein so I would feel it with every breath I took. Time wanted me to laugh at the past on the one hand and cry for the future on the other.

On the day when Uncle Küheylan told us there was a world in the sky where we were reflected and where we each had our double, I raised my head and saw a rainy, crowded, bustling Istanbul in the darkness. I heard the sound of the street vendors, the roar of the car engines that inhale exhaust fumes in heavy traffic, and the bells signaling the end of the working day. Istanbul, which extended from one end of the sky to the other, engulfed men and women, pulverized, then vomited them. Everywhere there was the stench of rotting meat. Everyone regarded everyone else as a stranger, no one spoke to anyone. Because people are like the cities where they live, they would wake up feeling cheerful one morning, and troubled the next. They worked from morning till evening and from evening till morning. They had accepted death and were prepared for everything, except coming face to face with the truth in their hearts. They flowed in the streets like a muddy stream, congregating in the squares when they tired. I too had a double amongst those people. My double, who walked alone in the crowd, tied a thin scarf around her neck. She was as much a reflection of me as a reversed image in a mirror. I was a man, she was a woman. I was troubled, she was serene. I was ugly, she was beautiful. I was evil, she was good. I was Kamo the Barber, she was my wife Mahizer. When we met we fit into a single shadow. We read poems that bound us to one another. Thanks to those poems, we invented our own private language within languages. We communicated in that language that no one understood, we joked, we made love. Even in our sleep we wanted to dream of a poem and start the next day with it. But time didn't allow our language to take root and bond with the earth. That bitch time.

When Mahizer abandoned me and left home, in the beginning it wasn't her I sought, but the poem of all poems.

The language I learned from my mother wasn't enough. I had grown up with my mother's language, memorized names, grown to know objects and people by their names. I assumed the information of language was the information of truth, and prepared myself for an existence like everyone else's. I spoke with a few words, and remained silent with the same number of words in my head. I had not invented language, my mother had given birth to me inside it. Until the day when, leafing through some notebooks in my mother's drawer, I found a series of handwritten poems, I had believed I wouldn't be able to step outside of that language. The poems written in faded ink were my father's. It was the first time I had seen his signature and his handwriting. Although my father used words I knew in his poems, he changed the sounds, giving the letters a new significance. He invented meanings that no one had thought of before. Like Lokman Hekim in his quest for the elixir of immortality, he was seeking the pure language of existence. He would make the stars descend from the sky and replace them with the stars of poetry. He swore that poetry and love had both suckled milk from the breast of death. He would open the curtain a crack and with his hand wipe the condensation from the window that opened out onto the truth. Like animals that are hunted one by one, he belonged to a species of poets that was becoming extinct. He died before I was born, but he left me a priceless inheritance. With his poems he saved me from the quicksand of desire. Desire was life's new God. Like God, it tried to reach all places and control all things. It knew no limits. Whereas God was false. Desire was the repetition of that falsity. When you added people's falsity to that, life became unbearable. Who was there, apart from poets, who could break that vicious circle? Who was there left, apart from poets, who spoke in the language of death and who promised people the infinity of truth rather than the boundlessness of desire?

I visited library after library, in the hope of finding the poets' most beautiful poem and laying it at Mahizer's feet. I pored over catalogues. I scoured series after series of journals and books in reading rooms. When the time came for children's poems, I crossed over to the Asian side one sunny autumn day and went into the courtyard of the Çinili Children's Library.

Like my father's lyrical poems, the library's small courtyard was alive with the music of birdsong. The shade of the ivy evoked the sensation of peaceful slumber. A wooden bench with flaking paint stood at the point where the grass and the side wall met. I walked across the cobblestones and the grass. Sitting on the bench, I waited for the beads of sweat that had formed as I climbed up winding hills during the journey from the Üsküdar Quay to here to dry. Beyond the wall there was silence. Everywhere was deserted. Just as my eyes were about to close, the courtyard door opened. A little girl entered. She was wearing a school uniform and carrying a schoolbag and glanced, first at the steps going up to the library on the next floor, then at me. I wasn't sure she was able to distinguish me through her thick glasses. She came and sat beside me.

"Whose father are you?" she asked.

"I'm not anybody's father," I said.

"Then who have you come to collect?"

"I haven't come to collect anyone."

"In that case are you the new librarian?"

"No. What happened to the old librarian, is he retiring?"

"She's dead."

I hesitated, wondering how to proceed.

"Was she old?" I asked.

"She was older than my mother. The night the librarian aunty died a burglar broke into the library. When he saw there was nothing here but books, he stole the wall clock. Now we have no clock."

"When the new librarian arrives she'll buy a clock and put it on the wall."

"The old clock was ten minutes fast. We'd got used to it."

"You can put the new one forward too."

"Forget about what's outside, the librarian aunty used to say, forget about the time outside."

"And were you able to forget it?"

"Sometimes."

I wanted to know how they managed it. Was it the stone walls dating back centuries, or the picture books, or the birds' chirping, or the librarian that had made them forget time?

"My name's Kamo, what's yours?" I said.

"Kıvanç."

"Kıvanç, how far can you see with those glasses?"

"You're just like all the children, Kamo Ağbi," she said. "You're making fun of my glasses."

"No, I'm not making fun of you. I just wondered if you can see the stars in the sky at night."

"No, I can't. The sky is so far away, it looks like mist. I look at stars in picture books. I scan the north on star charts and always manage to find the north star amongst all the others."

"When I was your age I was more interested in the south than the north. If you ask why it's because the south made me think of descending. There was a well in our garden, and I spent my childhood playing beside it. When I said the word south, it made me think of the bottom of the well, the depths of the earth."

"But the library is one floor up. You need to climb up ten steps to get to the reading room."

"I've grown up, I've grown accustomed to upstairs places too. Do you like counting?"

"Yes. I count steps, lines, windows. And I never forget."

"Kıvanç, who opens the library? Who supervises you?"

"The attendant in the hamam next door opens and closes up. She leaves us alone. We study. We haven't got up to any mischief since the librarian aunty died."

"Good girl. I'm going to study with you for a few days."

"This is a children's library, Kamo Ağbi. What are you going to study?"

"I'm doing some research. I'm going to check out the poetry books. What are you doing here, do you have homework?"

"I come here every day after school. I wait for my mother to finish work and come and collect me. I study until she gets here."

Kıvanç slid off the bench. She put her rucksack on her back. She walked toward the steps. I went after her. I climbed the steps. There were several children in the one-roomed, square library, studying, their books and notebooks open. The walls were lined with shelves. Everywhere was neat and tidy. The tables were clean. Apart from the marks left on the dome when the rain leaked in, there were no stains anywhere. Kıvanç sat at a table near the window. She indicated that I should sit on the chair next to hers. I glanced at the shelves. Ignoring the science, history, and geography books, I located the poetry books. I picked a stack of them. I sat on the chair that Kıvanç had pointed out. Taking paper and a pen out of my pocket, I put them beside the poetry books. I could see the circular mark left by the stolen clock on the opposite wall. The rusty nail above the mark hung there devoid of purpose.

That day I had the double pleasure of reading the poems of elderly poets missing their childhood and the pleasure of studying with children. I assimilated the silence. I turned the pages one by one. I went from one book to another. I jotted down brief notes on the pages in front of me until Kıvanç, who was looking out of the window, packed her things away. It was only then I realized that it was evening. I followed Kıvanç down the stairs. I watched her hug her mother who had entered through the courtyard gate.

"Kamo Ağbi," said Kıvanç, "this is my mother."

Seeing the paper and pen in my hands, her mother took me for a teacher. "I'm pleased to meet you, hoca," she said, holding out her hand.

"Pleased to meet you too," I said. I shook her hand. "You have a very intelligent daughter. Kıvanç is the most studious child here."

"Thank you."

Mother and daughter left, hand in hand.

Outside I heard her mother say to Kıvanç, "I've got a surprise for you."

I lit a cigarette. Taking a drag, I blew the smoke into the air. I left the library with a feeling of contentment I hadn't experienced for a long time. The street was deserted. The lights were on in the Çinili Mosque on the left and the Çinili Hamam on the right. The days were getting shorter, it got dark early. The colors of the evening quickly encircled the houses. The autumn wind blew the washing on the balconies skyward. Kıvanç, who padded beside her mother like a contented cat, looked up at the balconies as she walked. She tried to see everything she could through her thick glasses. When she turned her head to look at the far end of the road, she decided to play a game for the rest of the way. She let go of her mother's hand and started running. The scene looked like a painting I had seen somewhere years ago but had never forgotten. Yellow light shone onto black and white walls and the pavement. Naked branches of trees were elongating. Birds were poised on electrical wires like ornaments. Past the trees and the birds, a woman was waiting by an unlit lamp post. The woman stepped off the pavement and held out her arms, hugging Kıvanç, who ran into them. They remained locked together for some time, then they linked arms and spun like a windmill. Their skirts billowed out. This must be the surprise that Kıvanç's mother had meant. Turning into three shadows, they all disappeared together at the end of the street.

Once the street was empty again, when only the trees and the birds remained, I came back to my senses. I thought the woman who had thrown her arms around Kıvanç looked like Mahizer. She had been far away, the lamppost had not been lit and in the dark I sometimes mistook women for Mahizer. Although I was not certain, I tossed my cigarette away and raced after them. I looked down side roads on street corners, trying to work out where they had turned. I glanced at every window in the apartments that had their lights on, right until I reached the main road at the end of the street. Once I had hit the two-way traffic and the throngs of people on the main road, I realized I had lost them. I turned back down the same road, scrutinizing the same streets and the same windows. That night I walked up and down that road over and over again. I felt cold, I felt tired. When I met Kıvanç in the library courtyard the following afternoon, I couldn't hide the exhaustion on my face.

I was sitting on the bench. Kıvanç entered through the courtyard gate, her hair in plaits, and came and sat next to me. She chatted to me as though I were her classmate from year three.

"Why do you look so tired?" she asked.

"I worked until very late last night," I said.

"I have to work too, I have a lot of homework today."

"Do you want me to help you?"

"Would you really?"

"If you want me to, of course."

"Yes please."

"It's a deal."

"If I finish my homework I'm going to the cinema tonight."

"That's nice, is your mother taking you?"

"Yasemin Abla's taking me. My mother has to work the night shift tonight."

"Who's Yasemin Abla? Is she a relative?"

"No, she's my mother's friend. She arrived yesterday, and she's staying with us tonight."

"Was that the surprise your mother was talking about yesterday?"

"Yes, Yasemin Abla comes and spends time with me now and then."

"What do you do together? Do you play house?"

"We play house, we play hide and seek, we play cat keepers."

"And then you sleep together . . ."

"We sleep snuggled up together."

"Look, I've got a surprise for you too."

I took a bar of chocolate out of my pocket. I put it in Kıvanç's tiny hand. Her green eyes dilated, the transparent lenses of her thick glasses turned green.

I didn't read any poems that day, I spent it doing Kıvanç's homework. I ate some of the chocolate she shared with me. I helped her write a story in her notebook and to draw a picture of a mountain, a lamb, and a tree. I gave her small clues to the answers of a ten-question test. Before we had finished her homework I realized that the daylight streaming in through the window was beginning to fade. Excusing myself, I stood up. I left a bit earlier than the day before. I smiled goodbye to the children, whose stares were now familiar to me. All the children sat facing the clock. Even when it wasn't there they were dependent on it. Counting myself as one of them and going by the time on the nonexistent clock, I descended the ten steps with the sound of ticking in my ears. I went out of the courtyard gate, which was ajar. Crossing the road with large strides, I entered the courtyard of the mosque on the opposite side. I sat on a stool alongside feeble old men, and waited for evening.

From my vantage point at the courtyard gate I observed several women and children in the street; when I spied Kıvanç too, skipping happily outside, I stood up. Hiding in the shadows, I followed her. I knew she would run down the same road and go to the same unlit spot where her Yasemin Abla had waited for her yesterday. I maintained a good distance between us. I was close enough to be able to see them easily but far enough for them not to notice me. When Kıvanç had advanced a bit further, the woman beside the unlit lamppost stepped out and threw her arms around her. She was wearing the same coat as yesterday. It was my wife Mahizer, in all her glory. She was here, with her pink lips and large eyes. I leaned against a wall and observed them. I watched them embracing long and hard, feeling each other's warmth, nuzzling one another.

I knew that Mahizer had become a revolutionary after she had left me, that she lived in secret hideouts and constantly changed her name. So, her latest name was Yasemin. What a waste. Just as a flower opens oblivious of its own beauty, and a leaf falls unaware of death, my wife Mahizer lived oblivious of herself. She didn't know that she became a fairy in her sleep, that she cast magical incense on the sheets. She didn't know, but I did. Because she did not, I kept the image of her beauty alive in my mind for her. If I had come across the question "What is beauty?" whilst doing homework in the library today, I would have drawn a picture of Mahizer and written: "Unattainable beauty or love is like knowing what water is but going without it." That was my case. I knew what water was, but I was deprived of it. I could see Mahizer but I lived without her. I cursed time, Istanbul, and people, I hated everyone.

Leaving the narrow streets behind us we came out onto a main road, with them walking ahead and I following behind. We got into two taxis, one behind the other, and went to Bahariye Street. There we each had a toasted sandwich, then went in to watch a film I had not even seen the poster for. They sat at the front, I sat in a seat in the back row, near the door. I tried to remember when Mahizer and I had last gone to the cinema together. Throughout the film I looked at them as much as at the screen. While they were engrossed in the film I became lost in dreams of the old days. When we went out the weather had turned cold. The biting wind was more like winter frost than an autumn breeze. We walked in the crowd. We bought hot chestnuts from the street vendors. We looked in the shop windows. We got into two separate taxis and returned to our street. They stopped in front of a building with a green door, I got out at the next corner. I hid by a wall in the shadows and waited for the man in the gray raincoat who had been following Mahizer for hours.

A short man had been trailing Mahizer and Kıvanç since they had met. He had raised the lapels of his gray raincoat to give him an air of mystery, like the detectives in foreign movies. He too had got into a taxi, entered the cinema, and browsed in shop windows. Too busy chain-smoking and surveying the area, he hadn't realized I was following him. At the end of the evening he turned back down the same road. As he got out of the taxi he lit yet another cigarette. He strode toward the green door of the building. He slowed down and peered inside. He jotted a quick note on a piece of paper he took from his pocket. His work done, he raised his lapels once again and crossed the road. He entered an abandoned plot behind a low wall. The plot was dark. I went after him, and saw that he was waiting by a tree surrounded by darkness. I approached him and asked him for a light. He took his lighter from his pocket. When, after several attempts, he eventually managed to ignite the lighter, he brought it close to my face. No sooner had he seen me than his free hand flew to his waist. I was too quick for him; brandishing my steel knife, I held it against his throat. I hit his knees and made him get down on the ground. I confiscated the gun tucked inside his belt.

"Who are you?" I said. "Who are you following? Whose wife are you trying to snare?" Once the man had got over his initial shock he pulled himself together. "I am the state," he said, in a tone that exuded confidence, "if you don't let me go you'll regret it." I punched him in the face, knocking him onto his back. I pressed my knee down on his chest. "You are the son of Satan, a bastard of the state!" I said. Still unsated, I landed him another punch. He emitted some indistinct grunts that may have been curses or pleading. His puny body squirmed right and left. The harder I pressed the more he tried to wrench his chest free of my knee. He groaned in agony as his ribs broke. I felt his repugnant breath on my face. "Do you know what you are?" I said. "I'll tell you something you won't understand. My wife Mahizer is truth, you're a shadow out to destroy her. The shadow of the truth is worthless. Whereas anything that delivers the truth from worthlessness and recreates it is a beautiful poem. But what about you? You're the enemy of the truth."

After that night I started singing the song of the steel knives more frequently; in one week I rescued my wife from three separate shadows. My wife Mahizer was naïve. All the while she thought she knew the world and could change it she wasn't aware of my presence that was just a scream away. She roamed the streets of Istanbul with no idea of what lurked behind her. She shuttled back and forth between the two sides of the Bosphorus. She waited at bus stops, sat in cafés, wandered around libraries. Whenever the person she was meeting failed to arrive at the appointment she went away feeling anxious. She stayed in damp houses with moss-covered roofs in rundown areas of Üsküdar, Laleli, Hisarüstü. She went to bed late, and got up early. She looked after the plants and children in the houses where she stayed. When, one evening, she went to the street that housed the Çinili Children's Library and hugged Kıvanç again, it gave me as much pleasure as it did them.

Mahizer spent that night at Kıvanç's house and didn't go out the next day. She had looked tired and unwell for the past few days, her face had appeared thin. She needed to take care of herself and rest. I was glad that she was spending at least one day at home. I decided to go to the library and read poems while she was at home giving herself a break. I bought a bar of chocolate from the corner shop. Slowly I walked up the street, of which I was now a part. I waited for Kıvanç in the library courtyard. Before long Kıvanç opened the gate and burst into the courtyard wearing her broad smile.

"Where have you been for so many days? I was worried about you!" she said.

"I went to other libraries," I said.

"Yasemin Abla was worried too."

"Yasemin Abla? About who?"

"Who do you think, you of course."

"Does she know me? I mean, that I come here . . ."

"Of course. I told her."

"When?"

"You know we went to the cinema last week, well that night I talked about you. I told her you'd helped me with my homework."

"She's known for a week . . ."

"Yes."

"What did she say?"

"She said she knows you, that she loves you."

"She said she loves me? Are you sure?"

"Positive."

"What else did she say?"

"Last night she wrote you a letter. She put it in my bag so I could give it to you. Look, here it is."

I took the sealed envelope. I examined it front and back. Not knowing what to do, I fidgeted with it for several minutes. As all kinds of possibilities, good and bad, raced through my head, I noticed that Kıvanç was eyeing me with a teasing smile. I smiled back. I stroked her head.

"You're the prettiest girl in this library," I said.

"Today I have to write a poem for homework, will you help me?" she said.

"I have to go soon, do you think you can do your homework by yourself today?"

"Okay."

"Go on, up you go, start writing your poem."

"Okay, Kamo Ağbi."

"May the muses smile on your pen, Kıvanç."

"Thank you . . . but haven't you forgotten something?"

"What do you mean?"

"Haven't you got a surprise for me today?"

"I nearly forgot. I bought this for you."

"Chocolate! Thank you, Kamo Ağbi. I love chocolate surprises."

As I watched Kıvanç climbing up the stairs and going into the reading room, I realized that my hands that were holding the letter were sweating.

I opened the envelope. I stared at the single page filled on both sides with Mahizer's pearl-like handwriting. Love, it said, pain, wounds, and memory, it said. She lined up familiar words one after the other, creating a whirlpool in each one. She wrote regret, tears, anger, separation, tears, regret, forgetting, forgiving, destiny, death, loneliness, destiny, regret, tears, and forgetting, over and over again, repeating what she had already said a few sentences later. She used near for far, life for death, union for separation, and vice versa. In another time and place I knew what those words meant, but now I couldn't understand what Mahizer was saying. Her language was nothing like either my mother's or my father's. It made meaning meaningless. Like a flock of birds that takes flight in a panic, her words were all jumbled together. She broke the wing of each word by driving it into the wing of the one beside it. She destroyed what had made us what we were in the past, and with it, any chances of opening the door to the future. I want to be forgotten, she said. Inside this huge city, I feel as though I'm imprisoned in one room. Although I love you, our past is our destiny, Kamo, we cannot escape our past, she said.

What kind of a delusion was that? She placed the word love on the same level as all the other words, without attaching any more weight to it. I groaned with the pangs of my conscience. Oh, that old, interminable conscience! As I reread the letter I asked myself: After all this suffering, would I have any power over time? Would I be able to conquer my blind and deaf destiny? I was broken. I was lonely. Nightmares plagued my sleep. Ah, my defeated heart! Ah, that old, interminable conscience! Who could endure such terror? Who could go on resisting life's cruelty for so long? Mahizer was asking me for the right to be forgotten, when I needed the right not to forget. I couldn't get her face out of my mind for a single moment. Otherwise I would not be me. I would become soulless. I would become a dead man rejected by the grave. Oh, that old and interminable conscience that plunges its poisoned arrows into my soul! If I took Mahizer out of myself all that would remain of me would be a corpse. A corpse gnawed by maggots.

Mahizer had collected all the poems that we used to read each other and dissolved them into her letter. She was like an orphaned child. She was groaning with affliction. She said she was trapped inside a room and was asking me to open the door, to rescue her. "Open the door!" she said. "Open it and set me free! You go your way, I'll go mine!" She was struggling. She was banging on the door with her small fists. Bang! Bang! "Open the door!" She said I had the key that would save her, but I didn't know what to do. I forgot where I was. I could hear the distant sound of dogs barking getting gradually closer. I could make out howling in the darkness and recognized the distinct sound of the white dog. I was cold. My chest hurt. Voices echoed inside my head. Bang! Bang!

"Open the door! Guard! Open the door!"

Unwillingly, I slowly realized that the voice coming from somewhere very deep was Uncle Küheylan's.

"Open the door! My friend is dying! Help us!"

Bang! Bang!

I half-opened my good eye and looked into the darkness. I saw that Uncle Küheylan was standing bolt upright, pounding on the cell door. I couldn't call out to him. I couldn't move my finger. I wheezed as I struggled to breathe. I groaned.

Uncle Küheylan came and leaned over me.

"You're alive," he said, "my wonderful Barber, you're alive."

He straightened my neck, which was hanging limply. He picked up the cloth on the floor and wet my lips. He wiped my forehead. As he stroked my hair he talked, his words full of optimism. He said we would leave here one day and explore Istanbul together. Beautiful dreams were either for heartbroken lovers or those at death's door. As Uncle Küheylan held my hand he could see I was near the end. He realized that the time I had wasted aboveground was running out in here too.

I heard the sound of the iron bolt. The cell door opened. The guard's huge bulk appeared before the light.

"What are you shouting about, halfwit!" he barked.

"My friend is seriously ill, he needs help," said Uncle Küheylan, speaking more gently.

"He can drop dead, that way he'll be free and so will we."

"At least give him some water, a painkiller . . ."

"You'll need that painkiller yourself in a minute, moron. They're asking for you in the interrogation room. Come on, get up!"

I saw the shadow of the white dog next to the guard's huge feet. It had padded in gracefully from the corridor. It stood in the light like pure marble. Its neck was wide. Its ears were erect. Its fur flowed down to its tail, like a warm blanket. Its wolf-like eyes pierced through me, like in the old days.

Oblivious of the white dog, the guard grabbed Uncle Küheylan by the collar and dragged him outside. He bolted the door on me. He left the two of us alone.

The strength drained from me. My eye closed. I wanted to drift off into an endless sleep.

The white dog approached slowly, from its breath I could feel it lying down beside me, accompanying me. Its warm body reclined against mine. It wound its long tail around my legs. Our breathing was synchronized, our chests rose and fell together. It waited until I was warm. If we had time it would have lain like that for hours. But there was no time. It raised its head. It came closer. It licked my face. It ran its moist, pink tongue up and down my body as though it were caressing its baby. From my eye to my ear, from my chest to my wrist, one by one it healed all my wounds. It eased my pain. In this excruciating world, when a person closed his eyes he should at least be able to breathe without pain. Otherwise what would be the point of living. The white dog shifted its weighty body. It leaned more heavily on my shoulder. Sticking out its sleek tongue, it also licked away all the fears that had been building up since my childhood. It soothed me. It relieved me of every burden. I felt weightless. I felt as though I were floating in warm, calm water. If only life were as kind as the white dog. If only life had shown me another path when I had lost my way.

# 10TH DAY

*Told by Uncle Küheylan*

## YELLOW LAUGHTER

"Send me three apples, bite one of them before you send it. As the ship's elderly cartographer took the letters of his long-dead lover out of his little chest and read them he repeated the sentence he had just come across: Send me three apples, bite one of them before you send it. Doctor, have I told you this story before? Really? This time I'll tell you a different version. Listen. The elderly cartographer had devoted his lifetime to roaming the world's seas with the two fortunes he had inherited from his lover, one, loneliness, and the other, the small chest of letters. On each continent he drew new maps, on each island he added new names to the maps. On his final voyage, which he undertook as a gray-haired man, he planned to bid farewell to the sea and spend his remaining years on land. Much as he respected seamen who surrendered their souls to the waves, he dreamed of his own body being buried beside that of the sweetheart of his youth. He confided this to the compass master with whom he shared a cabin. For his part, the compass master didn't care whether it was at sea or on land, but he wanted to die going by the right time. I go by the time on this watch, said the compass master, taking out his pocket watch and lovingly caressing its cover. The ruby encrustations on the cover concealed a sign that he had never been able to decipher. Either that, or he liked to believe that such a secret existed. It was a starry night. When a rough wave crashed into the side of the ship they heard something crack outside. The elderly cartographer and the compass master rushed out of the cabin and climbed up the steps to the deck. When they saw the sky studded with twinkling stars, they stopped and stared with an expression that was more like that of children fascinated by the sky than of old men who had spent their whole lives at sea. They gazed as the milky way flowed in slow motion. The elderly cartographer pointed at a spot where the stars curved like a river. Look, he said to the compass master, doesn't that look like the patterns on your watch? They took out the pocket watch and compared. They saw that the red rubies on the cover were sparkling and that they were an exact reflection of the stars revolving in the curve in the sky. It's right, continued the elderly cartographer, the time and the signs on your watch are right. Clouds gathered rapidly, the sky became overcast. The sails howled, while the ropes whistled like whips. The ship bound for the ocean was tossed about by the wind, like a leaf. As the rain pelted down, the ship was assailed by a whirlwind from all sides. They grew alarmed. Following the instructions that the captain barked between panic-stricken cries, they struggled to set the wheel back on track and adjust the sails. They scuttled right and left, loosening and tightening the ropes. For three days the deluge continued, unabating, the clouds did not clear. They were flung hither and thither on the waves, dragged, perhaps to the ocean, perhaps to a previously unnavigated sea. When, at the end of the third day the sea grew calm, the wind subsided and the stars reappeared in the sky, they believed the storm was over. They tried to work out where they were. They searched high and low for a piece of dry land where they could repair their torn sails and replace the drinking water that had poured out of the smashed barrels. One by one the captain examined the maps spread out before him, he followed the stars. Eventually he observed that the shapes on one old map corresponded to the position of the stars. Placing his index finger on the sea at the corner of the map, he said, we're here, adding: And there's an island here that's a day's journey away, we can go there. The elderly cartographer and the compass master standing beside the captain looked at one another. They had their doubts about the azure blue island the captain was pointing at. Captain, they said, let's not go so far off course, it looks like one of those false islands drawn by love-struck cartographers. In the past, certain cartographers would draw an island on a blank section of their map and name it after the woman they loved. That way they would leave an imprint of their love on the world. Stories of disillusionment after ships sailed to false islands found on maps were rife on the seas. Although the elderly cartographer and the compass master seemed to have their doubts about this island they did not make any forecasts. They both knew it was the elderly cartographer who had put that island on the map when he was a young man. They couldn't say so openly for fear of the captain's wrath, they were afraid of being tossed into the sea bound and gagged. The two friends went down into their cabin and spent the night talking. I first saw the girl I loved in the village market, said the elderly cartographer. I was an adolescent. I wrote her letters. I read the letters she sent me in secret, for fear her no good brothers would find out, over and over again. When I departed for my first ocean voyage I told her I would bring her back a present she would never forget. My aim was to make some money from whaling and upon my return take my beloved somewhere far away. My beloved was beautiful, she was slender, she was delicate. She fell ill while I was away and lay in bed burning with fever for days. Death eventually defeated her body, which was as fragile as glass. When I returned from my sea voyage I went to her grave. I dug a grave for myself adjacent to hers. For several nights I worked on the map I had with me. I drew the most beautiful of islands on a deserted coastline, colored it blue and named it after my beloved. As long as the world continued to revolve I would search for that nonexistent island named after my beloved. I set sail with that dream in my heart. Baring her chest to the waves, the white ship glided through the sea minus her sails, heading for the deserted coastline on the map. At dawn the elderly cartographer and the compass master went to sleep. They drifted off to the land of dreams. When, toward evening, they reached the waters where he had drawn the false island, they woke up to the lookout's cries of land ahoy! Land ahoy? How could that be? The elderly cartographer couldn't believe his ears. He hastened to the deck. Shrouded in mist, he beheld an azure blue city that stood resplendent with its city walls, its domes and its towers. Istanbul, he said, murmuring the name of his dead beloved, my beloved Istanbul! He stared with wonder and admiration at how the island that his own hand had once drawn on the map could have become real. His knees gave way, he crumpled to the ground. The compass master held him in his arms, the elderly cartographer gave him a weak but satisfied smile, indicating that he was sated with life. Can what I'm seeing be real, he said. Is what I see before me the totally nonexistent island I gave my beloved Istanbul? Seagulls glided from the shore toward the ship as a gentle breeze blew. The elderly cartographer expired there and, according to seamen's tradition, his body was consigned to the waters' immensity. As the years passed, the Istanbul dwellers, believing their own city was real but the mist-shrouded ship an illusion, told an endless number of stories about the captain, cartographer, and compass master of the white ship."

I was alone in the cell, but I spoke imagining that the Doctor was sitting in front of me.

I offered the Doctor the cigarette I had painstakingly rolled with my crushed fingers. I took out my matches and lit first his, then my own.

"The Istanbul dwellers thought they were real, they didn't know that they lived on the white ship's map," I said. I took a long drag of my cigarette and blew the smoke up into the air. "What do you say, Doctor? How do you fancy drawing an island on a map and then getting a job on a whaling boat and setting sail for the boundless ocean?"

Ever since my childhood my secret island had also been Istanbul. On the winter night when my father told me the story of the elderly cartographer I took my map out of my schoolbag and drew an island on it, I dreamed happy dreams about it and loved it dearly. It was an era when I felt that people chose to see rather than understand. Everywhere the world was changing. People forgot how to love without seeing. They had no island to dream about, they didn't know what they were looking for. They couldn't comprehend how I could have loved this city for so many years from a distance; having deleted the idea of conquest from their memory they couldn't understand me. Every conquest clung to a dream and advanced along its own path. Jesus' path was different from Alexander the Great's. While Alexander conquered the city, Jesus wanted to conquer the people in the city. My dream was to conquer both the city and the people in it and save them both at the same time. Istanbul needed it.

Everyone talked of Istanbul's beauty, but no one managed to live there happily. Uncertainty, selfishness, and violence masked the city's beauty. The city was the manifestation of the beauty and integrity that people sought in the world. God had long been insufficient for that. In the city people strove to fashion a nature and wanted to find themselves inside it. Hadn't God done the same thing? Hadn't He created the earth, the sky, and people in order to discover His own significance? Eras passed. Things changed. Chaos started to push God out. If an "in" was needed in order for Him to be pushed out, people were building it in the city. People who were spreading their own nature were building a new time unawares. Melancholy too was born there. It was not the melancholy of people, but of God, who could not adapt to the new times. The thing He had feared since the Tower of Babel was coming to pass.

The members of a tribe beyond the seas slashed their children's faces and disfigured them so they wouldn't be abducted by the enemy and sold into slavery. That way the children remained free. In their language, ugliness and freedom meant the same thing, beauty and slavery were expressed with the same word. The Istanbul dwellers too lived in fear of losing their city and did everything in their power to destroy her beauty. Above and below ground they were plunged in suffering, they clung to evil. They called disfiguring the city freedom. They could not see that evil's ultimate aim was to destroy beauty. But Istanbul could sense it. She made a stand against people's foolishness. That great city resisted all by herself, struggling to defend her beauty.

Good was moralistic. Right was calculating. Whereas beauty was infinite. Beauty was in a word, a face, in the carvings on a wall soaked by the rain. It was in someone's daydreams even in the absence of an image, and in an unknown meaning. Ever since people, tired of discovering the wilderness, have started creating their own nature in the city, they have devoted their lives to glass, steel, electricity. They have acquired a taste for creation. They looked in the mirror and said to themselves, I'm not a discoverer of nature, I'm a creator of the city. They did away with the conflict between people and nature and joined the spiritual and the material. They brought all times and places together. When they contemplated the city, they saw not only the past but also the future. Then they grew weary of rushing around. They grew pessimistic. They became hopeless. They were swept away by the ugliness in beauty, the poverty in wealth. They were exhausted. Could they see that the beauty in the city was in the throes of death? In that case they would have to devote their lives to that beauty once again. Could they sense that life in the city was becoming worthless? They would have to make it worthwhile again. Was passion ending, were there no more secrets? They needed to surround the city with passion, and, instead of battering it, conquer it anew.

I told the Doctor all this, whilst gazing at the blank wall in front of me. I raised the make-believe cigarette between my fingers to my lips. I took a drag. When the ash fell on the floor, despite all my precautions, I sighed. I tried to pick it up with my fingertips. The ash disintegrated into tiny specks. I felt annoyed again.

My annoyance had started when I had returned from being interrogated to find Kamo the Barber wasn't in the cell. When I asked the guard what had happened to him he hadn't replied but had slammed the door in my face. The Doctor and the Student Demirtay weren't here either. I hadn't seen them for two days. I wondered if they had come to the cell while I was being interrogated. Had they had a rest and got some sleep? I couldn't see any signs of them. The empty water bottle was still in the same place. I felt the walls and the door with my hands, but didn't notice any fresh blood stains. The opposite cell was empty too. I had lain on the floor and thrown a button under her door but Zinê Sevda had not responded, and although I had stood waiting at the cell door on my only good leg for several minutes, she had not come to the grille.

I heard a loud crack in the distance. The explosion, which

came from beyond the walls, beyond the corridor, beyond the iron gates, sounded like a Browning. When I heard the same crack a second time I knew my guess had been right. I stirred from where I was sitting. Holding on to the walls, I managed to stand up. Dragging my wounded leg like a sack full of rocks, I limped to the door. I gripped the bars of the grille. I looked out in the hope of seeing something. The corridor was empty. There were no signs of rippling shadows in the white light, or a breath. Which direction were the gunshots coming from? More to the point, who were they coming from?

Two possibilities shot through my mind. Was the target of the gunshots the Doctor, who had said "Death is good too"? Was it the ingenious Demirtay, or the angry Kamo, or the obstinate Zinê Sevda? If one of them had seen their opportunity, grabbed a gun, and run into different corridors and started a confrontation, how far could they have got? How could they have found their way around the corridors?

There was a better option: The Istanbul above hadn't forgotten us. Others had joined the group of young revolutionaries who had survived the conflict in Belgrade Forest. They had sworn to end our suffering, to rescue those who were in pain. They were coming to our aid. The Doctor's young son and Mine Bade were with them.

The gunfire sounded again. One explosion followed another. Beretta, Walther, and Smith & Wesson bullets mingled with the Browning fire. Their echoes were heard in the corridor. I distinguished each gun as I distinguished the cry of each wild animal on the Haymana Mountain where I had spent my whole life. I strained my ears. I grew anxious when I remembered the wounds each bullet could inflict on a human body.

I was worried about my friends. What state were they in now? Were they alive or dead? I thought they could be both at the same time. As long as I couldn't see them, my friends were both alive and dead. They breathed, and at the same time lay lifeless on the floor. The walls between us made every possibility likely. The same was true of those battling their way toward us. Those who had leapt forward, armed to the teeth, were both those coming to rescue us and those trying to kill us. I didn't know anything else. And as long as I didn't know, all possibilities were equally likely. The appearance of our underground cell from the world aboveground was also the same. While Istanbul dwellers who heard that we were suffering here walked around feeling sad and desperate, they thought of two likelihoods for us. We might be alive, or we might be dead. Perhaps we were breathing, or perhaps we lay lifeless on the floor.

I put myself in the position of the people aboveground. I looked at myself through their eyes for a moment and didn't know what to think. I felt both alive and dead, as though I were both at the same time.

While I was lost in thought, drawn to the white light in the corridor, like a moth, the gunshots stopped. Everywhere fell silent. The cell became soundless, like before. I continued to wait, as though someone might appear from the end of the corridor at any moment. I held onto the grille bars so I would be able to stand on my one good leg for a bit longer. The light dazzled me and I blinked. I heard banging on a cell door in the corridor behind ours. "Guard!" shouted a voice. Someone in a cell behind ours needed help. "Guard!" I trained my ear on the corridor. I waited for the guard's footsteps. The guard would get up from his chair now, come out of his room and stride along the concrete on his hard heels. He would go to the rear corridor and stand at the cell door. He would slide the bolt, open the door, and start cursing. But the guard didn't move. He didn't get up from his chair, his heels didn't stride on the concrete. He left the voice coming from the back cell unanswered. The corridor, now silent again, fell into a bottomless pit. I was too exhausted to wait any longer. I leaned against the wall. Putting my weight on my good leg, I slowly slid down. I sat on the floor. Opening my legs wide, I took a deep breath.

It was only then that I realized my nose was bleeding. I picked up the cloth from the floor and wiped it.

I was not sleepy. I felt hungry. My mouth was dry from lack of water.

I decided that chatting to the Doctor would be better than killing time staring at the blank wall. I mimed taking my tobacco case out of my pocket. As I rolled a cigarette with my split and cracked fingers, I resolved to go to the Doctor's house and chat to him there. I fantasized that I was sitting in his favorite place with him, on his balcony overlooking the Bosphorus. I handed him a generously rolled cigarette. Then I rolled one for myself. I picked up the lighter on the table and lit our cigarettes. I took a drag and, after holding it inside my lungs for a while, released it into the blue sky that is such a rare phenomenon in Istanbul at the start of winter. I put the gunshots I had just heard out of my mind. I listened to the car horns, the ferry sirens, and the seagulls' cries coming from below.

Arranged on the lace tablecloth on the balcony were dishes of ezme, cheese, and pickles. The rocket was fresh. The yogurt was creamy. There was squeezed lemon on the radishes. There were flaked chilis sprinkled on the olives. The bread was sliced thinly, a few of the slices were toasted. The water jug was half full. There was ice in the rakı, served in long, delicate glasses, the cloudy rakı was nice and cold. The tobacco case, the lighter, and the ashtray were all lined up on the table. It was clear from the lace embroidery on the edges of the white tablecloth that it was an heirloom from bygone times.

It was a warm day. The Doctor seemed relaxed and

cheerful. A crackly recording of an old classical Turkish song drifted out from inside. The singer was the Doctor's wife, who had died many years ago but never left this house. You are my heart's master, she sang, in her powerful voice, that place is yours alone. Though my lifetime is spent and my hair is gray, you're everything to me, you are joy, you are life, she sang. The words of the song trickled down the balcony like water and flowed along the gutters toward the earth. There was nothing left in the apartment, nor in the garden below, nor in the street that did not evoke that longing. The street vendors called out in the same voice. The ferry propellers and the car wheels rotated with the same whirring sound. The roofs were lined up in rows, descending like steps to the sea down below. The sea's swollen waves rose and fell in tune with the song. One after the other, the captains sounded their horns, as though they could see the rakı we were drinking and hear the song we were listening to.

The Doctor raised his glass first to me, then to the sea opposite us. He smiled when he saw me imitating him. He took a sip from his rakı.

"I'm so glad you came, Uncle Küheylan," he said.

"I'm glad I came too," I said.

"Have you been able to see enough of Istanbul?"

"A long lifetime, plus ten days, that's enough for me."

"I'm happy to hear it."

"I can die in peace, Doctor. I feel quite tranquil."

"Why are you talking about death? Let's think nice thoughts. Let's make a wish to set this same table regularly, and to drink rakı every season as we gaze out on Istanbul."

"Let's drink to good days."

"To good days . . ."

We clinked glasses.

We looked at the empty deck chairs on the roof terrace

of the opposite building, at the washing lines, at the roof tiles. There was no mist. The sky was clear. Except for a tiny scrap of cloud at Çamlıca Hill, everywhere was azure blue. We could even see the houses and the groves on Kınalı Island. There was approximately an hour left before the sinking sun on the right would set, painting the sky a flaming orange.

"It will be evening soon, everything will be cloaked in a magical blanket," I said.

"Magical? What magic is there left in Istanbul?"

"Doctor, I've applied what you said about hope the other day to magic. Magic is better than what we have."

"Hope or magic, it doesn't matter which one we use, it won't suffice to save Istanbul's beauty. I don't say this to everyone, Uncle Küheylan, I'm saying it to you. People grow weary, they want to get away from here."

"Doctor, people give up on this place because it's not fit to live in. But what we should be looking at is whether Istanbul is a city worth creating rather than worthy of living in."

"What part of her is going to be created? Her ravaged beauty?"

"Just recreating her beauty alone justifies a conquest in itself."

"Conquest. . . . Are you still resolved on that?"

"Naturally."

"Even after everything you've witnessed for the past ten days . . ."

"Now I'm more determined than ever."

"I think we should drink to that."

"Let's drink to everything that springs to mind today."

We leaned back on our chairs happily.

We spied a red shawl floating above the rooftops on our right. The shawl was caught up in the wind and was heading toward the sea. At times it rippled, at others it flew straight. It glided like birds with outstretched wings. It didn't look as though it intended to land on a rooftop, it looked set on reaching the sea. Immersed in the shawl's captivating redness, we thought of places far away.

"Uncle Küheylan, sometimes I get confused. It's as though I've known you all my life instead of just ten days. Do you get the same impression?"

"I also feel as though we've been exploring all the nooks and crannies of Istanbul together and chatting for years, and that the longer we talk the more we have to tell each other."

"We must be getting old . . ."

"I'm already old, Doctor, you watch out for yourself."

"But your mind is like a razor. You're fitter than I am."

"I haven't forgotten the things I've learnt, it's true. For example, that book you mentioned has etched itself on my brain, I've been thinking about it for days."

"Which one?"

"The *Decameron*."

"You've memorized the title."

"Yes, I won't forget it now."

"You won't forget the funny stories it contains either."

"Doctor, all the stories you told us from that book being funny reminds me of something my father told me. On his return from one of his trips to Istanbul my father said he had stayed in the underground cells and he told us about an island he had heard about from a seaman in his cell. According to the customs of that island, when someone died everyone congregated in the home of the deceased, and wailed and lamented until the middle of the night, then everyone went back home. Then, once the family members in the house of mourning were alone, they would start talking and laughing and telling funny stories about the deceased. With each story they would explode into laughter, and as the stories went on,

tears would roll down their faces. They call it yellow laughter.
They think yellow is the right color for laughter that makes
people forget death. What do you say, Doctor? Do you think
it's their need for yellow laughter that makes the noble ladies
and gentlemen in the *Decameron* tell funny stories when they
can feel death breathing down their necks?"

"Maybe," said the Doctor, but didn't continue. He rose to
answer the telephone that was ringing in the living room.

Laughter too was better than what we have. That was one
of the lessons that life had taught us. Alone on the balcony,
I extended the expression to the food in front of me: cheese
and pickles were better than what we have. Whereas rakı was
better than everything we have, without exception. I chuckled
to myself. I took a sip. I put the glass down on the table and
nibbled on a gherkin. How wonderful it is to live in Istanbul,
I said. I contemplated the small fishing boats bobbing on the
waves like matchboxes at the point where the waters of the
Golden Horn merge with the Bosphorus current. As the sky
behind the minarets and the tall apartment blocks in the
west was turning different shades of red, I became aware that
the sudden mist that had appeared on the Islands' side was
heading this way, and that it would soon be hanging over the
fishing boats. I spread ezme on a slice of toasted bread.

The Doctor, who had now returned, and I drained the last
drops of rakı. We refilled our glasses.

"That was my son," he said, "letting me know that he
won't be home tonight."

"Our young doctor? I wish he'd come. I wanted to meet
him."

"He wants to meet you too, Uncle Küheylan. He sends his
regards."

"Thanks."

"Young people. They do exactly as they please. It's

impossible to understand them. Apparently he has some very important business to see to."

"How's his girlfriend? Mine Bade . . ."

"She's well. I haven't met her yet either. They were both going to come tonight and I was going to meet her."

"It obviously wasn't to be, Doctor. Hopefully next time . . ."

"Next time?"

The Doctor paused, as though he were feeling tipsy. He stared at the sea beyond the rooftops. He clutched his glass with both hands. He laced his fingers together. He slouched forward. He hunched his shoulders. He watched the current of the now docile Bosphorus. He cocked his head to one side so he could hear his wife's voice from inside better. He closed his eyes. He murmured the lyrics of the song with her. His head bent down so it touched his shoulder. His voice slowed down, he fell silent. He breathed deeply. He waited. Just when I was beginning to think he must be feeling sleepy he sat up and opened his eyes. He looked at me sadly. He examined me first from close up and then from a distance, as though doubting my existence. He took a sip of his rakı.

"Are you all right, Doctor?" I said.

"I wanted to meet the girl my son loves. I wish Mine Bade had come tonight."

"If there's a shooting star tonight we'll make a wish for them."

"I think we'll be seeing fog instead of stars, Uncle Küheylan. Your magical Istanbul will be shrouded in fog in a minute."

We heard several explosions, one after another.

We couldn't work out where they were coming from. First we glanced over at the houses opposite, then we leaned over the balcony railing and looked down at the street three floors below. The heavy evening traffic, the darting schoolchildren and the streetlamps that were coming on one by one, all seemed normal. There was no one else leaning over their balconies or windows. The terraces and drawn curtains remained unchanged.

"Were those gunshots?" asked the Doctor.

"I don't think so," I said, so he wouldn't worry. "Never mind what's going on outside, let's enjoy our rakı."

I knocked back half the glass. I had an urge to get drunk there and then. I gazed at the distant windows lit up by the rays of Istanbul's setting sun, as though seeing them for the first time.

"Uncle Küheylan," said the Doctor, "your father said there's a world in the sky that's just like ours. I told my son about it the other day. It amused him, but as usual, he had to think the exact opposite of what I thought. He said we need to look for the world that's like ours down below rather than up above. The underground isn't far, it's right next to us, he said. People there suffer and writhe and search for a way out. They are tired and weak. They raise their heads as though they're looking at the sky. They fantasize about us and call out to us. Each of us has a double who lives underground. If we listen we'll be able to hear. If we peer down we'll be able to see them."

"Maybe my father's double in Istanbul is your son. A born again version. What do you say, Doctor?"

We both burst out laughing at the same time. We leaned back on our chairs. My father was dead, his son was alive. The color of our laughter, turning yellow on the line between death and life, flowed toward the Istanbul Sea like a river. Rows of lights shone wherever we looked. While Topkapı Palace and the Maiden's Tower were lit up, Selimiye Barracks and Haydarpaşa Station were trapped behind fog. Ships slowed down, ferries sounded their horns for longer. The fishing boats were returning to the shore. Day and night, reality and illusion, were becoming confused. Everything hid its own opposite inside it. As night enveloped the color of day, illusion was announcing the tidings of a new reality. The city that was sprawling out with her naked body was wrapping herself in a silky, fleecy cover embroidered with silver thread. But if a village symbolizes a person's childhood and a city their adulthood, the Istanbul dwellers still lived in purgatory, like troubled adolescents. They could not put on the appropriate expression for beauty. They wandered around nervously during the day and went to bed anxious at night. They forgot that wanting a beautiful city was the same as wanting a beautiful life.

The Doctor, who waved his hands around as he laughed, almost knocked over the water jug. He just managed to grab it by the middle before it fell off the edge of the table. He started laughing again as he wiped his wet hand. Along with his yellow laughter, everything around us gradually became tinged with yellow. The water in the jug and the bread in the basket turned yellow. A yellow wind enfolded the chairs on the opposite terrace. The seagulls flying from the sea to the shore surrendered their wings to the yellow emptiness. As the ships in Istanbul Port unloaded their yellow cargo, the feet of the Bosphorus Bridge lit up with yellow light. Remembering was as long as ever, living was short. The Doctor's memory overflowed with memories with yellow shadows. Each part of the city transported him to a different time, each sip of rakı led him to a different memory. The color of the iced rakı also turned yellow.

When we heard knocking at the door we looked at each other.

"He's here at last," said the Doctor.

He put his glass down on the table. He got up without rushing. He went to open the door.

I listened to the voices at the door.

"Demirtay," said the Doctor, "where have you been?"

"There wasn't any decent fish here, I had to go all the way to Kumkapı," said the Student Demirtay.

"What was wrong with the fish here?"

"Didn't I promise to bring you the best fish in Istanbul?"

"It's six o'clock and you've only just got here."

"Six? Your clock is wrong, Doctor. My watch says ten to six."

"Stop your teasing, you imp. Take the bags into the kitchen."

"I got salad too."

"Your punishment for being late is to make the salad while I fry the fish."

"It will be my pleasure. Isn't Uncle Küheylan here yet?"

"Do you think everyone's like you?"

"Is he here? Where is he?"

"On the balcony."

Demirtay ran out excitedly to the balcony. Without giving me a chance to get up he threw his arms around my neck. He buried his head in my shoulder. I felt his heart beating. I thought how well life suited the young. Don't let death take him away, I didn't want anyone to wrench Demirtay away from my arms. I waited until his heartbeat had returned to normal.

I held his hands, cupping them in mine.

"You look well," I said. "You've put on a bit of weight. Are you growing your hair?"

"Yes, I'm going for a shoulder-length mane like yours."

"Then we can have our photo taken together."

"I'd love to. We haven't got any photos of the two of us."

"Your hands are like ice, Demirtay."

"As usual."

"Go in and get a jumper. You're going to sit on the balcony

with us and drink rakı. I don't want you to get cold."

"I won't put on one jumper, I'll wear two."

"Good idea."

As soon as the sun went down the balcony started to feel frosty, it was beginning to get chilly. If I hadn't been wearing a woolen cardigan I would have been cold too.

"Uncle Küheylan, I bring you gossip hot off the press. Once we sit down to eat I'll tell you which singer used to sell fish when he was young and has now given up music to go back to selling fish with his childhood sweetheart. I heard the fishmongers saying which palace the map of the treasure buried under İnönü Stadium is hidden in. And I found out who had rigged the latest horse races. All will be revealed."

"We'll listen to you gladly. But you'd better go and help the Doctor now or he'll give you a hard time again."

"I'll be right there."

Demirtay went into the living room, but the moment he was out of sight he came back again.

"Uncle Küheylan," he said, "I almost forgot."

"What's up?"

"When we sit down to eat, apart from all the gossip, I'm going to tell you the answer to the riddle."

"Which riddle?"

"The riddle about Jean Bey and Filiz Hanım that was the talk of the newspapers and had the ferry passengers intrigued for days. Filiz Hanım was Jean Bey's wife and daughter and sister. We heard that. But according to the latest news Filiz Hanım was also Jean Bey's aunt. Do you remember?"

"Of course I do."

"I've worked out how that can be possible."

"Really?"

"You'll be amazed when I tell you."

"I can't wait."

"But I want a prize."

"What prize?"

"Seeing as I'm getting punished for arriving late, I should also get a prize for guessing the riddle. Don't you think so?"

"It makes sense to me. I think you should. Let's see what the Doctor thinks."

"I'll persuade him in the kitchen."

"Good luck to you, you'll need it!"

The Student Demirtay went inside. He left me alone on the balcony. I became lost in the contemplation of Istanbul, who reproduces suffering and sorrow every day, but at the same time creates hopes and dreams. Like tortured souls who climb up to the Bosphorus Bridge to commit suicide and behold the sights for the last time, or lovers strolling hand in hand who stare, awestruck, as though they have never seen them before, I gazed at Dolmabahçe Palace, Sepetçiler Pavilion, and the Galata Bridge. I observed the gecekondu neighborhoods on the poverty-stricken hills of the Anatolian side preparing to be enveloped by white fog. Istanbul was a city with a million cells, and one cell on its own was an entire Istanbul. A part was in the whole and the whole was in a part. Near was far and far was near. Everything was sterile and fertile.

In this city every physical pain was accompanied by emotional pain. Crowds and solitude were equally oppressive. The pain of unhappy love competed with poverty. Difficulty making ends meet advanced at the same pace as old age. Epidemic diseases and epidemic fears went arm in arm. Children were growing up thinking there were fiber optic cables under their skin instead of veins, the number of old people carrying calculators in their pockets instead of mirrors was growing. Figures replaced the letters on their tongues. They said that love had turned into money, but much as they took out their calculators and tapped away, they couldn't work out why money never turned into love. Figures were not enough.

I heard the Doctor calling out from inside.

"Uncle Küheylan! We'll be there in a minute. You won't be lonely for much longer. Be patient."

"If you don't hurry up I'll finish all the rakı," I replied.

I refilled my empty glass. I added water and ice. There in the city of my dreams, in the company of the people I loved, on a balcony overlooking the Bosphorus, I sipped my rakı.

My father used to say that Istanbul created a different city every season, that she gave birth to other cities in the dark, the snow, and the fog. On a hot summer's day he once saw a group of students sitting in a row on the shore of Tophane, painting. Each student observed the Maiden's Tower, the seagulls, and the sea before them and applied paint to the canvas, but no two paintings were the same. In one the sea was blue, while in another it was yellow. In one the Maiden's Tower was young, while in another she was old. In one the seagulls were spreading their wings, while in another they died en masse. The canvases were not depicting the same city, but all kinds of very different cities, separated by several eras and great distances. They were bright or dark, cheerful or melancholic. But the city my father saw was different from all of them. It was only then I understood, my father had said. What made a city into a city was a person's look. People who gave her bad looks made the city evil, people who looked at her through good eyes rendered her beautiful. The city's changing and becoming beautiful depended on people's changing and becoming beautiful.

I looked at the Istanbul that my father had left years earlier. It had disappeared from view. The body of the Maiden's Tower was submerged in fog. The sea had turned as white as the rakı in my glass. Ferries and fishing boats had pulled up on the shore to rest. The only visible object in the clouds of fog was a red-winged seagull. The seagull had spread its wings wide and was gliding from sea to shore. It had let its body go in the void. Monopolizing the whole sky, it descended toward the rooftops. When it came a little closer I realized it wasn't a seagull but the red shawl. The red shawl appeared out of the fog one moment, and disappeared the next. Had I overdone the rakı? How many glasses had I had? I tittered to myself.

I heard a voice shouting, "Doctor! Doctor!"

It was familiar and came from downstairs.

I stuck my head over the balcony railing. I saw Kamo the Barber waiting on the pavement at the building entrance.

"Kamo!"

"Uncle Küheylan! It's so lovely to see you."

I waved.

"Come on up," I said.

"I'll be along later," he said.

"How come?"

"I'm going to Beyoğlu to meet my wife Mahizer."

"Bring her too."

"We're both coming. She wants to meet you too."

"Don't be too long, dinner's nearly ready."

"Has the student kid arrived?"

"Yes."

"What about Zinê Sevda?"

"She'll be here soon."

"I'd better go. I mustn't keep Mahizer waiting."

"Go on, go quickly so you can come back quickly."

Kamo put his hands into the pockets of his thick coat. He walked away with quick steps.

When he was almost at the corner I called out to him.

"Kamo!"

He stopped and looked. He looked like a shadow in the

fog. At the junction where existence and nonexistence meet, he was in between the heart's slow pace and time's speed.

"I've missed you," I said.

He smiled. He opened his two arms wide and embraced the air. He hugged me tightly from a distance. Then, turning away quickly, he took large strides and vanished into the fog.

I raised my glass in the air. "To your health, Istanbul," I said, "to your health."

As I was putting my glass down on the table I realized my nose was bleeding. With my handkerchief I wiped the blood running down to my lip. As I was checking to see if there was any blood on my clothes, I remembered a hot summer's day from adolescence. I was on a hillside on Haymana Mountain, passing by a mansion on my horse, who was stifled by the heat. I drove my horse toward the girl collecting water from the fountain in front of the mansion. The young girl's hair was plaited. Yellow lira coins hung from the ribbon on her forehead. Her fingers were hennaed. It was obvious she had recently been a bride. She brought a bowl of water and held it out to me. I drank thirstily, shedding my weariness in the cool water. My horse too drank his fill in the trough. Turning my back on the sun, I left. I climbed up the hill. As I was passing a wild pear tree I noticed the blood on my shirt. My nose was bleeding and the blood had dripped onto my white shirt. At that moment I realized that I had fallen in love with the recent bride. Blood was the sign of either love or death. I was at an age where I was still far from death, but near to love.

I took a cigarette paper out of the tobacco case. I put the paper between my fingers and added a generous line of tobacco on it. I rolled it. I wet the edge of the paper with my tongue and stuck it down. I dried the wet patch on the paper with the lighter's flame. I inhaled so deeply it was as though I wanted to finish the cigarette in a single drag. I blew the smoke out through my nose. The smoke would help the bleeding too, it would clot the blood that kept stopping and starting. I leaned back. I strained my ears to listen to the classical Turkish song drifting out from the living room. But not for long; the song's melody was drowned out by the sound of gunshots coming from outside.

The Browning, Beretta, Walther, and Smith & Wesson explosions resounded again. On one hand I wanted to blot out the noise, on the other it gave me hope. As the sound of each bullet came a little louder, I wanted to know what it was that was getting closer all the time. Was it life or death approaching? I raised my head. I looked at the bird of time gliding in the profound darkness. It had spread its broad wings, filling the entire space. It had released its body, worn out by the winds of the past, into the emptiness of the present moment. One of its wings was tinged with suffering, the other with beauty. If I stood up and stretched out my hand, would I be able to reach it? If I stood on tiptoe and stretched my fingers wide, would I touch the black feathers of the bird of time?

As the gunshots came very close, stopping just outside the iron gate, I wanted my generously rolled cigarette to stay between my fingers forever. I didn't want life, death, or suffering, I just wanted to feel the taste of the cigarette in my nasal passage. I wanted to think of the lace embroidery on the tablecloth, the color of the toasted bread, the smell of the iced rakı. I wanted to dream of the red shawl flying on the sea breeze just for the sake of it, and to sink my bare feet into deep pile rugs. I wanted to eat cheese and pickles. I wanted to turn up the music full blast so everyone could hear, and to sit on the balcony waving to the ships. It didn't happen. The sound of the iron gate started up where the gunshots had left off. The saw-like grating of the iron gate filled the corridor.

I waited without moving. I raised my hand to my neck.

It was painful. I stroked it. I moved my head right and left. I examined my long nails. I smoothed back my unkempt hair. I wiped the bloodstains from my forehead. I straightened my torn shirt collar and squared my shoulders. I touched the wall, running my fingers along the uneven concrete. I felt a cold wind spreading from my fingers to my arm, and from there to my whole body. The air smelled of damp and seaweed. My throat stung. My ears were ringing. A whirlpool was spinning inside my head. As the bird of time glided on its broad wings in the darkness, the sound of the iron gate permeated the emptiness.

Raising my head, I took one last look at the fog opposite.

The yellow fog was beautiful.

The fog that enclosed time in Istanbul, harboring both life and death within it, was so beautiful.

*"Hell is not the place where we suffer,*
*it's the place where no one hears us suffering."*
                                    Mansur Al-Hallaj

# GLOSSARY

| | |
|---|---|
| Abla | Affectionate term of respect used for an older female. |
| Ağbi | Affectionate term of respect used for an older male. |
| Balık-ekmek | Highly popular Istanbul street food, consisting of freshly caught mackerel served in bread, often with onions, lemon, and chilis. |
| Bey | A formal term of respect used for a man, equivalent to Mr. |
| Cacık | A side dish made from yogurt, garlic, cucumber, and mint, commonly known by the Greek name, tzatsiki. |
| Darüşşafaka | A charitable society founded in 1863 for the purpose of supporting the education of poor and orphaned children. |
| Ezme | A very spicy pulverized tomato salad, popular as a mezze, or eaten with kebab. |
| Gecekondu | Literally "sprung up overnight." A cheap, illegal dwelling constructed very quickly by people migrating from rural areas to the outskirts of large cities. |
| Hanım | A formal term of respect used for a woman, equivalent to Miss, Mrs., or Ms. |
| Haydari | A popular mezze dish made with thick yogurt, garlic, feta cheese, and herbs. |
| Hoca | Teacher. |

| | |
|---|---|
| Lokman Hekim | A mythical medical doctor and pharmacist who lived around 1100 BC and believed he had found the cure for all diseases, as well as the elixir of immortality. |
| Mansur Al-Hallaj | A ninth-century Persian mystic, revolutionary, poet, and teacher of Sufism. He was accused of heresy and tortured and executed. |
| Rakı | Turkey's national drink, made of distilled aniseed. |
| Simit | Bagel-like street food covered with sesame seeds. Very popular in Turkey. |